EDWARD W. ROBERTSON

OUTLAW

EDWARD W. ROBERTSON

OUTLAW

REBEL STARS, BOOK 1

EDWARD W. ROBERTSON

EDWARD W. ROBERTSON

Copyright © 2014 Edward W. Robertson

All rights reserved.

ISBN: 1501029894
ISBN-13: 978-1501029899

Cover illustration by Andrzej "Dugi" Rutkowiak.

Typography by Stephanie Mooney.

MORE BY EDWARD W. ROBERTSON

REBEL STARS:

Rebel
Outlaw

THE BREAKERS SERIES:

Breakers
Melt Down
Knifepoint
Reapers
Cut Off
Captives

THE CYCLE OF ARAWN:

The White Tree
The Great Rift
The Black Star

EDWARD W. ROBERTSON

To Grant Naylor and Iain M. Banks, for getting me hooked on the stars.

1

Jain prided herself on being a person who prepared for everything, but there was only so much you could do to prepare to jump across two thousand miles of open vacuum.

Within the walls, motors whirred and clunked. The air sucked from the lock with the hiss of water on sand. And then she heard nothing at all. The floor vibrated faintly. The doors parted on a sliver of blackness. It yawned wider and wider, speckled with colorless dots of light. The stars weren't twinkling. No matter how much time she spent outside the envelope of Earth, she still wasn't used to that.

She detached her shoes from the floor and jumped.

She craned her neck for a look at the ship, but the suit and her gear blocked most of it. A black oval shrinking behind her. Jain put her eyes forward and was immediately overwhelmed by the multidimensional vertigo of plunging into empty space. She had no sense of up, down, or across, and so she felt all ways at once. Her breath roared in the mask. The edge of her vision grayed. An insistent beep chirped in her ears, alerting her that her heart rate was dangerously elevated. She shut her eyes and breathed.

Once the beeping quieted down, she opened her eyes. Which insisted that space was in front of her. In fact, she was flying, exactly as she'd been doing a minute earlier. She just happened to be doing so in a much smaller vessel—an environmental suit.

Now that she was clear of the ship, it flipped on its tail and vectored away, making to separate itself from the asteroid by several thousand more miles. Ahead, she couldn't see the rock yet, but the readout on her visor insisted it was there. In all likelihood, this jump was paranoia. She had 24 hours until rendezvous; if she'd used the ship to deliver herself to the rock, the asteroid's solar orbit would have pulled her tens of thousands of miles from the ship's engine signature. But they were probably clever enough to check the trail, weren't they? After all, they practically owned half the system.

The stars burned across the black field, completely immobile. If she turned to her left, the sun glared through the darkness, but it looked too weak to be able to reach her. She checked her course. To her complete lack of surprise, the jump had been off. She told the computer to correct. Her thrusters engaged, tugging her body across all three axes. The stars swam. After a few seconds, the thrusters quit. With nothing more to do, she closed her eyes.

A polite beep startled her awake. The rock loomed above her, a gray, potato-shaped lump two hundred feet across. She was vectored to pass a few miles ahead of it at a very shallow angle. She muttered to her computer. As she neared, the thrusters kicked in again, aligning her path to duplicate the asteroid's. Once their orbits matched, the thrusters fired front, decreasing her velocity. Slowly, the asteroid began to gain.

More waiting. Over the course of an hour, it filled the display of her visor. Another beep, less polite, informed her when she was a hundred yards away. She fired her spike. It spooled behind her and plunged into the gray rock, deploying a sphere of dust. She reeled herself in. By the time her feet touched down, the microgravity was still pulling the dust back to the ground.

Jain secured herself to the surface, unpacked her gear, and began assembling the comset. Erecting it took less than an hour. Finished, she beamed a Needle to the ship, which was now matching course with the rock from a distance of twelve thousand miles. The ship—presently nothing more than a remote drone—confirmed the link.

Nineteen-plus hours until contact. She killed most of it watching the stars.

Yet another beep. As beeps went, this one was firm, like the bark of a dog. Through the Needle, her ship confirmed contact. The strange craft's outline was indistinct, which would have been unsettling if she weren't already as unsettled as she could get. The vessel came to and matched her ship's course at a point tens of thousands of miles away.

"Well," a male voice said. It had the too-clean sound of alteration, yet there was something familiar about it. No video to let her confirm her suspicions. "Fancy meeting you here."

"You too," Jain said into the comset, which Needled it to her ship, which then broadcast normally, as if she were inside it and not hidden on the surface of an asteroid that was useful only as the reference point for a meeting in the middle of nowhere. "Mind telling me exactly who you are?"

"First, how about you tell me why you dragged me out here?"

"Is this a trick?"

The man sounded somewhere between annoyed and amused. "To do what?"

"To determine if I'm the kind of fool who will spill your secrets to the first craft that comes along."

"It's not a trick," he said. "Is this?"

"To do what?"

"To get me to identify myself to the galaxy."

Down on the asteroid, Jain smiled. "Would you?"

"I'm going to move in a mite closer," he said. "Make sure you are what you look like. You, of course, are welcome to put me under the eye, too. Once we're certain neither of us is a Durant warship, or a bomb with wings, maybe we'll be comfortable enough to start answering questions."

"Roger."

Her visor fed her the fore camera, following the progress of the other ship as it powered closer, advancing deliberately, as if not to spook her. It took several minutes before it was in detailed scan range. To her lack of surprise, it was armed, with fearsome-looking banks of weapons her computer didn't recognize, but nothing too far out of the ordinary.

Except for its hull profile. This shifted and undulated, as if it were wrapped in a cloud of dust or spores. Despite this, it wasn't all that much bigger than her ship, which was as lean as it was fast.

Strange, no doubt about it, and probably capable of pulping her in under a minute flat. But that was why she was spiked to a lumpy rock and not onboard the shiny, vulnerable target.

Her ship indicated that it was also being scanned. This completed, followed by a few seconds of silence that might have been digestive. She waited. The cloudy vessel began a new transmission. No speech. Just a packet of ones and zeroes that comprised her original message, complete with recipient footers.

"So," she said. "You're you."

"I could have told you that," he said. "How much do you know?"

"Let's assume everything."

"I don't think that's a safe assumption." The man sighed. "This is your first rodeo, isn't it?

Listen, you've already *been* vague and ominous. That was the purpose of your first message. To convince me to go through with this ridiculous cloak and dagger business rather than swapping a few mails like normal people."

Jain gazed up into the wall of silver-specked black. "I know you didn't invent it."

He was quiet a moment. "Are you saying we stole it?"

"I don't know that."

"Irrelevant, I suppose. Let's take it before the Bones, here. What *do* you want?"

"I don't think you should release it."

"I was afraid that's what your note meant," he said. "My first thought was you must be a Golden Virus type. Yearning to go back to the good old days of crapping in pits and dying on each other's swords. But you show no connection to them whatsoever. So…why?"

She frowned at the image of the frothy ship. "Because I know where it came from."

"Listen, we are talking about a *major* step here. It's not just about putting real people back in the cockpit. It's about snipping the fetters keeping us tied to this star."

"Sounds like you've already worked out the press release."

He laughed, making no effort to conceal his contempt. "Let's set aside why you think *you're* the authority on the future of a matter you know nothing about. If I don't quash the project, what are you going to do about it? Go public?"

"That's about all I can do, isn't it?"

"I was just hoping to hear something a little more imaginative. Well, I'm not fond of the position you've put me in. I'm going to offer you a deal. I know you're going to want to reject it out of hand, because you're a crusader, but please, seriously—think about it."

She lowered her eyes to the gray, jagged surface. "Go on."

"Seven figures," he said. "*Or* an Earth island plus a lifelong monthly stipend large enough to cover reasonable living expenses. Not some ice cube within shouting distance of Santa's workshop, either. Tropical. Private. Yours."

"Cash and tropical islands? Like *that's* so imaginative?"

"Cash is liquid dreams. You supply the imagination." The man sniffed. "Take as much time to decide as you need. I don't really mean that. But take as much as an hour."

To her surprise, she did think about it. Not for herself. He wouldn't accept if he knew it was from her, but it would be easy enough to spoof him—trust fund from a bachelor uncle, say. He would look into it, naturally. But when you were staring a good life in the face, you didn't tend to spend too long hunting for wrinkles.

She couldn't, though. And the thought pained her as deep as deep got. Because it meant he was right about her.

"I'm sorry," she said. "But this is bigger than any of us."

"I know," the man said. "I have to say I'm highly disappointed. However, you can still help me."

"How's that?"

"Turn around."

Her blood went as cold as the vacuum. Instinct told her to spring up as hard as she could and kick the jets to max, but she was still spiked to the surface. Besides, she was already too late.

She turned. The man hovered above the surface thirty feet away from her. His suit was a mottled gray that shifted to match the landscape beneath it. The gun in his hand was dull black. Couldn't say at a glance whether it was lethal or suppressive, but she leaned toward the former. Lethal meant kinetic, and in microgravity, kinetic meant the user had better not miss—because the mass of the first shot was going to send them flying.

She let her hands hang from her sides, transmitting on the same band as before. "How did you find me?"

The man in the suit cocked his head. A black plate hid his face. "Of all the questions you can ask," he said, "you're going with that?"

"You're right. You bugged the ship, sniffed my trail, used some fantastic tech no one can afford but yourselves. Whatever it was, it was boringly mundane and I can't undo it now."

"That's more like the Jain Kayle I've studied."

"You guys are so *creepy*," she laughed. "Tell me what's next? What will you do with it?"

"Take the last step before the leap." He inclined his face toward the gray dirt. "For you, nothing more."

A sphere of flame erupted from the gun. Jain felt the bullet enter her body, but oddly, the reaction of its discharge didn't budge the man an inch. Not even when he fired a second shot and a third. Her brain wanted to puzzle through this, but she didn't need the panicked beeping of her suit to tell her she didn't have time.

Her last thought was of the cabin. The moment was as fleeting as a shooting star, yet it seemed like it would never stop, like a satellite passing out of the outer edge of the system, to fly forever into the ink beyond.

Yet she had prepared for this, too—something like it, at least.

As her heart stopped, and stayed stopped, a new Needle spoked between the comset and the ship. Within an instant, the ship relayed a prerecorded Needle of its own. It was capable of sending a packet containing the totality of human literature, but the information it delivered consisted of just twelve words.

Try as they might, the crew of the indistinct ship couldn't pierce Jain's computer. In the end, they had to do it grim and dirty: grabbing hold of her ship manually, towing it out a few hundred thousand miles, then flipping around and flinging it directly at the asteroid.

When it made impact, the others turned away, struggling with their expressions, but the man who'd shot her couldn't tear his eyes from the screen. A minute earlier, she'd been nothing but dead meat. Now, she was vapor, the tail of a comet being dusted across the Solar System.

Was there anything more beautiful?

2

Midway through the job, with all the struts welded in place and the panels still on their way up, Webber puffed over to the wing to tie down and have lunch. Not that it was much of a lunch. All-Paste, and watered down to keep it flowing through his tube. It wasn't much of a break, either. Mummied up in a suit that looked and felt forty years old. That always smelled like stale breath (him, probably) and even staler piss (definitely *not* him — faulty recyclers, most likely). It was crummy enough that he would have been happy to shell out for his own suit.

But if he could have afforded his own suit, he wouldn't have signed up for the *Fourth Down*.

Then again, as bad as the lunch and the breaks were, he wasn't much of a worker, either. Not a welder, at least. In his defense, he hadn't signed up as one. He'd signed up as the sweeper. Sometimes literally. All the shit work, also sometimes literally.

Porter, low-level maintenance, custodial. Nothing that should have put him anywhere near a torch.

It sure was pretty out on the hull, though. All that darkness, all those stars. The *Fourth Down* had a lot of charm to it, too. Apparently Captain Gomes didn't think so—the new struts and panels were purely aesthetic, there to smooth over some of the ship's more jagged, artlessly utilitarian patches—though for Webber's money, the fact it was old and showed as much made the boat far more handsome than something fresh out of the yard. A little heavy in the butt to account for the original engine design, yet more than compensated for by the fact it had wings. Extremely useless, but that's what made them extremely cool.

A figure detached from the skeleton of struts, puffed itself clear, then boosted over to the wing. A half moon glared from the forehead of his suit, slanted into an evil eye. Jons. He drifted over the wing, stopped on a dime, then pirouetted, spraying Webber with propellant.

He drifted down, clamped the soles of his boots to the surface, and grabbed some wing. For reasons known only to Jons, he transmitted the sound as he slurped down a sizable mouthful of All-Paste.

"Man," he said, flicking a hand at the view. "Does that ever spook you?"

"Every time," Webber said. "Like the eyes of a million ghosts who won't quit staring at you."

"That's not at *all* what I meant. Ghosts ain't real. I'm talking about what *exists*."

"Aliens."

"They could be looking down on us right now. Watching us on this wing, thinking, 'Man, they don't even *know*.'"

Webber sipped paste. It tasted mealy and beany with a slight tang of fermentation and a heavy aura of generic spice. "If they are, they're pretty good at keeping silent."

"That's the scariest part of all, isn't it? What have they been up to all these years? What are they preparing for?"

"Maybe we haven't heard from them because they're dead."

"Okay, turns out I was wrong about what's scariest. You know what's even worse?"

"If they're dead, what killed *them*?"

Jons laughed. "Exactly. If it wiped them out, what chance do we have?"

They finished a day and a half ahead of schedule. Because Gomes was a just officer, she decreed the extra time would be added to their leave, then hove away from the shipyard at Keens (which was more of a garage than a port) and toward Beagle Station, which was about as big as settlements got between Inner and Outer.

Most of the crew was ecstatic to be on the verge of nine and a half days among civilization. Webber was less sure. Civilization meant the chance for Gomes to increase or replace the crew, and as far as the current alignment went, Webber was the very bottom rung of the ladder.

Thus why he was prone to accepting assignments to weld things to other things when his only qualification for doing so was that he'd once spent seven months in the Martian warrens repairing bikes. That, and it was never an oxford idea to say no to the person who had the final word on your food, water, and oxygen.

On the trip to Beagle, he tried not to spend too much time dwelling on how much he had and how much more he owed.

He was still new enough that coming into a station felt like an event, and as they arrived, he made his way to the bridge to watch. Beagle Station looked like two long-handled hammers connected at the end of the shafts. To make do without the artificial gravity its owners refused to purchase, they'd spun it up to a sickening speed. Drone-piloted ships could dock at either head of the hammers without any trouble, but trying to come at them with live people onboard was a good way to run up your aneurysm bill. To solve this issue, one of the hammer-heads had affixed a long, long, long cable leading out to a platform reachable by a much gentler approach. Gomes was currently staring at that platform, slouched in her chair, swiveling side to side.

"You know how the Beagle got its name?" she said.

Lara, the pilot, didn't look up from her terminal. Webber glanced across the bridge. "You're talking to me?"

"Anyone else here?"

He shrugged. "Darwin's ship?"

Gomes frowned. "Who?"

"Darwin. Charles. Guy who figured out evolution."

"Never heard of him."

"Pre-Panhandler scientist. He worked out the theory by traveling to some weird islands on a boat called the *Beagle*."

Gomes took a moment to stare at him. "And you learned a thing like that where?"

"The School of Hard Knocks. Fortunately, it has pretty low entrance requirements."

"Beagle Station," she said, "was named after founder Richard Danson's beloved pet."

"A beagle."

"That was also named Beagle."

Webber decided the captain was being serious. "People get weird out here, don't they?"

"It's the lack of social accountability."

"Just wait until the first person makes it to Alpha C," he said. "They'll rename it Mittens."

Gomes snorted. Given how few conversations they'd had, Webber was certain it was the first time he'd made her laugh. He decided to leave the bridge before he spoiled the impression.

Back at his bunk, he buckled in. The ship came in at an angle, squishing his guts across an uncomfortable vector. Distantly, things clunked and whirred. His body lifted against the straps, suddenly in free fall; then he plunked down, pressed into his chair by the spin gravity. He unbuckled and headed to the airlock. The others filtered in, Jons and Vincent, Harry and Lara, Deen. No sign of the captain. The lock opened, feeding them into a rubber tunnel connected to the terminal. Inside the station, Webber got his first look at the modified profile of the *Fourth Down*.

It looked like a different ship. The irregularities of its hull had been smoothed out, particularly near its front, which was now nearly as wide as its butt. Stern. Whatever they called it. The wings were still there, but these had been blown out into blocky thumbs that might conceivably be extra stowage or living spaces. He didn't like it.

The terminal smelled like algae and strangers. Less water in the air than they were able to sustain on the ship. From an external perspective, they were docked on the underside of the auxiliary platform and the view past the station roof was dizzying: a thick cable climbing straight overhead, disappearing on its way to the two hammers a few hundred miles away. These appeared fixed in space, but beyond them, the stars streaked past like they'd just split their pants in front of their crush.

After passing security, which made a big deal of collecting everything remotely weapon-like, the crew piled into the elevator, which was fully transparent, obviously designed by sadists. As it whipped them upwards, they appeared to be floating in street clothes through empty vacuum. Webber closed his eyes, but that only made it worse.

Minutes later, with the head of a hammer looming above them, they braked to the point of free fall. The elevator entered the base of the station and glided to a stop.

The doors parted. A whiff of chlorophyll and loam whirled inside the elevator. Beyond, the ceilings were twenty feet high, a waste of space you could only afford in a foyer. Sunny light dispersed from the pale blue ceiling, showering down on the manicured shrubs and vines that pulled triple duty as park greenery, oxygen generators, and food.

"Gross," Jons muttered. He strode through the semi-circle of people waiting on the elevator. Webber followed.

Instead of a 24-hour Earth-style light cycle, Beagle kept each of its layers at a permanent level of illumination. The highest layer, with a skyward view of space, was deep night. After that, the second-highest layer was full "daylight"; as you descended toward the bottom of the hammerhead, it got progressively darker, until the second-lowest layer was back in full darkness.

Naturally, the bars, clubs, and hippest cafes clustered between Twilight and Midnight. Inevitably, the entirety of the crew (minus Harry) headed straight there.

First stop was the layer known as Sunset. Unusually wide streets between the buildings, some of which were painted to look brick. Webber was sure it was meant to evoke some Earthside city, but mostly it just looked Disney.

Jons had the best instincts for these things, so Webber followed him into a joint that was moderate in all ways: size, lighting, patronage. You didn't want your first stop too loud nor too dull. Could throw off the whole night.

Vincent, Lara, and Deen stuck with them. Even if he hadn't been the pup, Webber wouldn't have minded their presence. Deen was the hulking, quiet type; one glance at his forearms steered away trouble. Lara made it okay for women to approach them, and besides, she could match Jons shot for shot. Vincent had too many opinions about how the entire Solar System ought to be organized, and the drunker he got, the righter he became. But he was useful for running interference, and could keep the conversation going no matter the circumstances.

Jons, of course, was the one who made interesting things happen. Sometimes that meant trouble, but it was that or they might as well stick to their bunks and knit each other socks.

Jons insisted the first round of any stop be the local liquor. On Beagle, that meant something that tasted like licorice and bread mold.

"Next is on me," Vincent said, glancing across the table at the others. "Consider it my thanks for tearing through those hull mods."

"Wasn't much to it," Deen said.

"Right," Jons said. "Suit up, swim for hours on end, and do work that typically requires two certs and a diploma. No big deal."

"Must not have been," Lara said.

"Okay," Webber said. "Why?"

"*You* did it."

"I mean why bother changing up the *Fourth* in the first place? What did we accomplish with that?"

The four of them exchanged looks. Deen shrugged. "Bigger holds."

"Doubt it," Lara laughed. "Put anything heavier than a load of pillows in there, and the welds will rip off first time you try to turn. I say it's safety. A little more padding if we dock hot."

"You clowns," Jons said. "It's about looks. That ship is Gomes' baby. Her husband. Her ride. It's *her*. The way it looks reflects that. I cannot believe this is a serious question."

Webber looked around the table. A beat later, the others busted up with laughter. He smiled and bought the next round.

After that, they relocated to a place down the block, then dropped a level lower into Twilight, which was three times as rowdy. They were still feeling the cramp from the ship and quickly relocated to Last Light, where the ceiling was smudged with purple light and the people were downright demure, as if paying their last respects to the day. Vincent began to try his luck on the local girls. Next time Webber looked up, the man was gone.

When Jons suggested a descent to Midnight, Lara shook her head. "Not me. Too early in the trip for that."

Deen nodded his agreement. Jons raised his eyebrows at Webber. Webber was starting to get his stations legs under him and agreed without hesitation.

Midnight was actually two layers deep, but Jons stopped at Midnight-One, swinging into a bar Webber vaguely remembered from their last visit.

Total crewman's bar where even the darkest-skinned people looked pale and nine-tenths of the crowd wore black clothes—not for fashion, but to better hide the stains. Jons plugged them into a booth, strolled to the bar, and returned with four doses of the moldy licorice-tasting stuff.

"What's up?" Jons said after the first was down.

"Nothing."

"Don't 'nothing' me. We bunk together. I can read you like you were my wife."

"I owe." Webber traced his finger around the rim of the full shot. "Money."

"Who doesn't? Why else would you be crewing?"

"On a house."

"A *house*?" Jons peered at him, brown eyes sharp with disbelief. "Tell me it's not on Earth."

He nodded. He hadn't meant to say it, but most of what got spoken in Midnight was that way. "It's not mine."

"Definitionally, I can't say I agree with you! Whose is it, then?"

"Complicated." Webber lifted the little glass. He knew the devil was inside it, but he drank anyway. "I've been doing a lot of reading. Back channels on the net. I hear that once you owe so much, when you pass the threshold..." He looked past Jons' shoulder. "You disappear."

"You disappear?"

Webber opened his hands, revealing nothing.

Jons scrunched up his face. "Like they grind you into All-Paste?"

"They take you. Knock you out. You wake up in a hole on Triton, hauling rock. And that's where you stay until you die."

"If that were true," Jons said, "do you really think you'd have heard of it?"

As drunk as drunk logic got, but Webber was in the same headspace and had no trouble accepting it. "Maybe not. But the threshold, I'm coming up on it. And I don't want to see what's on the other side."

"Well hell, man. If you're that far underwater, what are you doing spending your money in a *bar*?"

They blinked at each other, then burst into laughter.

"It's never as bad as it seems," Jons said once they'd calmed down. "If it comes down to it, here's what you do. Cut a deal with Gomes. She reports you died in an accident somewhere off the Lane. A few months later, Bob Smith shows up on Titan. Boom."

The door banged open. A steroidal bald man entered, followed by two more men and a woman. All four were dressed in blue. The bald man headed straight to the bar, relocating several people along his way.

Webber turned back to Jons. "It's not as easy as that. Everything leaves a trace. If someone's looking for me and they see a smudge on the record, and they go check with Gomes about that 'accident,' how much pressure do you think it takes before she spills?"

They talked more, but Webber had accomplished his mission of turning his memory into a reverse terminator line, behind which lay only darkness. Next thing he knew, the bald man in blue was standing over another man so short and thin it looked like he'd been raised on a diet of imagination soup. Neither of them looked happy, but the bald man bore a fatalistic, half-amused expression.

"That," Jons said, "is the embryo of a fight."

The bald man's team was watching from their table, but between the noise, the gloom, and the booze, nobody else was paying much mind. The bald man said something. The short man shook his head. Before he finished, the bald man swung his fist.

If the measure of a punch was how hard it was to avoid, this one rated about an "Angry Toddler." The short man ducked, spinning away, lashing his left hand at the other man's balls. The little man's momentum was drawing him back, neutering his strike. But considering he was attempting to do just that to the bald man, it didn't take much.

The bald man dropped. As if connected to him by Newton's Third Law, the three members of his crew shot to their feet. The little man danced back. A bystander shoved him from behind, sending him reeling toward the crew. The woman stutter-stepped up and socked him in the cheek. He bounced back, tripping on a young woman as she scrambled to escape the burgeoning violence.

The bald man was still on the ground, thighs clamped tight. The blue-suited trio advanced.

Webber wiped his mouth. "Somebody should do something."

"Yeah," Jons said. "Little dude should run."

Webber downed the table's last remaining shot and found himself on his feet. Near the bar, the little man parried an incoming kick and swept the attacker to the ground. The woman came in from his side, driving her knuckles into his gut. This time, he fell.

The three standing members of the Blue Crew swarmed him, drawing back their feet. Webber burst through the ring of people surrounding the skirmish, fumbling out the Settler of Scores.

To both the naked eye and security scanners, the Settler of Scores was your standard-issue charge stick, a finger-sized portable power source whose universal ports could provide days of electricity for whatever gizmos you were carrying around. During a particularly rough stretch on Jindo, Webber had done some research, bought a few parts (one of which was quasi-legal at best), and converted his one and only charge stick into a much more versatile item.

The short guy had managed to kick the legs out from the paunchy guy, but the woman and the third guy were now giving him the ol' boots to the ribs. Now that the bald man was out of it, the woman looked like the nastiest contender, so Webber ran up on her, dug the charge stick into her back, and pressed the button.

A pattern of electric pulses discharged through the stick's needle-sharp golden pin. The woman went as stiff as an antenna, then dropped in a twitching puddle. The third man turned, mouth agape. The little guy slammed his heel into the side of the man's knee. The man's face got very serious. He fell beside the woman clutching a bundle of busted ligaments.

By this time, the paunchy guy had gotten to his feet. Regrettably, the Settler of Scores required a recharge/reset between uses, but Webber was feeling all right: it was now two on one in their favor.

The little guy pointed over his shoulder, crying out. Webber turned, glimpsing the bald man and a fist incoming straight at his jaw.

He saw stars. Not the fixed kind you saw on a starship monitor. These ones twinkled like crazy, alerting him that his brain was temporarily nonfunctional—and that more stars, comets, and darkness were soon to follow.

3

There was nothing Rada hated more than someone who flaked on a date. Sitting there, the scenery was pleasant to a fault—a real wooden booth with a clear view out the floor-to-ceiling windows, which displayed the curve of Mars in all its fiery glory—but she only had eyes for the clock. Her device. And its stubbornly empty inbox.

It didn't help that it was in Harrigan's. That's what her contact had requested, however, and given the nature of that request, Rada hadn't been about to say no. She could have lost herself in her device, as Simm was doing, but she forced herself to look at the bottles behind the bar. All the colors of the alcoholic rainbow: amber; green; rich, translucent brown. With one exception, it had been three years (and counting) since the murders on Nereid and hence three years (and counting) since her last taste.

Between then and now, she'd learned two lessons. The first was optimistic: mind trumped matter. Any internal problem was capable of being solved internally. You just had to want it. Hard enough to be ruthless with yourself. Over the last three years, she had starved that part of herself until it was little more than skin and bones in the back of a cage.

The second lesson wasn't so nice. She had starved it, weakened it to the point where she could toy with it without fear, but it was still there, wasn't it? That part of herself—the part that demanded more than the plain, unadulterated world could deliver—she didn't think it *could* be starved to death. It was a zombie. Weak, presently. But if she started to feed it again?

Darkness never truly went away. She should have known as much from the beginning. You were reminded of it every time you flipped off the light.

She checked her device for the ten thousandth time. Sipped her Fizzea, which had a hideous name but tasted wonderfully of tea and active bacteria. She people-watched. Gazed out the window on the dusty orange-brown sphere beneath them.

"I want to ping her," she said.

Simm didn't look up from his device. "Bad idea. Will seem needy."

"I know it's a bad idea. I said it out loud so I wouldn't do it."

He glanced up, scanning her. Eyes as blank as windows reflecting the sun. On the Spectrum of Unusual Personalities, he rated about a five, shading toward six: fully functional, but also capable of appearing inhuman. Robotic. Able to withdraw to a place of pure observation, untroubled by feelings or doubts. This creeped a lot of people out, but not Rada. It was a major factor in why they were together: she envied him. Tried to emulate his ability for herself. Didn't matter that she too often failed, blowing her stack at the worst possible moment. What mattered was that she made the attempt.

He came back to himself, personality returning to his eyes, and smiled at her. He looked back to his device.

She finished her Fizzea, stirred the straw around the melting ice, and waited to order another. She was finishing her third when the message came in.

It was total gibberish.

"Not necessarily." Simm frowned over his device. "It could be in code."

"For what, toddlers?" Rada laughed. "It sounds like a nursery rhyme."

"The words are arbitrary. An empty vessel for the real message embedded in the transmission."

"Or that." She slid from the booth. "Can you trace its source?"

He swept his fingers across the device's screen, scanning. "Maybe. It looks like it's been rerouted."

"Get cracking. I'm going to prep the ship."

"Isn't that premature?"

"Only if everything's okay."

He watched her a moment, descending back into scan mode, then dropped his eyes to the device. She jogged out of the bar and into the mall.

The air smelled dry, and though it looked clean, it carried the odor of dust, too. Better than the sweat that pervaded most stations.

Ares Orbital was about as old as old got, but it had been retrofitted with artificial gravity a few decades ago. Mars-standard levels, though, meaning her hard jog felt like something she could keep up all day. Her haste was pretty stupid—whatever was going on with Kayle was surely happening very, very far away—but Rada couldn't help it. She might not be able to understand what the woman's message meant, but that in itself carried meaning. To her, the words sounded like someone who'd just been bashed on the head.

She hopped a shuttle to the port. Beyond the massive windows, the *Tine* rested on the tarmac, a scalpel among hammers. She still couldn't believe it was hers. Profile of a skiff with the engine of a cruiser. The perks of working for a billionaire. Check that: an *eccentric* billionaire. Then again, they all were, weren't they?

She'd already ordered a tube hooked up to its lock. At the gate, she scanned her thumb and eye and was allowed into the featureless tunnel to the ship. The lock opened and she stepped inside. When she was living on it, she never noticed the smell, but she'd been away from it for three days and easily detected the unique musk of Simm and herself.

Onboard, she put the *Tine* through its paces. Could have done most everything remotely, but she didn't trust the automation the way she trusted her own hands. She'd barely gotten started when Simm pinged her, letting her know he was on his way. He wouldn't say more.

She had everything spooled and humming by the time he arrived. Aggravatingly, they weren't cleared to launch for another forty minutes. They settled into the control deck, which was too large to be called a cockpit but too small for a bridge. Simm was fastidious about belting himself in and she knew better than to start asking questions until the last strap was clipped tight.

"So you've got something?" she said.

"Yes and no."

"Give me the yes first."

He finished installing his device into his dash and leaned back. "I think I've cracked the code."

"What's it say?"

"Well," he said, "that would be the no. What it says is, 'Hey Pip: when the rabbit sees a shadow, where can he go?'"

She drew back her head. "You're saying there's nothing embedded in it? So what is it? A lyric? A quote?"

"I don't know."

"So search it."

A trace of annoyance colored his eyes. "That was the first thing I did, Rada. No matches. Some partials, but you can partial anything if you get vague enough."

"Then where does that leave us?"

He rolled his lower lip between his teeth. "Three possibilities. First, it *is* gibberish. Unlikely, but it could have been an accidental transmission."

She narrowed her eyes. "It's a grammatical, parsable sentence. How could that be an accidental send?"

"I *said* it was unlikely. The second is that it's a generic code phrase—you know, 'the condor soars at midnight.' The third possibility is it's the only type of code that's truly unbreakable: something that only makes sense to the sender and the recipient."

"Except she sent it to us," Rada said. "And we've never even met her."

Simm looked almost but not quite at her eyes. "That's why I thought we'd go ask her in person."

"You've got a read on her."

"On where the message was sent from, anyway. It's weird. It was routed around the entire system, like you'd do to disguise the source, but it wasn't hard to track at all."

"Sounds like she wants us to come find her." She glanced at the countdown. Another thirty minutes to go. "Punch up the course."

He did so. Not that this took any more effort than transferring the coordinates from his device to the ship. The *Tine* spat out a course. Closer than Rada had feared. Within the Belt. Simm pulled up the course's details, subjecting them to his usual rigor. Unlike Rada, who ran manual checks because she didn't trust them, he did so in order to learn to calculate such things himself.

Wasn't much else to talk about until countdown. Eight minutes to departure, Simms started to get twitchy. She tried not to smile. Once the seconds hit single digits, he squeezed his eyes shut.

She laughed and reached for his hand. "This isn't even the bad part."

"It's *all* bad."

There might come a time when she got sick of his flight anxiety, but that day hadn't arrived yet. With a lurch, the ship lifted, steadying itself with brief, automated blasts from its docking thrusters. She followed along in her head. The rear screen showed the platform of parked ships shrinking behind them.

As soon as they tilted away from the station, Simm's breathing went from audible to frantic. He clamped hard on her hand.

"Everyone was wrong about everything," he said. "We should never have crawled out of the ocean."

Once they were clear, the *Tine* blasted away, thrusting her into her seat. As soon as their vector steadied, Simm's breathing calmed. Around the time Mars was a red dot in their rearview, he opened his eyes.

Rada rolled hers. "We really need to get you an anesthesiologist."

Simm muttered something and checked his device. Jain Kayle still hadn't replied. Rada's good humor fell behind her as swiftly as Ares Orbital.

"Wake up," he said. "There's a problem."

She inhaled sharply and tried to sit up but was arrested by her harness. She scowled at the screens. "What? I don't see anything."

"Exactly. Our asteroid—it's missing."

"We're sure there's supposed to be an asteroid?"

He pulled up a navigational representation on the center screen. "See where it was supposed to be? And that's her engine sig. The *Ship With No Name*. When the Needle came in, her ship was in matching orbit with the asteroid's course."

"Okay, but she could have gone anywhere since then."

Simm eyed her sidelong. "We're just trying to find the asteroid. Once we've got that as a reference point, then we can see if we've got any vape trails to follow."

"Sorry, still shrugging off the sleep." She unbuckled and walked closer to the screens. "Any debris?"

"Some. But this is the Belt. Would be weird if there *weren't* any." He frowned over his device, which he'd detached from the dash so he could hold it on his knees. "Hang on. It's not gone. It's moved."

A map appeared in the 3D display above the main screens. It was off scale, with the asteroids represented far larger than reality. Two lines appeared across space: one red, one green. Toward the right side of the screen, the lines converged. The *Tine* was currently just a few thousand miles away from the end of the red line.

"Red is the original path," Simm said. "Green is the new. Based on this, it altered course a little less than 36 hours ago."

"Almost a day exactly before Kayle Needled us." She pointed to the green line. "Intercept the asteroid's new course. We'll see what's there, then follow the trail back to the inciting event."

He nodded and fed the orders into the ship. Rada buckled in. Once she was secure, the ship flipped around—they'd been approaching the asteroid's previous location tail-first—and accelerated toward the head of the green line.

"Should I upload the rock's new course to the net?" Simm said.

"Not yet. I want a better idea of what we're getting into before we let anyone know we were here."

"Getting traces of engine sigs. Wait much longer and they'll be gone."

"How much longer?"

"I don't know. That would depend on the sig."

He meant no malice, but if you were the slightest bit less versed on a subject than he was, his explanations had the tendency to make you sound like an idiot. Mentally, she bumped his SUP to a 5.5.

"We're operating on the assumption she sent the Needle so we'd come find her." As she said this, it struck her that it could also have come from someone pretending to be Kayle. "First priority is finding out whether she's here. She could be troubled. Disabled. For all we know, she's floating around with nothing more than a blanket and a plastic bag of O2."

"Well, I think we know enough to rule out *that* much."

Ahead, she saw nothing but stars. On the 3D map, the ship inched nearer the tumbling rock. It was gray, potatoid, rotating crazily.

"There's some debris around," Simm said. "Might not want to get too near."

That was about as close as he ever came to trying to give her orders. "Debris? What kind?"

"The kind that will shred us like something you put on top of a burrito." He frowned. "Lot of heat on that rock."

He flipped a map to infrared. The rock was largely a dull, deep red, but parts of its surface were a warmer orange. A few speckles were all the way to yellow.

"Oh stars," Rada said. "She crashed."

"We don't know that yet."

Typically, she appreciated his refusal to jump to conclusions, his dogged maintenance of an open mind until all the facts were in hand. But this time, she knew Simm was wrong. The ship flashed a warning about micro-gravel and suggested a course change. Simm glanced at her. She nodded. He punched it up. The views shifted dizzyingly; the acceleration pushed her into her seat.

Simm navigated to a clear spot above and to port of their initial approach, then parked the ship, matching the asteroid's trajectory. Rada floated against her straps. They were now close enough to see the heat signature for what it was: a messy crater. Scans confirmed the concentrated presence of minerals often found in starship engines and weapons arrays.

"We still don't know it was *her* ship," Simm said. "Or that she was in it."

"She's dead, Simm," Rada said softly. "Do you know what this means?"

"Not necessarily. It *could* be an accident. Coincidence."

"It means that whatever she was going to tell us was worth killing for."

Simm looked abruptly uncomfortable. "*Now* should we alert the authorities?"

"First, let's pick up those e-sigs. Right now, we are firmly in the Middle of Nowhere. Even if we can find someone to take on the case, I doubt they'll be top of the class."

He laughed and brought the *Tine* about, putting it on an intercept course with the red line that marked the asteroid's original course. As the scanner started scooping up the various ions left behind by the recent passage of other vessels—ions that were almost but not quite as unique as a fingerprint—Rada opened up a line.

Not to the cops, but to the net. Their current location was far enough out in the black that the poky lightspeed communications made for a frustrating lag, but she wasn't headed for the usual channels. She was going to the Labyrinth. Even with her connections at the Hive, establishing access was going to take a few minutes. The sooner she had that going, the sooner they could follow up on whoever else had been here.

Stressful as their current conditions might be, she found nothing more meditative than drifting through space, the stars steady on the screen, the engine humming like a whale in the middle of a note that would never end. It felt right. Like destiny fulfilled. In the long, troubled history of human existence, no one had ever made it to another star (excluding Weirdness, anyway, but he didn't count). It wasn't for lack of trying. Ships got out there, deep in the nothing, and then they just...disappeared. Not a word returned to tell their fate. Any rescue efforts, any drones dispatched to their last known coordinates—those too vanished into the eternal night.

Even so, Rada thought that someday, she might give it a try.

"Contact."

Simm said it the way you'd mention where you bought your new shoes, and for a moment, the word meant nothing to her. She glanced up from her pad, annoyed with everything, and stared at the unlabeled dot winking on the local map.

"Oh," she said. "Tell me that's a cop."

Simm shook his head. "They're not broadcasting any signal at all."

"Weapons hot." Rada checked her straps and found them firm. "Let's show them our teeth are more than paint."

4

Webber staggered, blinking against the stars dazzling his vision. He cringed, attempting to brace himself for the man's second punch.

Someone grunted. Webber was no gruntologist, but it sounded like a surprised grunt. The knockout punch did not arrive as expected. A second person grunted. He recognized that grunt. It was Jons, performing something physical and unpleasant. The first man grunted a second time. His tone was pained.

Thudding noises, capped off by a large and final one.

Abruptly, Webber came to. Jons stood in front of him, breathing hard, hunched over the immobile body of the bald man. Only one of the bald man's crew was conscious and he was too busy grabbing his blown-out knee to think about continuing the fight.

Webber rubbed his thudding jaw. "Where'd the sprite go?"

"He ran off as soon as I foiled Mr. Rock of the Scarred Dome here." Jons grabbed his collar. "And running is the best idea I've seen all day."

They dashed through the gawping bystanders. When they were halfway to the door, the crowd burst into applause.

Outside, the streets of Midnight-One were the typical scene of drunken laughter, shouting, and people depositing precious fluids into the gutters to be dutifully recycled by the machinery of the station. Jons settled into a no-nonsense jog toward the elevators.

"What the hell, Webber?" His face was clenched like a fist around the hilt of a knife. "I mean, damn!"

"I thought brawls were your idea of a good night."

"You didn't even know what it was *about*! For all you know, you just helped out the bad guy!"

"I don't care." Webber rubbed his face. Was already swelling. "You swing on a guy four to one, that makes *you* the asshole."

Jons laughed, looking angry with himself for doing so. "Next time, at least wait until day two to start throwing punches, okay?"

They found a room on Twilight where such things were cheapest. It was obvious neither of them would be able to sleep for a while, so while Webber held down the fort, Jons headed to the corner for a case of condensed beer. Webber took two, drinking one and pressing the other to his jaw.

When he woke in the morning, Jons was gone. Webber sat on the end of his bed and spent a long time reaching the conclusion he shouldn't start the day with one of the remaining beers. Last night made him feel like a giant idiot, but he knew that was just the hangover talking.

When he got around to checking his device, he found a dozen messages waiting. Most were from the crew, demanding the details firsthand, but two were from Captain Gomes. The first was dated four hours earlier. The second was from an hour after that. Both demanded his presence—on the ship.

Figuring he was already hours late, he took a blip of a shower, turning off the water as he soaped up to keep his meter down, then dressed and hit the street. Around him, Twilight partied on. He descended to Beagle's foyer and got into the elevator for the long ride to the docking platform.

The *Fourth Down* was dim, silent. He made his way to the bridge. There, Gomes was barking into her device. She glared him into a chair and went on with her conversation.

Five minutes later, she pocketed her phone and stood across from him, staring at him like he'd driven the *Fourth* into the nearest rocky body. "Don't you dare make me drag this out of you."

"Well, you see," he said. "There was drinking."

"I was drinking, too. You see me starting a brawl?"

He didn't say: *Nope, but I've never seen you spend more than five minutes with the crew off-ship*. "If you had, I'd be disappointed in the others for not having told me the story."

Gomes' jaw flexed. "Why, Webber? Did they spill your drink? Call your mother mean names? Or were you just pickled and looking to hurt someone?"

"Captain, what's going on here? We get into fights all the time. As long as we take care of the fallout, since when did we get called in here to be whipped?"

She pressed her fists against her eyes, speaking through gritted teeth. "I don't like to go into this shit, because it's as depressing as it is none of your business. This next delivery, it's make-or-break. As in, if we don't make it—"

"You'll break me."

"So we understand each other."

"Perfectly." He made to stand. "It won't happen again."

"I'm sure of it. Because you're restricted to ship until departure."

His jaw dropped. This hurt so much he snapped it shut, which hurt even worse. "Captain!"

"Shut up." She stuck a finger in his face. "And if you ever want to leave this ship, stay shut up until we're on our way."

Right then, he wanted to do some yelling, but he'd been on a streak of bad decisions lately and anyway, he knew he wasn't about to change the captain's mind. Not in the heat of the moment.

"Whatever you say." He tugged up his pant leg to expose his ankle. "Want to fit me for my bracelet?"

"Fuck off, Webber." Her language was hard, but he spotted a flicker of guilt in her eye. "Don't step off the ship. Otherwise, it's leave as usual."

He saluted. She ignored him, getting out her device and exiting the bridge. He felt like some pouting was in order—this was his first leave in weeks, and right after he'd pulled extra duty refitting the hull, too—but right then, he was too tired. He headed to the galley, ordered it to approximate him some bourbon on ice, then took the glass to his bunk.

After he'd added one third of its contents to his bloodstream, he started to feel better. Not that the conversation made any more sense. He and the crew, they'd gotten in plenty of fights in the past. Gomes was rarely *happy* about their scuffles (although she sure enjoyed hearing about them), but she rarely did more than grumble about discipline. She'd certainly never sentenced anyone to quarters for a week of leave.

And if it was the money she was mad about? If she was really as deep in the red as she claimed? Then what was she doing dropping tens of thousands of bucks on making her boat look marginally nicer?

Captains. There was no understanding them. He thought it would be smooth to be one some day—to set your own rules and your own course, going and doing as you pleased, the master of a portable nation of you and your crew—but even in his drunkest dreams, he knew he wasn't the type who would ever own a ship.

Ships cost millions. He couldn't afford a *house*. And if he couldn't come up with a way to pay it off soon, he wouldn't be around to be dreaming for much longer.

Jons came to see him later that day to see what had happened and to do some mutual griping about Gomes. Other than that, Webber was left to himself. He didn't even see the captain, though he was sure she was monitoring the *Fourth*.

He supposed it was a win that he wasn't out spending money he shouldn't be spending. But if it was a win, it was a real Battle of San Pedro. In exchange for his enforced financial responsibility, he was compelled to spend all day thinking about his prior irresponsibility. To visit his account, visualize his debt, and contemplate the gigantic gulf between the two.

He spent a lot of his time drinking. He liked to think he wasn't doing so alone, though. That, despite his sentence of isolation, he was joining the crew in spirit. What could be more noble than that?

Five days into his term, with three days to go until they shipped out, thumps emanated throughout the ship. When he went to investigate, he found longshoremen loading the lower bays with cargo and securing it tight against the upcoming journey down the Lane. As usual, they were more interested in insulting him than answering questions.

The afternoon before departure, he heard voices in the common area. Webber wandered from his room, drink in hand, and found the crew draped over the couches, looking worn-out but relaxed.

"What's up?" he said. "Don't tell me we're leaving early."

Lara laughed. "Gomes called a meeting. Must have figured there was no sense telling the monkey when she can just knock on his cage."

"Hilarious." He sipped his drink. "Let me guess, you've been out there curing hunger."

"Nah. Just loving life."

Webber found an unoccupied couch and installed himself in it. On a lounge chair, Vincent curled on his side and snored. Jons started telling Webber about a sholo singer down on Midnight-2. Webber didn't want to care, but it sounded amazing.

Ten minutes later, iron-soled boots thumped belowdecks and ascended the ramp. Gomes showed up first. She was followed by the blue-suited bald man and the woman Webber had taken down with his homemade taser.

"Whoa!" Webber bolted to his feet. "Captain, those are—"

"Webber!" She snapped her fingers and pointed at him like he was a misbehaving terrier. "What did I tell you about shutting up?"

The woman smirked at him. The bald man stared, arms folded. He was wearing sleeves, but his biceps filled them out to where Webber suspected he worked out in double gravity. Webber frowned and sat down.

"I'll get right to it." Gomes walked in front of the two strangers. "This is MacAdams," she gestured to the man. "And this is Tzavioto."

"Call me Taz," the woman said.

Gomes stared straight at Webber. "These are the new members of your crew."

A moment of silence enfolded the room. The others glanced sidelong at Webber and Jons.

Jons clasped his hands behind his neck and arched his back. "Just curious, but what exactly are they here to do? I thought you were strapped."

"That's right," Gomes said levelly. "That's exactly why they're here. This next delivery, I can't afford for anything to go wrong. Taz is here for logistics—that means she's working with you, Vincent. Got me? *With* you."

As quartermaster, Vincent did his best not to look insulted. "Gotcha."

"As for MacAdams, he's on electrical. That means he'll be poking around the ship. Maybe even opening parts of it up. All you need to know is to stay out of his way."

Jons raised his hand. "While we're doing what, exactly?"

"Delivery to Skylon."

Gomes moved to the wall and waved her device across it, calling up a map of the system: Inside, including Earth, Mars, the Moon, and a few hundred stations of all sizes; Outside, which started at Jupiter's orbit and extended all the way to the Kuiper Belt; and the Lanes, the safe roads between the two divisions of the Solar System. Skylon was a dot in orbit around Triton, Neptune's only moon of significance.

"Long flight," Jons said.

"Thus why it's valuable," Gomes said. "Everything else, it's normal parameters. Do your jobs, keep your heads, and we'll be back on our feet in no time."

Maybe it was the presence of the two new players, or maybe it was the hangovers, but nobody had any questions. The others filed out, headed back into Beagle to enjoy their last night of leave.

As Webber stood, MacAdams eyeballed him. Gomes watched them both.

"For the record," Webber said, "I had no idea what that was about."

The corner of MacAdams' mouth twitched. "Funny thing to get involved in, then. You in the habit of sticking your hand into dark holes?"

Taz stepped past MacAdams, putting herself chest to chest with Webber. "We're here on business. Business makes for short memories. But if there's *any* more bullshit, I will stomp you into something you can't scrub out of the floor."

She turned and walked away, boots thudding. Gomes gave Webber an odd smile and left with MacAdams, jabbering about wiring.

Webber went to the galley and had the machine dispense a double.

Whole thing was puzzling. Captain was in money trouble, yet not only was she modding the ship, she was hiring new crew. On top of *that*, she was taking a Lane. As far as Webber was concerned, the Lanes were about the biggest scam in the system. At one point they'd served a purpose, yeah. Way back when you couldn't make it through the Belt without stirring up five hives of the unassociated pirates who'd taken to the area the instant it became feasible for a small-count colony. Plenty of real estate in the rocks hollowed out by decades of mining.

Back then, the frontier had boomed. Intense as a gamma burst. Everyone had been so hell-bent on making sure there could never be another extinction-level event like the Swimmer invasion that they'd flocked to space like lemmings in bubble helmets. For the obvious reasons, Mars and the Moon had been popular destinations, but so many people had headed into the Asteroid Belt that nobody had a true count. There was no one government keeping things in order. People did what they wanted. What they had to.

Often, "what they had to" meant capturing the cargo of any ship that passed through their territory. Particularly after so many corporations had discovered that it was cheaper and more efficient to employ autopiloted ships that didn't require human personnel or the life support needed to keep that personnel breathing. Drones, though? Drones were dumb. Trickable. You could correct that by assigning them remote human pilots, but unless those pilots were relatively close, the lag in communications meant the pirates could carve up their ships like gouda.

Naturally, the corps had fought back, but the system was too huge for any one company to clamp down. And the fragility and expense of their navy meant that any losses put them in the red immediately. When they'd tried hardcore deterrents—nuking pirate enclaves, say—the PR fallout had been more lethal than their attacks. Two of the largest space-faring companies had been broken up and reassembled under new management. There had actually been a full-fledged revolution in the New Roman Alliance. Completely rewrote the corporate section of their constitution. Top executives had been executed for war crimes.

Pretty cool stuff.

Then some bigwig had gotten the idea for the Lanes. A series of stations in empty space that could serve double duty as defense bases and as remote-operation platforms for drone pilots. By staggering them across the void, you could provide a response to threats in very little time. The corps involved had recouped the massive expense by charging a toll for anyone who wanted to make use of the Lanes' safe passage beyond the Belt. Win-win.

Except that, during downtime, Webber liked to feed his delusions of owning a ship by reading up on logistical issues. People didn't talk about it openly, but if you found the right corners of the net, it was clear that a lot of people *didn't* use the Lanes. And were just fine. Could be Gomes would rather pay the toll and play it safe, but the more he'd learned, the more Webber felt the Lanes were insurance for a problem that didn't exist.

Whatever. Wasn't his call. Worrying about Gomes' problems was a much less interesting use of this time than getting tore down.

Figuring he'd be more motivated to do his job while drunk than hungover, he made his first round of launch prep, stowing, securing, and tying down anything that wasn't bolted, locked, or magnetically sealed in place. Among his duties, this was possibly the most menial yet also the most crucial. Get a pen whipping around during takeoff, or a glass of water left loose during the transition to zero G, and that was the way somebody lost an eye or a computer.

In the morning, he woke feeling groggy and crummy, glad he'd had the foresight to take care of most of his work the day before. There were benefits to having no illusions about your character.

The others returned in ones and twos, taking on their responsibilities with bleary-eyed competence. After the last week of quiet, the clamor of their work was deafening. Hours later, Lara made her final check—her eagle eye for that which was out of place made her a natural—and reported to the bridge.

A minute later, Gomes' voice reported across the ship. "Grab a chair or wave goodbye."

Webber was already in position, strapped down, as always, to his bunk. He had no duties during launch, and he figured if he was about to die, he'd be happiest doing so in bed. The screen on the ceiling showed the feed from the Beagle control tower, centered on the *Fourth Down*.

Lara began the count. At zero, flame and vapor swallowed the ship. It emerged from the flattened spheres of smoke and powered away from the landing pad. For several minutes, it operated solely on maneuvering thrusters. Safely removed from the station, it swung about and blasted toward the closest checkpoint in the Lane that would guide them to Skylon Station.

It would be six days until they arrived. With no responsibilities for several hours, Webber stayed in his bunk and watched the stars shining on the ceiling. They looked vacant, like graffiti on a warehouse wall, but he knew this was false. The illusion of a distance too far to grasp.

Hours later, his eyes snapped open. He had just…moved. Abruptly. Yet their route had been set hours ago. A course change wasn't totally crazy—the ship may have detected some unplotted rocks or debris in their way—but that wasn't exactly comforting. The ceiling had gone blank. He tried to call up the view from the bow, but the screen refused to budge.

The ship jarred again, pressing him into his bunk. Below him, Jons snored away.

"Jons. *Jons*." Praying they weren't about to get jolted again, Webber unbuckled enough to lean way over the edge of his bunk and give Jons' shoulder a knock.

Jons stirred, scowling in the darkness. "The hell?"

"That could well be our next destination. We're juking around out there. Can you pull up the screen?"

Jons sighed as if Webber had just asked to be taught how to put on a pair of socks, then got his device from its nook and began fiddling. The ship lurched again, squeezing Webber's stomach.

The screen on the wall flared to life. Space. Stars. And what appeared to be a burning ship.

"What the—?" Jons tapped his pad, to no effect. "Is this an SOS? What are *we* doing on it?"

Webber squinted at the array of stars. "Because there's no one else. We're out of the Lane."

"Are you still drunk? What would we be doing out of the Lane?"

"Man, I don't—" On the screen, a new star blazed from the darkness. The ship turned again, sloshing Webber's guts around. "Oh."

"What?"

"Shit."

"*What?*"

"We're out of the Lane," Webber said, "because we're pirates."

5

Inside the *Tine*, an orchestra of clicks, whirrs, and beeps announced the defense systems had just gone hot. To Rada, it announced something more: that she had a sword in her hand and it felt good.

She punched the broadcast button. "I don't know who you are or what you're up to. But I have taken a peek at what you're flying. Back off or I'll open you like a can of tuna."

Across from her, Simm frowned. "Why do you get fired up like that?"

"Like what?"

"Like you *want* to chew them up. That's not a drone. It's not a dot on a screen. There are real people inside."

"That means they can be scared." She sat back, eyes fixed on the screen. "It's more humane to drive them off than to let them come at us, isn't it?"

"Presumably." His hands hovered over the controls. "But it might work better to stick to the facts."

"That would convince *you*. Most people? We're dogs. Ninety percent of the time, you can avoid a fight through attitude alone."

A high-pitched boop indicated the unmarked ship was giving them a scan. It hadn't slowed down. They were nearing the threshold where Rada would need to launch the drones.

"Could this be them?" she said. "The people who hurt Jain?"

"I don't think so. So far, I've only got a partial e-sig on whoever was here with her, but whoever this guy is, he's way off."

"But he could be affiliated."

"I have no way of knowing that."

The other vessel hadn't yet crossed the threshold, but she had a pretty good look at it now. The computers had it pegged as an old *Serpent*-base, but it had seen a lot of modifications, including a large, cylindrical structure grafted perpendicular to the ship's long body. The age of the vessel and its accompanying mods meant it was almost certainly unaffiliated. In the Belt, an unaffiliated ship refusing to ID itself pointed to one conclusion.

"Launching drones." She tapped buttons. On the main tactical screen, four light blue dots materialized, inching forward from the larger, darker dot of the *Tine*. She braked, pushed forward against her straps, and guided the *Tine* to the computer-suggested safest spot behind her defensive screen.

It was a long time from the days of single-fighter dogfights. The sad, unromantic truth was that, in tight spaces, unoccupied drones could execute maneuvers that would pulp a human pilot. Her role in this encounter was less pilot and more admiral, overseeing her unmanned combatants against whatever the enemy could bring to bear. If she wanted, she could take manual control of any drone at any time, but it didn't feel the same as being in the seat yourself. Anyway, that could get dangerous. Ensconced in the perspective of a single drone, it was easy to miss the forest for the trees.

The drones spread out, staying close enough to support each other while covering enough space to put themselves in front of anything that came their way. The *Serpent*-class slowed. Light washed over its hull; a swarm of rockets appeared on tactical. As soon as these were out, the *Serpent* hooked and braked so hard its crew would be on the verge of passing out.

Rada smiled tightly. "Think they're bugging?"

"I can't read minds," Simm said.

"Bet you four hundred they're bugging."

He pressed his lips together. "No deal."

On tactical, 23 discrete rockets spread like puffball seeds. Two of her drones moved to intercept. Probably overkill—the enemy's looked like dumbfires—but you never could tell. The line between missiles and drones had gotten pretty blurry.

As the cloud neared, the three drones released dumbfire spreads of their own. These came in three waves. The first would directly engage the enemy rockets. The second would come in on the heels of the first, slamming into anything that slowed as it tried to outmaneuver the first screen. The third wave was comprised of high-explosive warheads that could zap huge chunks of space. Maybe not enough to damage a hardened spacecraft, but certainly enough to set off a fragile drone that was little more than a warhead with an engine on its tail.

The cloud of enemy dumbfires met the first cloud of drone-fired rockets. Two of the enemy missiles made it through the first wave. Zero made it through the second. Fire bloomed in round whorls of red and white. The exchange of fire was as sexy as it was expensive.

It had bought the *Serpent* exactly what it was looking for, though: time to stomp the brakes and haul ass away from whatever the *Tine* was.

Simm glanced over. "Should we pursue?"

She had no doubt the *Tine* was physically capable of chasing down the *Serpent*-class mutt. Problem was that the *Serpent* was already pushing itself to the limits of human physiology. Computer thought they could run it down, but that would take four hours, and would probably involve another fight. Assuming they came out of that unscathed, it would be another four hours to make it back here. By then, the e-sigs could have decayed beyond recognition.

"Fall back," she said. "No sense chasing. If they'd been involved, they would have taken the good stuff and bugged out long ago."

"Got a steaming hot sample of their sig." Simm smiled. "*Now* should I call the cops?"

"Get the other sig first. Then we'll worry about some two-bit pirates."

He punched up a course to intercept the red path signifying the original path of the asteroid Jain Kayle's ship had crashed into. A gentle pressure held Rada against her chair as the *Tine* swung about.

She sighed, staring at the exploded missiles' residual heat on the tactical screen. She had been born in the wrong era.

Once he had the sig, she took them back to the asteroid, stopping when the rock was on the very fringe of the *Tine's* sensor range. While Simm began to navigate the ad hoc e-sig database on the undernet and the Labyrinth, Rada punched up the closest thing that passed for a government: the 371st Conglomeration of Associated Asteroids and Habitats. After delivering the summary to a receptionist, she was transferred to one Boyd Huygens, a lighter-skinned man with deep bags under his eyes and a smile that apologized in advance. It was a low-band vid link with just enough of a distance-lag to result in awkward pauses between each response.

"Like I told your assistant, we didn't get a name," Rada said. "We did pick up a signature."

She sent it over. After a second-long lag of blank staring, his eyes snapped to his screen. He punched something into his device.

"We have records of that sig," he said. "Problem is, the vessel that sig is attached to is unregistered. And after a squabble like this, you can be sure they'll have it altered."

"You can't alter your engine signature."

"Not whole cloth. But you only have to change it enough to argue in court that it isn't a perfect match." Huygens thumbed his hat up his forehead. "They'll change their profile, too. Either that or claim their comms were down and you were coming at them with hostile intent."

"You would *believe* that?"

"Hell no," he chuckled. "But I can't prove otherwise, can I? Take a look at what went down: two ships meet in blank space. You make a threat. They fire off enough missiles to cover their ass, then turn said ass and haul it away at suicidal speed. That sound like an act of piracy to you?"

"Maybe they're just really terrible pirates." She pressed her lips together. "What about Jain Kayle?"

The officer sobered. "That is unfortunate. Going to ask you the same thing: What do you see when you look at it from a remove?"

"Two ships rendezvous in blank space. Get real cuddly. A short time later, Kayle's ship crashes into the rock."

"But there's no evidence of gunplay. Nor of overt foul play."

"It's hard to believe it's coincidence," Rada said. "Her ship wouldn't have *let* her crash into an asteroid."

"Unless the nav conked out. Or she turned off the nav to fly manual. Or stars know what else." His apologetic smile took on a grim note. "I'm not saying we won't do anything. I'm saying there's little we *can* do. Unless you can give us something more."

"Such as?"

"What brought you out to that rock in the first place?"

Rada shrugged. "We were scheduled to meet with Jain Kayle on Ares. When she didn't show, we checked around. Discovered her last known broadcast had come from the site. Went to check her out."

"What was the subject of your meeting? The one she missed?"

"I honestly don't know."

Huygens pushed out his lower lip, narrowing his eyes to slits. "You're supposed to meet. No idea why. But you *do* know it's so important that when she misses her meeting, you immediately track down her last known whereabouts and fly straight there. Have I got this right?"

"On the nose."

He leaned back in his chair, rubbing his eyes with his fingertips. "I'll send someone out to do a sweep. In the meantime, if you can remember anything more, I would suggest you let me know. Assuming you want to learn the truth."

He smiled and signed off.

Rada swore. "Was he blackmailing me for intel?"

Simm was nose-deep in his device. "It sounded more like the self-awareness that his institution would be unlikely to turn up any results without more of a lead. Also, he's a detective. Detectives can't stand when part of the story's being hidden from them."

"Well, that settles it. We'll continue to look into this ourselves."

Simm looked up from his screen and regarded her with naked amusement. "I wasn't aware you had any intention of stopping."

"What's our next step? I say we follow whoever Jain was meeting while the trail's still hot."

"Agreed." He gestured to his device. "Somebody on the net's got a line on the e-sig. The match isn't perfect, but the signature was decaying for more than a day before we got here. Could be our bogey."

"Yeah?" They were currently at a dead stop, zero-G. She grabbed the handle on the ceiling and squeezed forward, activating its magnets; it skated across the ferrous ceiling, dragging her behind it. "What are they asking for the ID?"

"Twelve point five."

She snorted, halting directly above him. "Talk him down to eleven."

"That would be exceedingly difficult," Simm said. "As I've already paid him."

"Are you joking? Why?"

"Because he had it, we want it, and that's what he was asking. Besides, what's fifteen hundred to Toman?"

"Fifteen hundred he didn't have to spend. Running this ship across the system is comically expensive as it is."

He stared up at her. "Well, there's good news, if you care to hear it. The ship's owner is right down the block. Less than a thirty-second lag from here. Want me to dial her up?"

"Punch it in." She was already hand-skating back across the ceiling toward her chair. "We're going in person."

Simm nodded and fed his coordinates into the ship. Rada pushed off the ceiling, got a hold on her seat, and buckled in. The ship accelerated gently, sticking her in place. For a moment, she felt guilty about burning time and fuel when they could speak to the ship's owner via radio. But there were advantages to seeing someone in person, even if "in person" only meant getting close enough to talk in real-time, without a minutes-long lag between each response. Having a conversation in real time meant there was no opportunity to perfect every response. If somebody was lying, it was far easier to catch them.

Besides, so much of what the Hive accomplished was done from desks, screens, and private rooms, removed from the action by millions of miles. That's why Toman was paying to put them out in the field, right? To give the org a presence in the physical world to match the one they kept on the nets. This was their job.

She dislodged her device from the armrest. "I'm going to put everything we've got into a Needle and zip it to the Hive. Sealed, for now—EOMD."

Simm sat back from his device, eyeing the rocks dotting their course ahead. "Shouldn't that be in the event of *our* death?"

"I assume you have a plan to back yourself up and live forever among the ones and zeros."

He chuckled. "Trust me, if I could, I would."

She rolled together everything they'd learned so far and Needled it into the darkness. She had a lot of faith in herself, and even more in the *Tine*, but if Simm was right about the sigs, they were on their way to see whoever had been with Jain Kayle at the time of the incident. And that was enough to plant a seed of doubt in her gut.

Maybe it was the prospect of meeting with a potential killer. Maybe it was the lingering adrenaline of the pirate attack less than two hours earlier. Whatever the case, her biology was asserting itself in a major way.

"So," she said. "Want to take advantage of gravity while we've got it?"

Simm glanced her way, then did a double take. "Yes. Yes I do."

She unbuckled her seat, stood, and walked toward his station, drawing down the zipper of her flight jacket. Often, she resented the urges of her biology. It rarely knew what was best for her.

After what they'd been through in the last few hours, though? She was happy to be its servant.

The e-sig of the ship Simm had identified at the crash site was registered to one Ophelia Major, resident of Taub's Pebble, one of hundreds of asteroids hollowed out for raw materials, then refitted as habitats. Entry to it was invite-only, and while it and eighteen other nearby rocks were organized within a loose confederation, Rada had her doubts that its police force would give a damn about her unofficial, outsider investigation of one of its citizens.

She drafted a message and sent it off. Simm ID'd their ship to Taub's Pebble and was granted clearance to park a few hundred miles away. While Rada waited for a response, she floated to the galley, which was really more of a closet with nozzles, and dispensed herself a bag of espresso. As she did so, she glanced at Simm, who always asked why she didn't simply order pure caffeine—the answer being that she enjoyed participating in a cultural ritual that was now well over a thousand years old. But he'd fallen asleep in his chair, hands and feet drifting like the weeds in the shallows of a quiet pond.

The call came in before she'd drained half of the little bag. She dropped the bag, clipped herself to the wall, and got out her device. The caller had no face or name attached, but it was the same address Rada had pinged.

She enabled video of herself. "Ms. Major?"

The woman's voice was gravelly and exasperated, as if she stayed up too many nights complaining about the laziness of her kids. "You said you're interested in the *Piper*?"

"That's correct," Rada said. "If you don't mind —"

"You're too late."

"Too late? For what, exactly?"

"To see it. Buy it. Whatever you had in mind. Six days ago, it got pounced. Pirates. Nothing but scrap."

"Gods," Rada said. "But you're all right?"

"Wasn't on it. If I had been, we'd be talking at those jackals' funeral."

"May I ask who was piloting it at the time?"

"Nobody," the woman said. "Flying drone. They hijacked it. Tried to ransom it to me. I did my all to negotiate, but sometimes I'm more stubborn than oxford. Yesterday, I gave them an ultimatum. This morning, they sent me a rather nasty reply." She laughed raspily. "So I pushed the button."

Rada's jaw dropped. "You had it rigged to blow?"

"And they were too damn dumb to shut down my comm to it."

"When it was taken, did you report it to the police?"

"For all the good I knew it would do."

Rada chuckled ruefully, then let her expression grow serious. "Ms. Major, I'm afraid that while these criminals were in possession of the *Piper*, they may have done some bad things. If you can tell me anything about them, I can help prevent them from hurting anyone else."

"Can't," Major said. "Completely anonymized."

"Can I have a look at the files? Our software may—"

"Can't and won't. Ma'am, I don't know you. For all I know you're working *for* them. Here's the facts: they took my ship, and now they're dead. Far as I'm concerned, I got my justice."

"Ms. Major—"

The line went black.

Rada hurled her device across the cabin. It cracked into the wall and rebounded, skimming toward Simm. He cried out and ducked behind his chair. The device knocked against its back and spun away. Rada pushed off on an intercept course, snagging the device and inspecting it for damage, absently catching herself against the ceiling.

Simm floated from behind the chair. "What did *that* accomplish?"

"It successfully rebooted my emotional state. Now: dissect."

"It's a plausible story," he said without a moment to reflect. "With lower-value ships, it can be more profitable to steal and ransom them than to reconfigure them. It's also logical to use a stolen ship in the commission of a crime you don't want connected to a ship you do own."

"But?"

"But she refuses to provide any hard evidence that this actually happened. Her story is extremely convenient. It then becomes possible she was somehow involved in the crash of Jain Kayle's ship."

"My thinking exactly." Rada rubbed a scuff on the corner of her device. "But it's also possible the pirates stole the *Piper* with the express purpose of hurting Jain."

Simm frowned. "Unlikely. *Piper* had some defenses, but nothing like Jain's *Ship With No Name*."

Lacking adequate gravity to throw herself despondently into a chair, Rada settled for flinging out her limbs and flopping on her back. She spun slowly, gazing up at the ceiling.

"If anything, this just opened up more questions. Could be Major was involved. Could be pirates. The e-sig you picked up, were there any other matches?"

"Nothing I would consider remotely probable. Bear in mind, however, that the databases are user-generated. Plenty of ships don't appear there."

She was approaching a wall. She drew her limbs trunkward, getting her feet under her to absorb the coming impact. "Could it be IRT? Payback for the *Rebel*?"

"We haven't had any problems with them since then," Simm said. "Besides, they'd have to know about Jain and her extremely recent and equally tenuous connection to us. It would be a highly convoluted scenario."

"Well, keep it in the back of your mind. For now, let's dig up everything we can on Ophelia Major. Check in with the cops regarding local pirate activity. Offer a bounty for anyone who can ID our e-sig."

Simm scratched the back of his head. "Alternately, we could quit."

Rada caught herself against the wall and swung about to stare at him. "Simm, she was *murdered*."

"We don't know that. We don't know her, either. We don't even know what she was going to tell us."

"All signs are it was pretty damned important! We haven't even been on the case for two days. If Toman wants to recall us, he can recall us. Until then, I want to get hold of the local cops and—"

Her device dinged. She blinked at it. "Speak of the devil." She glanced at Simm, then switched the feed to the receivers implanted in her ears.

Toman Benez's face appeared on her device, which indicated they had an eight-second lag. "Hey Rada. I don't have time for an extended chat. But I wanted to let you know I got your message. And I read it."

"What?" she said. "That was event of death only!"

For eight seconds, he fiddled with a second device. When her words finally reached him, he looked up and grinned. "So imagine how relieved I am to see you're alive! Listen, I'm sure you're busy, but if you're not in the middle of anything too sticky, can you swing by the Hive? I'd like to discuss our strategy in person. See you soon!"

He winked and blanked off.

Rada tethered the device to her leg. "Change of plans. We're headed to the Hive."

Simm raised his brows. "That was Toman, wasn't it?"

"Sure was. And when Toman Benez suggests you drop by for a chat, you strap in and punch it as hard as you can stand."

6

"Pirates?" Jons leaned from his bunk closer to the screen. "Where do you get *that*?"

"Because that ship is burning," Webber said. "And we're dodging."

"Could be what we're dodging is burning pieces of ship."

"This is what the mods were about. MacAdams and Taz, they're not electrical engineers. They're security. Marines."

The ship juked again. Jons rocked and swore, grabbing at his back. "Okay, well, if you frame it like that, it makes kind of a lot of sense. Except for the part where it's totally fucking crazy."

"It's only crazy to a sane person. Gomes is on the brink of losing everything. How cohesive do you think she is?"

On the screen, a spread of rockets leapt from the bow, engines igniting in silvery starbursts, and spiraled toward the flaming vessel. Sparks fired from the rear of the wounded ship. Four flashes of light signaled the death of one rocket after another. One went off beside the crippled ship, followed by a second. Rather than being torn to shreds, however, the ship simply went silent. No lights. No launches. No nothing. Just a cape of flames that was already dwindling to nothing.

"Pulsed out their power," Jons said.

Webber inched to the edge of his bed. "Can't be that simple. What about backups?"

"Judging by the way that thing defended itself? Full-on drone, baby. It's got its maneuvers, its defensive algorithms, but that's never going to stand up against a pirate who knows their way around a fight. Bet you two grand that's how Gomes' new crew is earning their keep."

Webber's head bobbed down; they were accelerating. Nothing too intense. On the screen, the disabled ship slowly drew nearer, continuing to coast on its momentum even as the *Fourth Down* moved to close.

"Gomes is more desperate than she's let on," Webber said. "Check it out. None of us are in on this, right?"

"Can't be. I've played way too much poker with these guys to miss when they're bluffing. Nobody had a clue."

"There's no alarms. No announcements. She hasn't even turned on the seatbelt light. We're not supposed to know this is happening."

Jons poked his head from the side of his bunk and met his eyes. "Where are you headed with this?"

"Every one of us is in debt, right? Past the eyeballs and up to the scalp. Bet you anything her Plan B is that, if anyone figured her out, she'd buy them off." Webber pressed his palms together. "But what if we unionize?"

"Is that a fancy word for mutiny?"

"She just made us accessories to piracy. If she's going to expose us to that kind of risk? She'd better make it worth our while."

Jons tented his fingers over his nose, eyes hooded. "Or we shut this off. Pour ourselves a drink. And pretend we didn't see a damn thing."

"That sounds like a good way to stay stuck here for the rest of our lives. Getting put to use by someone who sees us as nothing more than human cogs. With nothing more to look forward to than the next time we can get drunk and, if we're really lucky, get in a fight with some other sailors." Webber swung his feet over the edge of the bunk, careful not to bonk his head on the ceiling. "I say we round up the others. Tell them what's up. And demand our cut of the action."

Jons laughed and ejected himself from his bunk. "When did you start believing there was a future, you son of a bitch? One condition: before we rally the troops, we stock up at the galley. No way I mutiny without a cup full of grog."

Their door was sealed—Webber was looking forward to Gomes' explanation for that one—but Jons delved into his device and went to work. Two minutes later, with the other ship filling half the screen, a cylindrical pod launched from the *Fourth*.

Webber tapped Jons on the shoulder. "See that?"

"Life raft," Jons said. "What do you want to bet Taz and MacAdams are on board? Ready to snatch up the loot?"

"Better move fast. While Gomes is alone."

Jons stuck his tongue between his teeth and resumed work. A minute later, the door slid open.

"Let's get them one by one," Webber said. "Will be easier to win them over."

Jons nodded. "Lara first. If we convince her, the others will fall like dominoes. While I work on her door—"

"I know." Webber saluted. "The grog."

The hallway was dark, quiet. He tiptoed to the galley, punched up an order of dark rum, and watched the thick, syrupy liquid pour into his plastic jug. Finished, he sealed its sippy lid and jogged toward Lara's quarters. The door was closed but opened to his touch. Inside, she stood with her feet planted shoulder-width, separated from Jons by three feet. She snapped to face Webber. Her expression froze.

"Oh no," she said. "You guys are serious."

He took a drink and thrust the jug Jons' way. "I don't like it any more than you. If you want to go back to bed, we'll pretend we were never here. But Gomes, she just put our future at risk. Our lives. Roll over, or come with us to the bridge—your choice."

"Way to make me sound like I'm a pussy if I say no." She stuck out her hand. "Give me that bottle."

Next was Harry. As their local fixer—a glorified diplomat—he saw which way the wind was blowing. He didn't even ask for a full explanation.

After that, they went to Deen. To Webber's surprise, the big man shook his head. "Guys, you're talking about *mutiny*. We signed a contract."

"Yeah," Jons said, "and Captain just flushed it down the tube. How can you stand behind someone who just made you an accessory?"

"Because either way, this is pure dirt. I choose to wash my hands." Deen crossed his thick arms. "I won't back you. But I won't get in your way, either."

Webber nodded. "Might want to lock your door until it blows over."

That left Vincent. Appreciative of logic, but highly contrarian. Webber readied three different arguments. When they sprung his door, he stood on the other side, amused.

"So," he said, twirling a knife. "Finally figured out what those mods are intended to hide? They're made of lead for a reason, you know."

"I'm just the one who welded them down," Webber said. "You with us? Or would you rather mock us from afar?"

"I'm assuming you saved me for last. Where's Deen?"

"Switzerland."

"Huh?"

"He's decided he's above both sides."

"That's because he doesn't understand that, when the revolution comes, standing back looks the same as standing with the enemy." Victor sighed and reached for the jug. "I'm with you on one condition: first, we negotiate. Gomes is no fool. We'd be wise to hear her reasons for her course of action before we fling her out the airlock."

Webber glanced at Jons. Jons winked. Webber sloshed the jug. "I'll drink to that."

They advanced toward the bridge. The doors were locked, but Jons parted them with the same trick he'd used to spring the others. Webber entered first. Gomes was alone. Eyes locked on the screens. Muttering into her comm. Brown face turned pale by the light of the displays. For a moment, Webber's confidence receded like a tide. On screen, the lifeboat was docked to the cargo ship's airlock.

"We need to talk," Webber said. "It's about you being a total asshole."

She whirled. Her cheeks twitched, gaze shifting past him to the others as they filtered through the door. "Vincent. After I plucked you out of the gutter?"

Vincent shrugged his bony shoulders. "Believe it or not, I am but a remora here. You're looking right past the shark."

A cloud crossed over her face. "Webber?"

"I might be dumb, but you're the one who hired me." Webber stalked forward, bottle in one hand, galley knife in the other. "Talk. Bleed. Your choice."

"It's not how it looks." She stood, palms raised. "When we made the delivery, I was going to announce a bonus."

"How generous," Jons said. "Is that our idiot pay kicking in?"

"Wait until you hear the numbers."

Harry cleared his throat. "Before we start dividing up this manna from heaven, might we discuss who we're currently robbing?"

"Nevedia," she said. "Next-gen meds. Tailored to knock down whatever mutations Jupiter's magnetic field induces in the locals' bacteria. So sizzling they wouldn't even trust the formula to Needles."

"*Nevedia?*" Harry said. "Third-largest drug manufacturer Nevedia? Top-forty fleet in the system Nevedia?"

"That's exactly why they were arrogant enough to cut out on the Lane. Speaking of cuts, you know what we're looking at? Fifteen grand."

Jons beetled his brows. "You knocked off a Nevedia cargo cruiser for fifteen grand?"

"Each," Lara said. "Dumbass."

A startled silence washed over the bridge. Webber lowered his knife. "How were you going to explain a 15K bonus?"

"With great difficulty," Gomes laughed. "Got lucky speculating on the tritium market. Something like that. Might have had to spread it over multiple deliveries."

"How much are *you* taking?"

"Well," she said. "I'm the captain. I knew what was happening. The rest of you would have had plausible deniability."

"How much?"

"You have to consider expenses. Your cut. The new recruits. Mods, materiel, bribes. Savings against potential damages to the ship. Adds up. The net's a lot slimmer than the gross."

Webber tightened his grip on the blade. "Don't make me ask a third time."

Gomes swallowed. "Six hundred."

"Grand?" Lara honked with laughter. "I'm guessing that's conservative, too."

"And you get fifteen. Each. All you have to do is keep your mouths shut."

Webber moved to rub his mouth, caught the gleam of the knife, and arrested his hand. Fifteen thousand. That was three months right there. Enough to get his head above water—for now. But after it was gone, he'd be right back where he started.

"Question," he said. "Is this a one-time thing?"

Gomes met his eyes. "Do you want it to be?"

Harry laughed in disbelief. "Might I remind you this is Nevedia? Who exactly was on board?"

"No one. Drone. Only potential casualties were Taz and MacAdams."

"And us," Jons muttered.

"And us." Webber stepped forward. "Taz and MacAdams, what are they getting?"

Gomes glanced at the screen. "Depends on expenses."

"Points on the net? Then what's what we get, too."

"Come on. You can't ask points for staying in your bunks and squeezing your eyes shut."

"We'll earn our points the same way they are. How much are they getting? Ten?"

"Fifteen," she said. "Each."

"Then we'll take ten. Each."

Gomes drew back her chin. "That leaves me with twenty. As *captain*."

He shrugged. "A lot better than twenty years in the brig after one of us decides being accessory isn't worth 15K."

"Eight," she growled. "Each. This is the only time I'll make the offer."

Webber glanced between the others.

"Drones only," Harry put in. "I'm not blowing a hole in anything with a crew. No amount of money is worth murder."

"Second," Lara said.

"And we discuss the targets in advance," Jons said. "Nevedia's not so crazy. They've barely got a presence Outside. Some of the others, you're talking suicide."

Webber nodded. "On the flip side, I don't want to be stealing Ma and Pa's yearly harvest. I only want to take from people who can afford it."

Gomes' gaze moved across them. "For freebooters, you make a lot of moral demands."

Webber set down the knife. "Even pirates got to have a code, don't they?"

Jons hefted the bottle. "I'll drink to that. Captain?"

Anger danced in Gomes' eyes, but a smile spread across her mouth. She stepped forward, took the jug, and tipped it up.

She returned it and wiped her mouth. "Christ. First order of business once we sell those pills? Buy something worth drinking."

On the screen, the lifeboat disembarked from the Nemedia vessel and thrust back toward the *Fourth Down*. Once it cleared, the cargo ship burst from stem to stern. Webber put up his fist and cheered.

After, as always, he felt dumb. Yet also, as always, he knew the feeling would pass. He was well beyond the normal rules. When you were drowning, you grabbed hard to any opportunity to surface. No matter how it would look to those watching from the safety of dry land.

The lifeboat returned to the *Fourth*. MacAdams and Taz appeared on the bridge and halted, staring in surprise at the crew. Both bore pistols on their hips.

Gomes smiled. "Welcome to the shareholder's meeting. We have decided to rewrite our business plan to focus on our most profitable enterprises. Speaking of, how'd the robbery go?"

"Great." MacAdams fished a baggie of pills from his pocket and lobbed it toward Gomes. They were currently under light acceleration, and in the low gravity, the baggie sailed through the air like a spear.

Gomes nabbed it and held it up for inspection. "Wonderful. Everyone, buckle up. Time to get out of here before the dragons show up to reclaim their treasure."

The crew strapped in. The course was already planned and ready, but Gomes let Lara do the honor of punching the button.

The *Fourth* blasted away. Behind them, the ruin of the Nemedia ship faded into the darkness.

7

The most widely-told story of how Toman Benez came to own the Hive—known, in those days, as the Eye of Julia—was that it had been a hostile takeover.

By itself, this wasn't remarkable. Space being space, i.e. a gigantic yawning nothing much too vast for any single government or corporation to control more than a hair-thin slice of, people reached out and took things from each other all the time. Even things as significant as stations and habitats.

What was remarkable about the taking of the Eye of Julia was the method. Toman hadn't come at it with a fleet of dreadnoughts and twelve tubs of marines. He hadn't swarmed it with drones and nukes. According to rumor, what he'd done was convince its security that they were playing for the wrong team. Not through bribes, blackmail, or strong-arming them. He'd simply reached out to them, one by one, and explained why they needed to switch sides.

And when he showed up with his fleet, they opened the door and rolled out the red carpet.

To Rada, it sounded exaggerated. Another example of the cult of personality around Toman Benez. But after working for him for the last three years, she could almost believe it was true.

Unlike many habitats, the Hive was built to be mobile. Its present location was in a heliocentric orbit in a quiet patch of space about twenty million miles behind Mars. Originally, it had been a run-of-the-mill spinning ring, but after installing artificial gravity, its previous owners had drawn it to a stop and expanded its docking port. Once Toman had gotten hold of it, he'd negotiated purchase of a nearby asteroid and dragged it over. Then the bastard had sealed it inside a spherical dome. Dumped fertilizer all over it. Added ponds, greenery, animals. And connected the dome to the Hive.

On the *Tine*'s screen, the installation looked like a silver ring about to pass over a tiny, pocket-sized Earth.

They docked and debarked. The air inside the port smelled moist and earthy. Rada still found the whole thing ridiculously extravagant, but she had to admit it was relaxing. A cart waited for them at the empty terminal. On autopilot, it carried them straight through the tunnel bisecting the ring and into the spherical dome housing the microplanet.

Which had a separate gravity system from the ring. As the cart neared the sphere, gravity dissipated until the vehicle began to float. It exited the tube, flipped about on a puff of air, oriented its wheels toward the ground that awaited them two hundred feet below, and passed into the rock's puny gravity well.

It fell. A parachute shot from its center, its air-capturing cells so fine the whole thing had a gauzy, indistinct appearance, more like a cloud than solid matter. The cart descended gently, touching down on an X-marked pad, retracted the chute, then drove them to the rendezvous at Lake Mars, a (relatively) large body of water whose bed was lined with genuine Martian red clay.

Toman sat on its bank, fishing. Hearing the cart, he reeled in his line and stood, brushing off his pants. He was shorter than she always remembered him. Younger, too—early thirties, and he was the rare tycoon whose apparent age was the same as his actual one. He had a way of moving that was difficult to describe, though. Flowing. Like a dancer, or Simm's Rainese knife fighting, or someone born to near-zero gravity.

"Rada!" He threw aside the fishing pole and rushed toward her. "Please—tell me the *Tine* is okay."

"I'm afraid it…it went down, sir. We had to swim vacuum all the way here."

He gave her a look, then turned to Simm. "Is it okay? Your message said you'd been attacked."

Simm smiled, looking past Toman's shoulder. "You will be gratified to learn the aggressors turned tail the instant the *Tine* showed its teeth."

"I *am* gratified." He patted Simm on the shoulder and gestured Rada to a nearby rock. "Pull up a chair. And tell me exactly why I'm putting my people—and my ship—at risk."

She sat on the large, flat stone, warmed by the artificial sunlight. There was even a bit of a breeze swirling around. Flies jounced on the surface of the lake. It was almost more than she could stand.

"I thought you read our message," she said.

"And I judged that it was too flimsy a reason to keep you out there. Not if it means dogfights and lengthy, unsatisfying murder investigations." He lowered himself to a boulder across from her. "So: convince me."

"First off, our contact on this is—was—Jain Kayle. Ex-professor, physics and astronomy, emphasis on exosolar colonization. Several years ago, she left that post for the private sector. One of your rivals, as I recall."

"I wouldn't call Iggi Daniels a rival," Toman said. "Rivals have to be able to beat you."

Rada let a moment pass. "Point is, Kayle was tops. She dedicated her life to getting us out of here and into the galactic neighborhood. Two years ago, there was a rumor that they'd done it."

"She hadn't spent long enough with Iggi to get anywhere."

"If true, they'd be the first ones to get outside the Oort. In this case, the middle of nowhere is a major somewhere. After she contacted us, we did some serious digging. Every corner of the undernet we could find, including some isolated networks in the deep Outer. Every twist of the

Labyrinth. We didn't find any hard evidence of the mission, but there was talk. A lot of it."

"That is because talk costs nothing." Toman shifted on the rock. "Unlike deep space missions designed to thwart an unknown threat that's vanished everything else sent its way."

"You told me to tell you everything we know."

He closed his eyes. "Go on."

"Backing up, Kayle contacted us two weeks ago. To prove that she was talking to me, and not someone pretending to be me, she made me go on video with a paper sign, gave me a key phrase, and watched as I wrote it on the sign. After that, she asked for a meet."

"To tell you what?"

"Well." Rada drew her feet in to sit cross-legged. "She wouldn't say. Not until we were in person, on one of your ships."

"The topic can be inferred by context," Simm butted in. "She was into deep space. We're bug-hunters. Presumably, she found something out there—something alien."

"Yes, it's all very tantalizing," Toman said. "And it's just like Iggi to send the entire Solar System on a wild goose chase."

"Before the crash, Kayle tried to clue us in," Rada said. "She Needled us one last message. Routed it all the way across the system to hide her tracks. Delayed its delivery by a whole day."

"Why would she delay her final words?"

"Best guess?" Simm said. "She didn't want us to arrive on the site while whoever killed her was still there. However, it was timed so that we arrived in sufficient time to get a read on engine sigs, flight paths, et cetera."

Toman's shoulders bobbed with laughter. "So you agree she was murdered, Simm? I thought you needed more proof than that."

"The evidence isn't conclusive. But it deserves further resources."

"I looked into her message. The thing about the rabbit. Not a single reference to it anywhere."

Rada sighed. "That's why we went after the e-sig instead."

Toman turned to gaze at the yellow light gleaming on the blue water of his private world. "I want you to back off that angle. I'll task some worker bees to it. They can pry into police records, pirate chatter, and anything involving the *Piper* from a safe distance. If their panning turns up any gold, I may redeploy you to the field then."

"And in the meantime?"

"You're headed to the most boring place in all the universe: Earth."

She glanced at Simm. "I'm not following."

Toman stood and stretched his back. "Jain Kayle, astronaut extraordinaire, is a born-and-raised Earther. Her funeral's already been scheduled. If her last words mean anything to anyone, chances are you'll find them there."

"That's a hell of a way to condense the search." Rada got to her feet. "When's the date?"

"Two weeks. They have to make sure everyone has time to fly in." Her boss turned and smiled at her. "In the meantime, I want you to think long and hard about what you almost did to my *Tine*."

~

The funeral was to be held on the beach at Founder's Bay. Rada arrived early, taking a chair near the back. The air smelled like salt and kelp and water. Out to sea, the Invasion Memorial rose from the waves, silent, titanic, a black plane of startling size. She knew it had been restored many times over the centuries—not to mention stripped of anything interesting and/or useful long, long ago—yet gazing at the alien ship, she couldn't shake the feeling that it could lift off at any moment.

And finish what it had started.

As the guests arrived in ones and twos, she gave them a good long look. Following along remotely through the lens cam in her right eye, Simm identified each in turn. Kayle hadn't had much in the way of family (a daughter, an ex-husband, two cousins), and most of the arriving mourners were either former colleagues from her university days, or employees at Valiant, Iggi Daniels' naval company.

No one paid Rada any mind. By the time the ceremony began, fewer than half the seats were filled.

A priest took the short platform, his back to the sea. He said some bland pleasantries and stepped down. He was replaced by Kayle's boss, Mikela Rolf, a fortyish woman with the musculature of an Earther. Rada didn't pay attention to her words so much as the strength of the relationship they hinted at. Fairly personal. She made a mental note.

The next to move to the stage was Kayle's daughter Dinah. She was only 28, but she looked twice that, frail and shuffling, dark circles around her eyes, knobby knuckles. Grief rarely did anyone any favors in the looks department, but Rada thought it was more than that. On her way to the platform, Dinah faltered and had to be helped up by a young man with the no-nonsense motions of a professional caretaker.

Dinah moved to the podium, looked down, cleared her throat. She put her hand over her eyes and gestured offstage. The caretaker bounded up and helped her off.

In the receiver in Rada's ear, Simm said, "Kudos for trying."

From anyone else, it would have been an insult. From Simm, she knew it was sincere.

A middle-aged man Simm ID'd as Bill Watkins shook Dinah's hand, leaned in to say something in her ear, then ascended to the podium. He was decent-looking, in an over-sunned way, and though he looked plenty sad, it was in a less severe way than Kayle's daughter. Watkins had been Kayle's boyfriend for several years, but they'd parted ways during the same period she'd left the university for Valiant. Rada wondered which event had precipitated which split.

"It's been a few years since I saw Jain," he said. "But I'm not too proud to admit I've thought about her far more frequently. She got under your skin — in the best possible way. Passionate, but rarely angry, and never hurtful." He grinned wryly. "Well, *rarely* hurtful."

A speckle of quiet laughter.

"She did better than most of us, though. Better than I did. I think it was because she believed so much in her work that it lent her a clarity of purpose that most of us lack. I don't think it's a stretch to say that, while we'll all miss her, so will the world."

Watkins bowed his head. Got some applause. Things wrapped up after that. People milled around, chatting in hushed tones. Rada got to her feet and, feeling more than a little ghoulish, approached Watkins.

"Touching speech," she said. "I think she would have liked it."

"Thanks." He smiled at her, eyebrows raising fractionally. "Were you a friend?"

"We shared mutual interests. That's what I'd like to ask you about, actually." She frowned at the sand. "This may sound strange, but does the name Pip mean anything to you?"

Watkins' face darkened like a squall. He blinked and glanced out to sea. "In the spirit of Jain, I'm going to leave before I can say anything unkind."

He turned and strode away.

"I am *so* glad I'm not down there," Simm said.

"Yeah," Rada muttered, trying not to make it look too obvious. "But you know what my humiliation revealed? That he recognized the name."

"I was too busy being incinerated with embarrassment to piece that together."

"Wish me luck. About to fling myself into the volcano."

She crossed the dry sand, grateful for the steady wind as a counter to the sun's heat. Mourners clustered around Dinah like Jupiter's moons. While Rada waited her turn, she kept her eye on Mikela Rolf, who had been approached by a tall, narrow-limbed man. Rolf looked as wary as a dog figuring how to climb a staircase occupied by an irritated cat.

The last of Dinah's moons smiled sadly and broke orbit. Rada moved in before another could take her place.

"My name's Rada Pence," she said. "I'm so sorry."

Dinah nodded, dislodging a fresh pair of tears. "How did you know her?"

"We were…colleagues."

"Colleagues." The woman nodded. "Seems like that was all she had."

"I think the fact she had so many of them speaks volumes. Bill did, too."

"I wish I could have."

Rada crinkled her eyes. "I think you said more than words."

"Oh," Simm said in her ear, "that's a good one."

Dinah smiled and dabbed at her nose with a tissue. "I appreciate that."

"Question for you." Rada took a deep breath. "This might be upsetting, but it's vitally important to something your mother was working on when she…suffered the collision. Can you tell me who Pip is?"

"Pip? Peregrine?" Within the dark circles surrounding them, Dinah's eyes blazed like flashlights. "He was my brother." She drew back her chin. "Why would you bring this up now?"

"It's complicated. It was—"

"Stop. Right now, stop what you're saying. You know what? Get the hell out of here. You don't get to do this to me! Not today."

Every eye in the place turned her way. Rada felt her cheeks glowing. "Dinah, this involves your mother's final—"

"Get *out*!" Her wrath cracked and she broke into tears, sinking halfway to her knees. People moved to her from all sides. Others glared at Rada.

"I'm sorry for your loss." Rada spun on her heel and headed for the path lining the base of the hills overlooking the beach. "Simm, why do I have the feeling I need to fly up there and strangle you?"

"Peregrine Lawson," Simm reported. "Her half-brother. Deceased. How was I supposed to tie him to 'Pip'?"

"Peregrine. Pippin. *Pip*. Like the little knight from the *Book of Good Acts*?"

"Never read it. I'm not exactly the religious type."

"Then how about for the story? Even heathens read the *BOGA*!"

"You're talking about fiction. It's not real. Why would I read about fairy tales when I can read about things that really happened?"

"Because it provides you with the common cultural background required to understand your fellow humans!" Rada bared her teeth and rubbed her eyes. "So basically, at her mother's funeral, I came up to ask her about her dead brother. It's a wonder I'm not being tied to a stake."

"I'm sorry," Simm said. "At least we've made progress, right?"

"If you can call discovering that Jain's final message was to her dead son 'progress,' then yes, we've made a shitload of progress today."

"On your six."

Reflexively, she turned. Behind her, Mikela Rolf strode through the sand. The woman lifted a palm. "What happened back there?"

"I stepped on a land mine," Rada said. "One planted by my partner." From somewhere in orbit, Simm sighed. Rada gestured back toward the ceremony. "Who were you talking to? You looked like you couldn't decide whether to run away or shoot him with a silver bullet."

Rolf laughed and rolled her eyes. "Asshole from FinnTech. No one you'd want to know. Listen, you're with the Hive, right?"

Rolf had surely ID'd Rada the same way Rada had ID'd her, but it was still nice to be asked. "That's correct."

"Awkward question time: What was she going to see you about?"

"We don't know."

The woman gritted her teeth. "I know Toman doesn't think much of us, but this is critical. We're not sure Jain Kayle's death was an accident. If not…"

"Then it could involve whatever she was coming to us about," Rada said. "I'm telling you the truth. She refused to be specific until we met in person. Your guess is as good as mine." She eyed the other woman. "Better, actually. What had she been working on leading up to the crash?"

"I can't get into that. You should contact our main office. Or better yet, have Toman call Iggi."

"I may do that." She extended her hand and shook. "If you find anything you can share, we'd appreciate it. We may be competitors, but this is a woman's life."

Mikela Rolf smiled, glanced back at the funeral, then headed for the stairs up to the street. Rada stayed where she was. The sun beat down from on high. Out to sea, the wreckage of the alien spacecraft watched over all.

"So?" Simm said. "What's next? Or are we no longer on speaking terms?"

"Jain's message, it sounded like something from when Dinah and Pip were kids. What's next is I make another run at Dinah."

"Then what are you waiting for?"

"To grow a pair of balls."

Simm laughed. "How come you can fly straight at a pirate without breaking a sweat, but a distraught person yells at you and you freeze like Enceladus?"

"Because millennia of evolution have trained my brain to fear social conflict."

"This isn't about you, is it? It's about a woman's dying wishes. What could make Dinah feel better than helping us fulfill them?"

"Sometimes, you're not a *complete* idiot," Rada said. "Even if it's only when you're trying to undo your past acts of idiocy."

She walked back in the direction of the ceremony. People in black passed her on their way to the stairs, stealing glances at her face. Rada reminded herself she didn't live within a hundred million miles of these people. Back at the gathering of chairs, Dinah was ensconced in a pocket of sympathizers. Rada did some more waiting.

When the others finally dispersed, Dinah wandered toward the surf until she was standing in it, foamy waves rushing past her ankles and shins. When the water receded, bubbles popped in the sand, fingernail-sized sand crabs scrabbling to hide themselves from the gulls.

"Dinah?" Rada stopped ten feet behind her. "I came to apologize."

The woman turned in profile. "Can't you leave me alone?"

"After this, I promise I will. But I want you to know I never meant to cause you any extra grief."

The woman's eyes became bright. "Then why would you say something like that?"

"Because your mom did. Right before the accident, your mom sent me a message about Pip. I didn't know that was your brother's nickname until I asked you."

Another wave hissed over Dinah's feet. "What did she say?"

"'Hey Pip: when the rabbit sees a shadow, where can he go?'" Rada raised her eyebrows. "Does it mean anything to you?"

"No." Dinah turned away. "But thank you for coming back."

"If you remember anything later, please let me know. I'm sorry for your loss."

Rada turned and walked across the sand. Sunlight reflected from it, dazzling her. "That's it, then, isn't it? It's over."

"Not unless you want it to be," Simm replied. "We can talk to Iggi Daniels. And I think we should talk to the woman Peregrine Lawson was with at the time of his death."

"Wife?"

"Nothing that formal. But they were together three years. You can get to know a lot about a person in three years."

"Sounds like a long shot," Rada said. "But I'd like to take it. For Dinah, too."

She trudged on, shading her eyes from the sun. She already knew she would dream of Dinah that night, the young woman who looked old, too frail to climb a step to a stage. Who had once lost a brother, and had now lost her mother as well.

The narrow-limbed man watched from afar as the woman climbed the steps from the beach.

"It's very heavy here," he said, although he was alone.

"That's Earth for you," his employer said into his ear. "Do you have something?"

"The Pence woman was here. Should I remove her?"

"Because?"

"Because she has taken a personal interest."

"That's it?"

"Interest is bad."

"I would agree it's not a *wonderful* state of affairs," the voice said. "But you can't just kill everyone who causes you trouble."

He considered this. "I think that you could."

"You know, maybe I could. For now, I would like to preserve the few remaining shreds of my humanity. But keep an eye on her, will you?"

The spindly man smiled. "With pleasure."

8

As far as Webber knew, the Locker was the only openly pirate station in the system. Despite that—or, more likely, because of it—it had the tightest security he had ever seen.

As soon as they entered Uranian space, an automated message directed them to a rendezvous point, where they were scanned and inspected by a virtual fleet of drones. After passing that, four drones detached and escorted them to a small station twenty thousand miles away from Ariel, one of the larger moons. There, they were boarded by a team of two inspectors and six armored marines, who had free rein of the ship. The team confirmed the *Fourth Down* wasn't carrying anything capable of mass destruction besides its weapons systems, then installed a bug on the computer to ensure those systems could be shut down by the Locker's command center if need be.

Finally, the *Fourth* progressed to the Locker itself. From the outside, the city resembled a large, featureless sphere in orbit around Ariel, a channeled orb of brownish ice and rock. But that sphere was just the thin shell around the small captured moon that supported the city proper.

They docked on the outside of the sphere and passed yet another round of security before being allowed into the terminal.

"Here's what I don't get," Webber said as they waited outside the elevator that would take them down to the surface. "The Locker's pirate central. Everyone knows it."

Jons sniffed. "So why don't the powers that be nuke it into a glass marble?"

"Pretty much."

"Two reasons. First, this place actually got safer when the pirates moved in. The corps used to do a lot of jockeying around Uranus." He paused to laugh at the joke that never got old. "Not only did the Locker put an end to that, but it's happy to provide services for anyone looking to do some mining, water extraction, whatever."

"For a fee."

"Of course for a fee. That's the beauty of it. Rather than two or three of the biggest dogs running everyone else out of Uranus, with the Locker, you got all kinds of crews doing business."

Webber glanced up at the timer on the elevator in time to see it tick down to sixty seconds. "So if anyone comes for the Locker, they stir up the whole swarm?"

"Not just the affiliated traders," Jons said. "Mostly, the groups at the Locker prefer to stay indie. Autonomous. But if you threaten them, they can put together a fleet big enough to take Mars."

"They couldn't take *Mars*," Lara said.

"Only because they wouldn't want it."

The elevator arrived and they filed inside, including Deen, who wasn't scheduled to ship out until tomorrow. Webber had conflicted feelings about the big man's departure. You couldn't expect him to stick around against his will. They were turning *pirate*. Some people—boring, responsible people, people with hope for the future—would have reservations about such a career change.

Yet this was the first departure of personnel the *Fourth* had seen since Webber had signed up. Losing Deen felt like breaking up the band.

Or like kicking out the bassist who didn't want to go on tour when the band was primed to break out.

The elevator halted and opened. Beyond, the buildings rose in solid blocks, occupying as much as two-thirds of the space between the ground and the ceiling. Many were the brutalist minimalism of the frontier. Balconies were common—space was at a premium—and these threatened to overgrow the street like a jungle canopy. Passing beneath them, Webber was privy to more than one conversation.

To a great deal of smells, too. If they were going to stay here for long, he was going to have to pick up a nasal filter.

Gomes moved with the surety of someone who'd been there before. The streets were too cramped for vehicles, so Webber wasn't surprised when she took them below the surface. They hopped a tube and were spat out three minutes later. Not a long trip by any measure, but when they got above ground, he stopped cold.

"I don't mean to alarm you, Captain," Vincent said. "But we seem to have stumbled into a magical forest."

"First week's all paid. After that, if you decide you want something cheaper, be my guest." Gomes flashed a grin. "Me, I wanted to be able to wake up every morning, look outside, and be reminded why I do what I do."

Trees climbed on all sides, branches drooping with round fruit Webber didn't recognize. The smallest were the size of his fist, red and blue and purple and yellow. The air smelled like apples and uncooked dough. Within the boughs, patches of leaves and branches glowed with spectral purple light.

"The hell is that?" Jons said, pointing at one of the patches.

Gomes undid her ponytail and tied it back behind her head. "Scrubbers. Bacteria."

"Yeah, but why are they glowing?"

"Why not?" She beckoned them down a paved path. "Look all you like, but do *not* touch. Unless you want to spend the next five years picking them on a chain gang."

After a few hundred feet, she diverted to a path between rows of trees that were two hundred feet tall if they were an inch. Their trunks were numbered. At 64, she stopped and smiled.

"Welcome to your new home."

For once, Webber felt free to gape.

They spent the next hour settling into their treehouse — their level of it, anyway; the trees were massive enough to support as many as ten "floors," with screens of leaves between each to provide some measure of privacy — which involved a fair measure of squabbling, as there were nine of them and only six bedrooms. Webber had zero interest in the arguments and politics and was happy to discover Jons had accepted a roommate (him) in exchange for second choice of rooms. He took one looking inward over the park with clear views through the branches.

Webber was in the act of dismantling his bags when Gomes popped in the door. "Webber. Downstairs. On the double."

"What's up?"

"I said get your ass downstairs." She withdrew.

Jons unrolled a shirt with a snap. "Looks like I made the right choice of roomies. If she murders you for forcing her hand during the attack, I'll have this joint to myself."

"I hate you." Webber grabbed the Settler of Scores from his drawer, pocketed it, found his shoes, and headed out.

At the base of the tree, Gomes waited alone. Webber put his hand in his pocket.

She rolled her eyes. "Come on with that. You think I'm mad at you?"

"Aren't you?"

"Initially? I wanted to tear your head off and jam it in a torpedo tube. After sleeping on it, however, I decided that things have turned out for the best."

He withdrew his hand from his pocket. "Because there was no way you could keep hiding repeated acts of piracy from us."

Gomes had a good laugh. "Thought I was going to have to start drugging you lot. Or swap you out for a crew of lesser scruples. Never thought you'd all go for it." She gestured down the path. "Let's walk."

He fell in beside her, glancing up at the ethereal purple splotches on the trees. "Where are we off to next? A volcano temple? A castle in the clouds?"

"To fence the goods."

He sputtered with laughter. "And you want me there? Your dauntless janitor?"

"Jons seemed like the logical option." She smiled with half her mouth. "But MacAdams insisted we take you."

This pleased him more than he would have liked to admit. They descended to the tube, popping out several stops later. Aboveground, amidst a tangle of buildings that all climbed to what was clearly the maximum allowed height, MacAdams and Taz waited on the corner.

Gomes fell in beside them. "All set?"

MacAdams nodded. "Cargo's moved and we're on sched. Site's right around the corner."

Webber scowled. "Before we strike a deal to offload our small fortune in booty, you think you ought to clue me in as to what we're doing?"

"It's a standard meet," Gomes said. "Four-and-four. I do the talking. You three stand around and look mean. I expect his side will be doing the same."

"What kind of arms are we bringing? Stunners? Toothies? Poison fingernails?"

"Nada."

"And just so we're clear, 'nada' *isn't* pirate lingo for 'the biggest guns we can stick up our asses'?"

"Nada is nothing is what we were born with."

"Check me if I'm being stupid," Webber said. "But these guys are professional criminals? Robbers, looters, strong chance they're murderers?"

"If they're any good," Taz said.

"And we're supposed to believe *they* won't be armed?"

MacAdams chuckled. "Tell me this isn't your first time in a Nude Room."

"Nude Room?" Webber glanced between them for signs of a joke. "Man, last week I was swabbing the decks. Everything we're doing is my first time."

Gomes gave him a look. "Do you think we're the first people in the history of crooks who wished they could know if they could trust their business partners? This is the Locker. They solved the trust conundrum a hundred years ago."

A block later, she stopped in front of a clean white building whose first eight floors were blank cement. They entered a white reception room. Webber sat while Gomes transferred her paperwork from her device to the receptionist's.

After processing it, the young man behind the desk smiled. "Right through that door, Ms. Gomes."

A door slid open in the wall. She thanked him. Webber and the others followed her into a short hallway not unlike an airlock. The other side opened into another white room with benches and cubbies. Before the door was done closing, the other three had seated themselves and begun to strip.

Such things weren't wholly out of place on a spaceship, but just in case they were messing with him, he waited until Gomes had peeled her top off before he started undressing. As the others finished, they went to a cubby and deposited their clothes inside. The cubbies sealed with a hiss. A second hiss announced their contents had been sucked away deeper inside the building. Naked, Gomes glanced at him, eyes trailing down his body, then gestured to the door in the far wall.

The next few minutes of his life involved navigating a labyrinth of scans. Once the machines decided he was completely unarmed of weapons and chemicals, and that his handful of mods and implants weren't housing anything aggressive, he was allowed into a room resembling the one they'd stripped down in. Here, the cubbies held white jumpsuits and slippers. The team dressed.

They exited into another reception area and were greeted by a smiling employee. "Are you ready, Ms. Gomes? Or do you need another minute to discuss matters with your people?"

"Let's go," Gomes said. "As I was just reminded, I'm not getting any younger."

The woman chuckled and pointed them down the hallway. "It will be the door on your left."

Gomes padded down the hall, stopped at the door, gave them a final look, and entered.

Inside, a man stood from a table. Three more men were behind him, backs to the wall. All were dressed in the same uniform white.

"Glad to finally meet you in person, Captain Gomes," the man at the table said. Webber couldn't place his accent. He smiled, eyes crinkling. "Perhaps one day such measures won't be necessary."

"I look forward to that, Captain Ikita." Gomes swung out a chair. "I suppose it all depends on how things go today, doesn't it?"

He smiled tightly. "I am not in the habit of attending a Cleaner in order to *not* make a deal."

"One-point-two, then."

"Was that our agreement?"

"On delivery of goods matching Nevedia's manifest." She scooted forward. "We've got the goods on site. The Cleaners have already inspected them to confirm."

"So I was told." Ikita tapped the tips of his thumbs together. "Since reaching our agreement, however, my buyer on Jupiter has decided that perhaps these meds are not worth as much as he first proposed."

"That sounds like your problem."

"It is a problem for us both. If my profit on the items is so minimal, it is hardly worth the bother to purchase them from you. You see?"

"Why don't we quit with the bread and get to the butter?"

He narrowed one eye. "An even million."

Gomes let out a long sigh, stood, and turned to the others. "Let's go."

Ikita rose halfway from his chair. "Captain, walking out is no way to reach a deal."

She snorted. "Neither is trying to job me down to a mil."

"And how much of that is raw profit? Half? I have run ships like yours, Captain Gomes, and I know the costs. Your expenses are the lowest in the chain."

"Mine aren't as low as you think. I had to take on unanticipated crew."

He lowered himself to his seat. "Crew is a drop in the bucket."

"Not this crew. They each pull a percentage."

"A *percentage*?" Ikita spread his arms, planted his palms on the table, and leaned forward. "Why would you pay them a percentage?"

"Does that contravene some unwritten Law of the Inky Void?"

"The only law against it is common sense. Why pay points when you can walk into any bar on this rock, announce you're paying 3K for a cruise, and walk out with a full team?"

"Because I don't want crewmen worth 3K." She stared into his eyes. "I want people worth a percentage."

He leaned back, tucking down the corners of his mouth. "As they say, your business, your party. Then again, offering a percentage was your decision. I do not see why that should compel me to pay more than I am comfortable. Otherwise, I am squeezed on both ends, you see?"

"Oh, quit whining," Webber blurted.

Every eye in the room turned his way. Ikita's eyebrows drew together. He chuckled, confused. "I am sorry, but did you say *whining*? In the manner of a dog?"

"No." His face burned. "Could be a little kid."

From the back wall, the three men in white jumpsuits pushed forward, moving to sweep around the table. MacAdams and Taz stepped to either side of Webber. MacAdams looked amused; Taz looked pissed. Gomes stood up fast enough that her chair squeaked.

Ikita held up a hand. His jaw was tight, but his anger had receded from his eyes—for the moment.

He turned on Webber. "For a man like you to say such a thing to a man like me, there must be a great truth shouting from your heart. Insisting you speak no matter how great the risk. Am I correct?"

"I sure hope so," Webber said.

The man laughed. "Then speak."

"It's just like you said: a matter of risk. In this equation, we're the only ones absorbing any of it. If someone gets hurt in the attack, it's us. Afterward, if Nevedia comes after someone, it's us. We're on the hook coming and going. But you? All *you* have to do is load some shit on a ship and fly it off to meet your buyer."

"You make it sound very simple."

"I'm sure there's a world of shit I'm not privy to," Webber said. "No pun intended. But I'm also sure those meds are worth cash money. Otherwise, we wouldn't have had to put our lives out there to get them."

"You are correct," Ikita said. "There *is* a world of shit of which you know nothing. Not only that, but you are disrespectful."

"It'll probably get me killed some day. I can only hope it isn't right now."

Cracks manifested in the man's stony expression. "It helps that you have raised a fair point. Doubly so because, in doing so, you expose yourself to yet more risk. Such an act demands respect."

Webber's heart began to slow. "When you're born with nothing, eating risk is the only way to get somewhere in life, right?"

Ikita inclined his head, sat, and shifted his gaze to Gomes. "If I have not misidentified the captain here, where do you stand, madame?"

"Though my bosun is shipping for a whipping, I believe he has a point." Gomes folded her arms on the table. "And I am sure that someone will be willing to pay you full price for those meds. If they won't, people start dying. It's Jupiter."

Ikita's mouth showed signs of a smirk. "Why do I get the impression I am about to be told to fuck myself?"

"Because you're canny. A fellow worth knowing. Or I wouldn't be here." Gomes lifted her brows. "And that is why, despite feeling insulted that you're trying to dicker me down on a price we'd already agreed to, I will accept 1.15."

He tapped his lower lip. "Perhaps you are worth knowing, too. I accept." He glanced at Webber. "Your first drink tonight, make it a toast to me, yes?"

Webber saluted. "No doubt."

Outside, back in his own clothes and shoes, he waited with MacAdams and Taz while Gomes made calls to finalize the transfer of the meds. Taz produced a straight, finger-sized pipe and inhaled green clouds of sweet-smelling vapor. She prowled the front of the plain white building, glaring down any pedestrian who came too near.

Whatever was eating her, MacAdams didn't look too concerned. He stood beside Webber, arms folded. "Who are you?"

"Mazzy Webber. Maintenance and custodial. What do you mean?"

"I know. Webber, the simple janitor. Who is suddenly unionizing his pirate crew and then busting the balls of one of the nastiest gangsters on the Locker."

Webber craned his head toward the building. "Who, Ikita? He looked like somebody's tailor."

"A tailor who's got more bodies under him than the Tri-Bay Bridge."

"If he's so big and bad, what's he doing negotiating with nobodies like us?"

MacAdams shrugged the hillocks that were his shoulders. "Maybe he sees an opportunity to add Gomes to his roster. Maybe he's tight on cash and needs a quick play. All I know is he was there in that room with us."

Webber considered this. "Gomes didn't seem too concerned about him being apt to take me down."

"Maybe she just doesn't care about you." He chuckled, frowning. "Or maybe she wanted to see how well you handled yourself. And that's what I'm asking: where'd you come from?"

"Like I said, the supply closet. Everyone has to start somewhere."

"Whatever you say."

"Hey, as long as we're clearing up mysteries, why were you trying to pulverize that little guy on Beagle?"

"Oh, the night we first met?" MacAdams laughed. "Wasn't nothing. The runt cheated us at cards."

"In that case, I'm sorry I helped him out."

"Water under the bridge. Listen, tonight we're meeting at the Hook and Claw. Hashing out the next hit."

Webber glanced up. "Another one? We just finished up the last one."

"Then what better time to start planning the next?" MacAdams clapped him on the shoulder, knocking him forward. "Eight o'clock. See you there."

He shoved off, gathering Taz in his wake. Aromatic vapor spiraled behind her. Webber tipped back his head to take in the buildings, the artificial sky just three hundred feet above him. He was wheeling and dealing under the roof of one of the freest places in the system. He was about to get more cash dumped in his account than he'd made in the last year. Maybe there was more to life than he'd let himself believe.

"You angling for a promotion?" Gomes walked up on him, stowing her device in her pocket. "Or a keelhauling?"

He shook his head. "MacAdams just clued me in. Had no idea Ikita was such a big knife."

"You're lucky I'm high on a million bucks. Otherwise I'd boot you out on your ass."

"Sometimes ignorance is the best advantage you've got, right? If I'd been smart enough to know better, we walk out of there with less."

She squinted at him. "Or we walk out into a mess of heavily armed gangsters. *Or* we walk out with the exact same 1.15, because this is my show and I'm not about to roll over."

Webber bobbed his head. "I got you."

"Do you? You're an asset I hadn't counted on, but you're proving to be an even bigger liability. Quit barging in on my scene. Watch and learn. Know your place. You got input? I'm all ears. But you provide that input in the appropriate ways at the appropriate time. Otherwise? You think you know better? Go get your own damn ship."

"I'm sorry, Captain. This is all new to me. From now on, I'll be more mindful of the chain of command."

"So you *do* know the concept. Next time it happens, you're back on mop duty. Got it?"

"Got it," he said. "But he *was* whining."

Gomes laughed, shaking her head. "Get out of here before I come to my senses."

He ducked his head and walked off. Away from the park, the air had the stale, recycled smell of all closed environments, but at that moment, it tasted like it had been pumped in fresh from Fiji.

He had a few hours until the meet at the Hook and Claw, so he figured he'd do some exploring, get a feel for the place. Captured moon it might be, but it was also tiny, small enough to handle artificial gravity. He figured he could see a decent slice of it before his appointment.

He stopped at a stall for a packet of fried starch. Feeling rich, he splurged on a bowl of curry made from local fruit. He took his meal down a side street and sat on a vacant stoop. The curry tasted like strawberries and half-cooked bread.

"New in town?" A man stood over him, dressed in a long, thin coat and a short-brimmed hat.

"This your apartment?" Webber stood, crumpling the wrappers of his meal. "Was just looking for a place to sit while I ate."

"More of a rhetorical question. I know exactly who you are, Webber." The man pulled his hand halfway from his pocket, revealing the dull black of a pistol. "Care to come with me?"

9

As it turned out, the ex-girlfriend hadn't moved since the breakup. She lived in Neucali, an old Martian warren near the water supply of the northern icecap. At the moment, Mars was on the opposite side of the sun from Earth. About as long as Inner trips got. After Simm confirmed the autopilot's course, there wasn't much to do besides catch up on correspondence and rake over what they'd gathered to date. She Needled Toman about their progress and to request he reach out to Iggi Daniels. Simm, as usual, occupied himself with the net, gathering up all traces of Peregrine Lawson and compiling them into one master file.

Toman replied within an hour, a prerecorded video. He congratulated her on cracking the first part of Jain Kayle's message and let her know he'd drop a line to Iggi, but didn't expect his rival to start spilling secrets.

Simm's automated search software hadn't turned up anything interesting in the Pip File, but with nothing better to do, Rada searched it by hand, combing through years-old message board posts about video games and genealogy. She didn't have any more luck than Simm's bots, but she came away with a better sense of the dead man: pleasant, though occasionally acerbic, and wishful for something more.

Halfway to Mars, coasting at cruising speed, Simm said he was picking up engine signals on the long-distance scanners. They kept their eyes sharp, but nothing came of it.

Around the time they began to brake, a video came in from Iggi Daniels. She wasn't much older than Toman. Like him, she had no interest in a traditional appearance. Blue hair done up in a wing. Dark eyeliner. A single point of light traced the black lines, making it appear as if each eye were being orbited by a tiny, glimmering comet. Rada thought it must be very nice to be so wealthy and successful that anyone who judged you would be accused of being jealous.

Iggi's message was prerecorded, too. "Hey all. What with the whole rivals thing, I can't get too deep in the guttyworks. Besides, we're all over this too. I can tell you this much: Jain's recent assignment involved a long, hard look at what's outside the Outer. Well-trodden ground, I know. But sometimes, the only way to break a case is to confront it with a fresh set of eyes."

She smiled into the camera and lifted her brows. "Dunno if that's enough to help, but I hope it does. She was a big part of the team. Appreciate the interest. Iggi out."

The message ended. Rada unbuckled and floated to the galley. "That doesn't do much. Besides reinforce our assumptions."

"Yeah," Simm said. "Nice of her to get back to us, though."

A day later, Mars grew on the screen, a dirty orange ball. The *Tine* was capable of atmospheric flight, but it was cheaper to dock in orbit and take a shuttle down to the surface. To stay on Toman's good side, Rada made the arrangements. A few hours later, the shuttle landed at Neucali Station. Outside the dome, wind whisked the powdery dust into scouring whirlwinds.

They descended to the warren. The tunnels were cramped and smelled like earth and fungus. Rada rented an electric two-seater, called ahead to Xixi the ex-girlfriend, and pedaled down the hallways. Things were very quiet except when she flashed by an intersection opening to a public cavern; then, voices and laughter rang loud.

Xixi lived in a hole a few bends of the tunnel from one of these caverns. She made Rada and Simm ID themselves to her door scanner before allowing them inside.

She wasn't as old as Rada had expected. 27, 28. The neutral resignation in her face looked much older. She offered them a seat on the dusty-smelling couch.

"So," Rada said.

Xixi stared. "Ask what you came to ask. It's been years. I'm not a flower. Down here, we endure."

"We're trying to decipher something Peregrine's mother said before her accident. It could be very important."

"Or it could be nonsense," Simm said.

Rada scowled. "Either way, it would be nice to understand her final recorded words. If only to know that there is no understanding them."

The woman closed her eyes. "Talk or don't. It's all the same."

Rada repeated Jain Kayle's message about the rabbit, then lowered her gaze to the plain stone floor. "Ring any bells?"

"No. You couldn't have asked me through the net?"

"Please, just take a minute to think about it. He lived in the warrens with you. Some Earthers call *you* guys rabbits. Does this bring back anything at all?"

"Let me think." Xixi nodded, gazing at nothing. Ten seconds drabbled by. Finally, she shook her head. "Down here, you get a lot of talk about rabbits. But I don't remember anything related to that phrase."

Rada sighed. "I see."

Simm tapped his knee. "Did you call him Pip, too?"

"Sure," Xixi said. "He hated his real name."

Rada glanced at Simm. "What does this tell us?"

"Nothing, probably." He folded his hands. "Curious if the message could have originated with anyone else."

Xixi shrugged. "I got friends who knew him. You might check with them."

"That would be great," Rada said. "Before we go, could you tell us about him? Anything could help."

"He wasn't the kind of guy who would knock you out of orbit. You had to spend some time with him before you started to see what was special. He was sturdy. Loyal. Hard-working. Every extra bit he made, he sent it off to care for his sister. For Dinah."

"Sounds like a sweet guy."

Xixi laughed wryly. "Sure. If you were his sister."

Rada glanced at Simm. "Did you think he was…too generous?"

"She's sick. Needs help. I get it. But I wanted a family too, you know? And I couldn't bring myself to start one until we'd paid off this hole. At least enough to know we wouldn't starve."

"Was that what broke you up?" Simm said.

Rada gaped. "Simm!"

Xixi waved a hand. "It's a fair question. There was more to it. He got angry sometimes. So did I. Dinah wasn't the only reason we split. But it sure didn't help."

"Well," Simm said. "I'm sorry."

"Maybe it's for the best. Thanks to her, we learned we weren't right for each other before we made the mistake of dragging kids into the mix." The woman shook her head. "You ask me, the rabbit business is probably something Jain and Pip joked about when he was little. Once he got older, they weren't on good terms. Her last message was probably a reminder to herself that it wasn't always like that."

Rada's stomach sank. "Do you know why their relationship was strained?"

"He thought she worked too hard when she should have been caring for Dinah. Resented having to shoulder the load himself."

"I see." Rada couldn't bring herself to make eye contact. "Well, the people who knew him. Would you mind drawing up a list?"

The woman nodded, got her device from the coffee table, and started tapping its cracked screen. A minute later, she looked up sharply. "Look, this is a long shot."

Rada leaned forward. "Lately, that's the only kind of shot we've had."

"Well, this part of the warren, it's pretty close to the surface. But there's another place. Way down deep. We're supposed to go there if there's ever an attack or an asteroid or anything that could compromise the upper level."

"The kind of place a rabbit would hide if it saw a hawk."

"Renters have communal shelters. But everyone who owns a hole gets a cabin of their own." Xixi got up and shuffled to a dresser. "Got the key around here somewhere."

"Do you think there might be something there?" Simm said. "Something Jain left?"

"I don't know. After we moved in, I haven't been to it since."

After a detailed search, she located the key — a small magnet set to the same frequency as the lock — and transferred the list of Pip's friends to Rada's device. At the door, Rada thanked her, smiling wanly. Xixi nodded, expressionless, and closed the door.

They started off to the elevator to the shelters. Simm glanced back down the tunnel. "Well, that was depressing."

"But we've got something. That's worth every moment, isn't it?"

"No doubt."

She felt lighter than she had in days, and it wasn't just the undemanding Martian gravity. As they navigated the tunnels with the aid of her device, moving deeper and deeper into the warren, she told herself that there was a good chance the shelter was nothing more than coincidence. Even if there was an answer in it, like Xixi had said, it would probably turn out to be nothing more than Jain reminding herself of better days.

There was hope, though. It sounded like Jain Kayle had been devoted to her work. To the point of alienating her own kids. Tragic, to be sure. But it gave Rada the idea that Jain would not allow her life's work to be lost.

The tunnels grew dim, quieter yet. Even when they opened on large caverns, the spaces were subdued, occupied by worn-looking people drinking from bottles and fiddling with their devices. Rada hurried along.

Two turns later, Simm slowed, gazing behind them. He murmured, "I think we're being followed."

"By who?"

"Not sure. Do you want me to go ask?"

Simm being Simm, she took a second to ensure he was being sarcastic. She forced herself not to look back. "Have we committed any crimes since getting here?"

"To the contrary, we've been model visitors."

"Then we can reasonably assume that crimes are about to be done to us." She detached the button-sized camera from her device, breathed on its back to activate its adhesive, and thumbed it to the wall. "Let's get a look, shall we?"

Simm bit his lip. "Why don't we call the cops?"

"Because they won't get here in time. But if it makes you feel better, go ahead."

"*That* sure doesn't make me feel better," he mumbled, punching something into his device. "How about we hurry?"

"I don't think there's any getting out of this," she said. "Not when it's their turf. But if you've got ideas, I've got ears."

They turned another corner. At their current pace, Rada's device estimated they were less than three minutes from the elevator, but the system was so old it wouldn't allow her to summon it to be ready on their arrival.

Her video feed flashed, insistent. She switched over. The wall-mounted camera showed four figures striding down the tunnel, faces concealed by the red-orange bandanas favored by Martians whenever there was a chance they'd be exposed to the planet's powdery dust. She thought they all had male builds. One carried a pipe or a club. The others appeared unarmed, but that didn't mean much. They swept past the camera in perfect silence and turned down the same corner Rada and Simm had taken seconds before.

"Too late," she said. "Hope you're wearing your scrapping shoes."

Simm turned around and glared down the hallway. It was dim and slightly curved. "This is outrageous. What do they want with us?"

"They look like hoods—or someone who wants us to think they're hoods."

"Armed?"

"It's a safe bet."

They planted themselves in the tight hall, spaced three feet apart. The four men rounded the corner. Eyes glittered above the bandanas. Two of the men flicked out batons, the heavy synthetics clicking into place.

One of them took a step forward. A beard bristled beneath his orange bandana. "Let's not make this hard."

"Agreed," Rada said. "In my pocket, there's a card. On the card, I've got four hundred and change. Here's my proposal: I give you the card, you turn around and walk away."

"You can't just give him your card," Simm said. "What'd he do to deserve it?"

The man narrowed his eyes. Rada rolled hers. "Simm, the sooner this is over, the sooner we can resume the rabbit hunt."

Simm folded his arms at the hoods' leader. "In that case, I insist you take the card."

"Four hundred," the man said.

Rada nodded. "And change."

"Pretty good haul for fifteen minutes of work," Simm said.

The man turned to his crew. "What do you think?"

To his left, a short man lifted his nose to the air and sniffed. "Hey. Hey, Pads. You smell that?"

"What've you got?"

The short man inhaled deeply. "Smells like money."

The leader frowned, sniffed. "Know what? I think you're right." He turned to Rada. "We'll take all of it. Cards. Devices. Everything you got."

"You're one shitty fortuneteller," Rada said. "And I'm rescinding my offer. Here's my new one: walk away with nothing."

"Okay," the bearded man said. "Let's show them how we do in Neucali."

His crew advanced like they'd choreographed it. Rada's heart shrank. She lowered her stance and raised her hands. The bearded man jerked his chin at the short man, who shuffled toward Rada. The other three, including both of the guys with batons, headed for Simm.

Sadly for them, they would have been better off coming at him unarmed. Simm was every bit as nerdy for Rainese fighting as he was for his space empire simulation games.

A man came at him, swinging the baton down at a three-quarter angle. Simm shifted toward it and lazily whipped his forearms at the incoming weapon, keeping his arms so loose that he seemed to be trying to throw his fingertips across the room. The baton cracked into his arms a short ways above the elbow. He dropped his left palm, grabbing the arrested baton, and swung a right backfist at the man's face.

The punch landed with a thud. The man groaned. Something small and white tumbled through the air and clattered on the stone floor.

Then Rada stopped paying attention, because the little dude was coming at her, and he suddenly looked very serious.

He shuffled, feinted, and threw a left jab at her jaw. Rada sidestepped stiffly. She had practiced just enough with Simm to recognize the short man had some training. She was either going to have to hang on until Simm finished with the others, or put the guy down before his advantage in skill won out.

He jabbed again. She slapped at his fist, knocking it to the side of her head. He threw a right, stepping into the punch; she pulled the same trick, deflecting it with her right hand. As soon as she did so, opening a hole in her guard, he drove a left hook into her gut.

The wind left her in a whoosh. Beside her in the dim tunnel, a baton struck bone with a distinctive crack. The yelp that followed was not Simm's. Two men fell back and Simm followed them in.

The short man hit her a second time. Her stomach was clenched, but it still hurt. She dropped, gasping for air, unable to get more than a tiny swallow past her uncooperative throat.

Her opponent was wearing shorts. His shins were almost white, speckled with dark hairs. As he drew back his right leg to kick her in the head, she clamped her teeth down on his left calf.

He shrieked, jerked, and fell. Rada tasted warm iron. She released her jaw, spitting blood, and swayed to her feet. The short man clenched his leg and swore. Rada's diaphragm had finally quit squeezing her and she took deep gulps of air. Her opponent scrabbled away, finding his feet.

Behind him, Simm knocked his last foe to the ground, spun, and charged the short man. He jabbed the hood in the kidney. The man yelled and staggered. Simm grabbed his wrist and bent up his arm, forcing the man to point his face at the ground.

Simm shoved his baton across the man's elbow. "Who do you work for?"

"Pads," the man said. "Guy who's snoring behind you."

Simm bore down harder. *Who?*

"Sonny Marbles!" the short man gasped.

Rada pulled the name up on her pad. "He's local. Nobody chased us here, if that's what you're thinking."

"That's a relief." Simm released the man, then struck him in the gut, crumpling him. "Now where are those damn cops?"

It was another ten minutes before the authorities rolled in on their closed-roofed cart.

They cuffed the thugs who were conscious and lifted those who weren't into the cart's back. A second vehicle carried Rada and Simm down to the station, which was blindingly bright after the dark tunnel. The cop who took their statement was overweight and had a habit of holding his elbows straight out to the side as if he were trying to balance plates on them.

"You said you're from the Hive," he said.

Rada nodded. "That's right."

"And that you were on your way to the Sanctuary."

"That's right."

"Problem," the cop said. "Only residents of Neucali are allowed in the Sanctuary."

"We have a resident's permission," Rada said. "Xixi Wells. Check with her."

"Think I'll do that." He reached for his device, called up Xixi, held a brief conversation, then clicked off and eyed Rada. "Why do you want to go to the Sanctuary?"

"We think one of your former residents may have left something in his shelter. Something his mom was asking for."

He frowned. "And if I call Ms. Wells back, she'll confirm this?"

"The resident in question is her ex-boyfriend."

"This sounds about a hundred times more convoluted than I'm obliged to care about." The man breathed out, deflating. "Officer Barres will escort you down. For your safety."

"What about the hoods?" Simm said. "Will you need us for the trial?"

"Trial?" The cop hooted. "You already beat them to hell and gone. You think we're gonna waste space boarding those idiots?"

Simm frowned. Officer Barres showed them out, loaded them into a cart, and brought them to the elevators down to the Sanctuary. At the bottom, an open airlock fed them into blank tunnels gritty with dust. He led them to Xixi's auxiliary apartment and Rada keyed open the lock.

The shelter consisted of three rooms: a bedroom, a bathroom, and a combined kitchenette/lounge. Sheets and linens waited in vacuum-sealed bags. So did the food. Rada made a quick sweep, turning up nothing else, then reconvened in the lounge with Simm.

She brushed dust from her pants. "See anything?"

"Nope."

"Check the computer."

"That was the first place I looked."

"Well, look again."

He rolled his eyes, stooped over the terminal, and swept his fingers across the controls. A minute later, he stood up, shaking his head. "Nothing but an operating system. Mailer hasn't sent a single message."

"That can't be true. It has to be here."

"No, it doesn't. This shelter, the warren, it's just a coincidence. Doesn't have anything to do with Jain Kayle's message."

"I mean that it has to be here." Rada lowered herself to a chair. "Because if it isn't, I don't know where else to look."

She made a second pass, then a third, then Officer Barnes informed her their time was up. She wanted to argue, but there was no point.

They spent two more days in Neucali interviewing Peregrine's friends. This turned up nothing of obvious interest, but Simm filed away the conversations anyway. With no other leads, they hopped a shuttle back to orbit, then launched the *Tine*.

"Do we have anything left at all?" Rada said once they were underway.

"I think we've exhausted our end of things. According to Toman, they haven't turned up anything with regards to the *Piper*, either. I'm thinking that's a dead end."

"Then we're done, aren't we?" She leaned back, gazing at the stars on the screen. "Nothing else to do but file it away, leave a few spiders on the net to be watchful for references, and see what other jobs Toman has for us."

"I hate this," Simm said. "There is nothing worse than feeling like the answer's slipped through your fingers."

"It's only a dead end for now." The words were far more optimistic than she felt. "Maybe we can pass it off to someone smarter at the Hive and they'll bring it back to life."

Simm frowned, staring at the screen as well. "We should turn this off. All those stars make me believe anything is possible if you hunt hard enough."

"What would you rather look at?"

"A big black box," he said. "That would be closer to the truth."

She snorted. "You're cute when you pout."

He smiled, but a distracted look had entered his eye. He bent over his device and resumed work. Dead tired, Rada closed her eyes and napped. She didn't wake until hours later, when the ship quit accelerating and she began to float up from her reclined chair.

The cabin was dark except the instrument lights and the glow of Simm's device. He was still hunched over it, tapping and scrolling. Seeing her stir, he blinked, returning to the physical world. An odd grin took control of his mouth.

"Oh no," she said. "You have a new idea."

He cleared his throat. "I think we've been going about this all wrong. Why tear around the system chasing down friends and relatives for answers? Why not just find Pip Lawson?"

"So your grand idea is we retire as bug-hunters and start hunting ghosts instead."

"You are making the worst assumption of them all: that what we understand to be true is actually true."

Rada raised the back of her chair to get a better look at him. "What have you got?"

"A whopper of a question," Simm said. "What if Pip isn't really dead?"

10

Webber slowly raised his hands. "Hey, there's no need for this. I thought Ikita and I were cool."

The gunman gawked in equal parts outrage and scorn. "Webber, you idiot. Don't tell me you did something to piss off Ikita, too."

"What would you care?"

"Because it would be significantly more difficult to collect our money if he puts you in cement shoes and flings you into Uranus' gravity well."

Webber lowered his hands. "You're with collections. You're here for money."

"Aren't we all?"

"Something wrong with mail?"

The man stared at him. "We tried that. You ignored them."

"That's because I didn't have any money."

"You think I don't know that?" The man gestured down the street. "Time to figure out some other way to settle your debt."

"That won't be a problem," Webber said. "I just got paid. I mean ten minutes ago. Right before you pulled a gun on me."

The man located an expression even less impressed than his previous one. "How convenient."

"It really is, because I feel like it's about to save me from a broken leg. Which would have been a counterproductive move, by the way. How am I supposed to pay you back when you add a hospital bill to my debt?"

The gunman sighed. "If this is a put-on, it's not going to make any difference."

"What's your goal here? To extract money? Or a pound of flesh?"

"Cash. Unlike flesh, it never goes bad." He gestured down the street. "Let's find somewhere quiet, shall we?"

"Why bother?" Webber said. "This is the Locker. If you rob me in the street, someone will probably offer you a job."

The gunman brought him two blocks to a plain apartment building. The collections agent swiped his key and tromped up the stairs to a third floor apartment that sported a few chairs, two tables, two devices, and a whole lot of nothing. Webber sat at a table and logged into his account.

His balance showed a smidge under two hundred. Enough to get by for a couple weeks in most places, so long as you had a place to stay. He was used to being financially embarrassed, however, and under normal circumstances, the numbers wouldn't have fazed him.

"Funny story," he said. "It isn't here."

The gunman leaned in for a look. "That isn't enough to pay the interest on your interest."

"My captain hasn't had time to make the transfer. Know what, she probably hasn't finished tallying expenses. I'm working for a percent of net."

He meant this to be impressive, but the agent didn't bat an eye. "Or you are a weasel in a human body. Know what farmers do with weasels?"

"Feed them cookies?" Webber spread his hands. "Hey, I'm as mad as you are. I should be out getting drunk and convincing women I'm rich, not sitting around a hovel having a gun pointed at me by somebody who wants to take all my money."

"This isn't a hovel."

"Call my captain. Kiri Gomes. She'll confirm everything I've told you."

The man gritted his teeth, paged through Webber's contacts, and transferred the number to his device. Staring daggers, he called up Gomes, setting the device on speaker.

"This better be an emergency," she said.

The gunman leaned over it. "That all depends on how much you like Mazzy Webber."

"My ex-janitor?" Gomes laughed into the camera. "He can't seem to keep himself out of trouble, can he?"

"Much to my disappointment. My name is Winslowe. I'm with Universal Debt Services. I'm here with Mr. Webber right now. I'm calling to confirm that he is indeed to be the recipient of a pending payment."

Gomes leaned forward, staring into his eyes. "Are you intending to hurt him?"

Winslowe looked aghast. "Well, not if he's got our money!"

"He doesn't. But he's telling the truth. Webber?"

Webber leaned into view. "Yes, Captain?"

"Just ensuring your head and your body are still attached. Will 20K cover your present difficulties?"

He smiled tightly; now Winslowe would know exactly how much he could take. He supposed it was all UDS' anyway. "That'll do just fine."

"Wonderful. We'll handle the rest once I've nailed down final expenses. Anything else, Mr. Winslowe?"

The company man waved at the screen. "Thanks for your time, ma'am." He clicked off, holding his smile until the connection died. Then he snapped his eyes to Webber, snarling. "You better pray the transfer comes through soon. You're cutting into my evening, dick."

"Then let's make the most of our time together," Webber said. "Want to play *BombZone*?"

Winslowe scowled. A half hour later, with his balance unchanged, Webber called his bank. They informed him a transfer was pending but could take a while longer to confirm. Winslowe sighed, got out his device, and sent Webber a friend request.

Two hours and seventeen games of *BombZone* later, the transfer cleared. Webber stared at the numbers as if they were revealing the secrets of the universe to him. "How's 10K sound?"

Winslowe stared him down. "Like you need to respect the man who just kicked your ass up and down the sector."

"15K," he said. Winslowe didn't budge. Webber sat back and folded his arms. "Eighteen. You saw what I'm working with. You want anything more, and you're going to have to make me another loan."

"Eighteen will be just fine, Mr. Webber."

Webber set up the transfer, contemplated adding the code that indicated it had been made under duress, then sent it through.

Winslowe checked his device, stood, and put his hand on Webber's shoulder. "Don't make me see you again, okay? Not unless it's to stage a rematch."

"You'll need more practice."

Outside, the artificial light had faded, indicating the coming of night. Webber pulled up directions to the Hook and Claw and jogged toward the nearest tube station. He felt…he didn't even know what he felt. It didn't bother him that Winslowe had extracted eighteen grand from his wallet; Webber owed what he owed, and anyway, Gomes' payment hadn't lasted long enough to feel real.

Besides, he still had two Gs. Technically, that was also UDS', but that could wait for another day. Right now, for the first time in his adult life, he wasn't broke. And the craziest part of all? Gomes still owed him more. A small fortune. Granted, that small fortune would go toward paying the actual fortune he owed UDS—but he'd been expecting to labor under its weight for the rest of his life.

If Gomes was serious about their new occupation, however, and they were able to pull off three hauls a year, he could pay off his debt within five, six years. Double that pace, striking a new ship every other month, and he'd be down to three years. If they could pull a hit every month—he had no idea if this was plausible, but he just wanted to think about it, to rest the possibility in the bed of his mind—and he'd be free in a little over a year.

And after that? He'd be rich.

He didn't so much walk to the Hook and Claw as float there. His head didn't snap back to reality until he stepped inside. It was dark and crowded, people standing around tables stacked with bottles and glasses, the space between their heads and the ceiling swirling with a Venusian atmosphere of vapors. He stepped to the side of the entry, scanning the patronage. A laugh boomed through the crowd, hard but not unfriendly. He traced it to MacAdams and threaded his way to their table.

As he approached, MacAdams glanced up, assessing the threat, then registered it was him. "You're late."

Webber nodded. "Next round's on me."

"You're right on time," the big man smirked. "Order up and get over here. We got a lot to discuss. Like whose barge is providing our next paycheck."

~

The basics of piracy—"crackin' tubs," as MacAdams called it—was very simple. Most drones were automated, and as sophisticated as that automation was, it meant predictability. Exploitability. Plus, after the drone-initiated nuking of the *Entonces* and the *Frequent Flyer*, two civilian cruise vessels that had drifted within the proximity of an unmanned cargo ship, system-wide laws had been passed to restrict how aggressive drones could be toward nearby ships. As with all such laws, enforcing them should have been a challenge, but they were propped up by widespread distrust of corporations, along with cash-strapped governments happy for the excuse to appropriate any company that stepped out of line. Anyway, avoiding such problems was what the Lanes were for.

The point was, through careful use of spoofing, camouflage, and jamming, you could typically get close enough to a drone to blind its sensors or damage its engines. Once either of those systems was compromised, it was game over. All you had to do was circle your wounded prey, pecking away at it until it was defenseless.

Externally, anyway. A sprinkling of ships had internal defenses as well, however, and since hulls were hardened against radiation of all kinds, the only way to disable the inner defenses was to go inside.

That's where the marines came in. And Webber had just been recruited.

He got a gym membership. The yearly plan was much cheaper, but as he wasn't yet ready to trust his recent financial promotion, he stuck with the monthly. In the mornings, he went there to work out, building up his strength and endurance for his new role.

In the afternoons, he logged time in the sims, practicing breaches one after another—both airlock-standard, and intrusions through holes blown in the hull. He mixed in some combat versus automated defense systems and a bevy of emergency scenarios. He trained on everything from skiffs to the whaleships capable of hauling a small mountain of ore. The sims were right on the cusp of life-real. Miles beyond any video game he'd ever played. When he asked, MacAdams informed him they were military-grade, straight from Earth. Taz opined that, rather than being stolen, they'd been provided to the Locker in exchange for discouraging the piracy of certain outfits and encouraging attacks on others.

In the evenings, Webber went out. He didn't spend like the drunken sailor he was. Kept it modest, restricting himself to a budget that allotted the vast majority of what he had to debt payments.

Even so, it was incredible to be able to buy what he liked without worrying about every last cent. It felt like everything he'd done in life to date —all the failures, setbacks, and screw-ups—these weren't actually mistakes. Instead, they had been part of the necessary process to lead him to this time and place. The only thing that had felt comparable was the first time time he'd shipped out with the *Fourth Down*.

Deen made preparations to depart. There was a nice farewell party. Gomes and Vincent got a little teary. Deen wished them all well, then got so drunk he fell asleep in the bar, smiling into a puddle of beer.

A week into their stay on the Locker, Webber stumbled into the treehouse around midnight. Usual stuff. Had to be up in time to hit the gym. Unusually, Jons was in, watching his device. They exchanged hellos.

Webber brushed his teeth and flung himself into his bunk. "Figured you'd be out on the town."

"I like to pull myself off the rotation now and then," Jons said. "Makes getting back to the front lines all the better."

"Nothing can be fun when you do it every day, right?"

"Precisely." He paused his device. "What are you up to tomorrow?"

"The usual," Webber said. "Training. Gym. Then, just when it feels like my body's about to melt, go train my brain instead."

"Gyms and sims. Man, you're taking off like a rocket, aren't you? Reminds me of that one book. About the orphan kid who goes on to become pants-droppingly wealthy."

Webber frowned at the ceiling. "*Oliver Twist*?"

"What? No, man. I'm talking about the one with the giant lizards."

"*Johnny Tapdance Versus the Godzilla Twins*."

Jons grinned and nodded. "That's the one!"

Webber laughed. "If you're in tonight, does that mean you're heading back out tomorrow?"

"You got a better idea?"

"Nope. Thought I'd tag along."

"I should be rolling out with *you*," Jons said. "Upgrade to the cool soldier bars."

Jammed as they were with activities, each day passed in a blink, yet Webber began to feel impatient, hemmed in. Their first mission hadn't really counted. He'd been asleep, unaware of what was happening until Gomes, MacAdams, and Taz had already brought the target down. For him, the next time would be the first time.

A good mission took time to arrange, though. You had to look at flight paths, cargos, the capabilities of the ship being targeted. That was Taz's domain, and Taz didn't answer questions.

A month passed. He made another payment to UDS, smaller this time. He began to leave more modest tips, then quit going out altogether. His life-altering new trajectory began to feel less like a rocket blasting free of orbit to sail forever and more like an arrow arcing inevitably back to earth.

Gomes called a meeting. Not at the treehouse. Instead, she'd rented a Black Room. Only way for spies to hear what was going on inside was to put their ear against the wall and pray the people inside broke into a rowdy argument.

"I'll get right to it." She stood in front of a blank screen; the others sat around a table. "We've got a new target. Won't be as fat as Nevedia, but it won't be nearly as risky, either."

"I'm good with low-risk," Harry said. "So long as it's not low-risk because it's Farmer John's only cattle car."

"Cooper Imports. Check their financials, if your bleeding hearts compel you. Luxury goods suppliers. We'll be taking a load of coffee."

"*Coffee?*" Jons glanced across the others. "Why, we'll be billionaires!"

Gomes shook her head. "Not printed crystal bullshit. Genuine Kana'ali beans."

"Never heard of it," Webber said. "I'm guessing that means it's expensive."

"It's a rare year that any of it gets off Earth. We're working with Ikita again. Contract's all hammered out. All we have to do is go grab it."

Vincent sniffed. "What kind of payout are we putting our lives on the line for this time?"

"Your share should come in around 20-25K, depending on how expenses shake out." Gomes gave them a moment to absorb this. "Some jobs will be bigger, some will be smaller. You don't get to pick and choose which are worthy of your time—you trust my judgment as captain, or you jump ship. Anyone want to jump?"

Nobody made a peep.

Gomes touched her device. "I've sent briefings to your devices. You'll have the next three hours to study them. Before we leave this room, the briefings will be wiped. You won't be able to access them again until we're in flight. Paranoid, yeah—but if you can't get to them, then neither can anyone else."

Webber called the file up on his pad. It included ship schematics (a *Painter*-class stuff-haulin' base trussed up with a sexy exterior to better match Cooper's brand), expected defenses (minimal), and the location and expected route of extraction for the cargo.

MacAdams glanced over his shoulder. "In the sims, be sure to not spend too much time on *Painters*. The corps, sometimes they drop worms in the program, hire spies to infiltrate the staff. If they spot somebody spending all his days on the same model, it's a dead giveaway."

"Man," Webber said. "Who ever knew that stealing stuff would take so much work?"

"The joys of an information-rich society," Lara put in. "Sometimes I think the only way to get by is to never do or say anything you wouldn't want everyone to see."

Jons raised a finger. "Or be so disgusting that no one can stand to watch you for more than five minutes."

Just as Gomes had promised, after time ran out, Webber's files deleted themselves from his device without a trace.

Four days to launch. He'd already quit the bars, but he spent every waking moment preparing.

The morning of, Gomes warned them that, although she intended to return to the Locker, you never knew how things were going to go down once you hoisted the black flag. Webber didn't have much in the way of possessions, but he made sure to pack everything he couldn't stand to lose.

They took an elevator up to the landing platform. Out in the vacuum, the *Fourth Down's* profile had been modified again. A third wing now ran down its ventral line. The fore was corrugated, as if to provide extra protection against tiny spaceborne rocks, or to provide more surface area for solar panels. He wondered if Gomes had modified its engine signature as well.

They strapped in and blasted off. Once they leveled into a cruise, Gomes restored access to their briefs. This time, it included a course. Their quarry was leaving Mars at that same moment, en route to Neptune. To intercept the ship without rushing past it or being left in the dust, the *Fourth* flew sunward. After several hours, they hooked cloudward and anti-spin toward Neptune's current position. For the moment, they were dawdling, but once the target was six hours out, they'd punch up a hard burn. By the time the other ship neared, they'd be traveling at virtually the same speed and vector.

The first day passed without a bump. Near the end of the second, as they prepared to burn, the crew gathered on the bridge and buckled in. Lara counted down. The engines ramped up, pressing them against their chairs. The extra Gs were tolerable but exhausting. Every hour, the ship eased off for a fifteen-minute break of standard G. Webber napped intermittently.

"This is the part I don't understand," Vincent said, waking him. "Right now, they're on our scans, yes? And we're on theirs. Why don't they insist we ID or move the hell out of their way?"

"They've already ID'd us," Taz said. "We're clean. Just another junk-hauler out of the Lanes."

"Surely this claim will grow less and less plausible as we get closer to missile range."

She gripped her temples. "You think?"

"Excuse me for never having robbed another ship before."

"The answer is a lot of boring computer shit," MacAdams said. "Ideally, we spoof 'em into thinking we're not actually getting nearer. If that fails, we shift to phase two—distress call, ID ourselves as a fellow Cooper vessel, whatever's been working lately."

Vincent squinted at the screen. The target wasn't visible yet, but it was indicated by a green dot. "And if they get spooked and bug out?"

"The ship can compute within instants if we can chase them down." For once, Taz was smiling, hunched so close to the readouts Webber probably could have made out the numbers reflected in her pupils. "If no, we fly away. If yes? Make sure your straps are tight."

Messages pinged back and forth on one of the screens. The green dot grew closer and closer. Webber got the feeling he used to get in bars when he was chatting up a woman who seemed into him but a part of him hoped she would wise up, pay her tab, and walk out. And then, on the highest-magnification screen, he could see the ship. Its nose was sleek like a river fish. The *Fourth* was still ahead of it in space, slowly losing ground as the other vessel continued along its predetermined course.

Taz pumped her fist. "Shock range. Captain, permission to deploy."

"Granted," Gomes breathed.

Taz hit a button. On the rearview screen, three tiny rockets fired into the black, turning tail to accelerate toward the Cooper ship. A flurry of communications appeared on another screen. Collectively, the crew held their breath. The mini-rockets streaked across the gap between the ships. A single point of light burst from the vessel and lanced toward the *Fourth's* rockets. As they closed on each other, the enemy countermeasure split into an anemone of smaller missiles.

"Those on proximity?" Gomes said.

Taz didn't turn from the screen. "Do you need to ask?"

"Do you need to ask, *Captain*."

Taz glanced halfway back. "They are indeed on proxy. Captain. Pulling up effective range."

A translucent green circle expanded from the green dot of the other ship. The three rockets arced apart, each one chased by a number of the enemy interceptors. They began to spiral and juke, doing little to throw off their pursuit. The nearest rocket veered back toward the Cooper ship. Before it had crossed halfway to the wide green circle marking what Webber guessed was the range at which it became useful, one of the enemy missiles closed on it. The instant before impact, a white flash burst from the *Fourth's* rocket. Then both missiles exploded in a blue-white sphere.

Taz swore. The other two rockets continued on, nearing the translucent green boundary. The enemy vessel began to veer, but its forward momentum was so immense it was hardly changing course. A swarm of countermeasures hemmed in a second rocket. It went off, following the same burst pattern as the first.

Still several seconds from effective range, the third rocket neared the interceptors. Gomes glanced at Taz. Taz only had eyes for the screens. The red pinpricks denoting the enemy missiles closed on the *Fourth's* last rocket, blotting it out. Webber let out his breath.

There was no burst. The rocket leapt free of the screen of red and streaked toward the Cooper vessel. Red specks turned tail, trying to follow. The rocket cleared the translucent circle, streaked forward, and vanished in a white flash.

Taz leapt to her feet and pumped her fist. "Hell yeah!"

On screen, the enemy began to zigzag wildly, exactly the way a guy might if you were to box his ears and poke him in the eyes. MacAdams clapped once. Another missile zipped away from the *Fourth Down*, taking the straightest route toward the blinded ship. It wouldn't kill it—just knock out its engines.

"Let's suit up," MacAdams said. "The sooner we launch, the sooner we're out of here."

Webber followed him toward the exit. Jons fell in beside him and slapped him on the shoulder. "Go get 'em."

"There better not be any 'em to be got," Webber said. "Listen, if anything happens to me—"

"I know. Make sure to pull your pants back up before they see you."

He laughed, regarding the floor. "There's a file on my device. EOMD. Take care of it for me?"

Jons nodded slowly. "Of course."

The words removed a cold shard from his heart. He jogged to catch up with MacAdams and Taz on their way to the shuttle parked in the fore of the *Fourth*. They already had their suits on; before the excitement at the bridge, Jons had prepped the shuttle. Outside the airlock, they affixed their helmets and double-checked their seals. Webber hadn't worn one since he and Jons had been tasked with welding duty over a month ago, and inside the confined space, his breathing felt tight and loud.

"No worries." MacAdams tapped him on the side of the helmet. "Most likely, we get in there and stroll straight to the loot. If anything gets ornery with us, follow our lead. Remember all the hours you've simmed. And trust your team to get you home safe."

"Got it," Webber said.

They entered the lock. As they waited for it to cycle, Gomes piped up: "Engines down. It's all yours, marines."

"Damn right," Taz said.

Past the shuttle's empty cargo bay, the cockpit was as tight as Webber's helmet. Taz settled in at the controls, MacAdams at copilot. In all likelihood, they wouldn't have to touch a thing. Webber wondered what it must have felt like back in the days when autopilot had been the exception rather than the rule.

The shuttle clunked and eased forward from the *Fourth*, thrusters pushing it up and away from the mother vessel. A zoomed-in screen showed the Cooper ship drifting at high speed but zero acceleration. Its tail burned wimpily, debris tumbling into the void. The shuttle's computer registered each piece, determined their course, and adjusted its own route accordingly. The shuttle reached safe distance and blasted forward, jamming Webber into his chair.

They looped over the expanding debris field and came at the crippled ship from above. It was prettier than most, a teardrop of smooth curves. The hull even appeared to sport windows—almost certainly fake. The shuttle neared, hosing down the few remaining embers, then clamped tight, jostling them about.

With physical contact made, Webber finally felt the full measure of what he was doing. He was scared—so scared that, although he was strapped down, he had to grip the arms of his chair to stop himself from trying to stand. But even more, he felt a sense of destiny, that his past was a pyramid and this moment was its peak.

A light on the main screen switched from red to green.

Taz punched her fist above her head. "Let's *do* this."

They were no longer accelerating, and as the Cooper vessel was a drone, it had no artificial gravity. The three of them unbuckled. MacAdams and Taz launched themselves toward the shuttle's hatch. Webber bunched his feet, admonished himself not to screw it up, and leapt after them, grabbing onto one of the rungs around the door.

MacAdams confirmed they were ready, then popped the hatch. The other ship hung not thirty feet beneath them, dark and still. With the skyscape of stars fixed behind it, it was easy to forget they were racing along at thousands of miles per minute.

MacAdams braced himself and fired a line toward the Cooper ship. Its magnetic tip struck the hull and held fast. He pushed off, secured to the line by a strap, and coasted across the gap, reaching the KO'd transport and locking his soles to the hull. He gestured.

Webber's turn. His heart had never beat harder. Nothing to do but to do it. He tied himself to the line, took three deep breaths, and pushed off.

Too fast. Coming at the hull like a meaty rocket. He clamped the hand brake on his strap and slowed with a jerk. He was afraid he'd lost too much, but he continued to slide forward. The ship loomed above/below him. He swung about and landed with a click. The world reoriented itself.

Taz zipped down, flipped over, and stuck. MacAdams consulted the device built into the forearm of his suit and led the way. Rather than attempting to enter the breach opened by the missile, he circumnavigated a quarter of the hull, stopped at a hatch, scanned it, planted a charge, and waved them back. The blast was hardly more than a puff of smoke. The hatch sprung open.

As usual, MacAdams was first inside. Webber followed into an airlock so minuscule that, if it hadn't already been open, would have required two cycles to pass the three of them through. MacAdams lobbed a thumb-sized black object past the lock and into the depths of the ships. The mini-drone scooted into the bay beyond.

Thirty seconds of exploration later, MacAdams gave a bulky thumbs up. "All clear."

Beyond the airlock, a shiny stripe marked a ferrous lane through the cargo hold. MacAdams walked along it into a room that would have felt large if not for the fact it was all but filled with modular cargo cans. The big man was halfway down it when a port in the far wall opened fire.

11

"You think," Rada said, "that the guy who everyone thinks is dead—including his dear, beloved sister, who he cherished above all else—isn't really dead."

"I don't *think* that," Simm said. "That would imply a level of confidence I'm nowhere near."

"But you think it's possible."

"It would patch a lot of the holes in the fabric. Like who's paying for Dinah's care?"

Rada laughed in disbelief. "I don't know, her mother's estate?"

"*Before* Jain died. Xixi said that Jain never gave enough. So during the years between when Pip died and now, who was paying for it?"

"His life insurance."

"I've been searching around. He did have life insurance, but the payment was nothing exceptional."

"There's probably a trust. They would have to make sure Dinah would still be cared for in case she outlived them."

"I might see that as further evidence that Pip had no intention of outliving her." Simm pressed his index fingers together and held them against his upper lip. "Regardless, I don't see records of any such thing."

She stared across the darkness of the ship, adjusting her weightless body within the straps. "Let's say your idea is worthy of exploration. How would you start?"

"Financial systems are going to be locked too tight to do much from the ship. I'd go to the Hive."

"Wrong," Rada said. "You'd ask Toman if he's okay with using the Hive to sneak into institutional financial data."

He stared at her. "We should probably do that instead."

He put his theory into a ten-minute-long message complete with sources and links. Just as he was ready to send it, Rada locked down the Needle.

"Are you crazy?" she said. "You're sending a message to *Toman Benez*. He doesn't have time to plow through ten minutes of your rambling nonsense. Summary first. If that catches his interest, then he can plow into the rest."

Simm bobbed his head, edited down a quick summary, and sent it on its way. They were currently working with about a six-minute lag (and closing), but there was no telling how long it might take Toman to get to the message. He replied within twenty.

"An exciting theory," his prerecorded response said. "If only because it's so outlandish. I suggest you make a cursory run at it. Before you use the Hive as the centerpiece of a criminal hacking spree, however, how about you try some legal methods first?"

In response, Simm sent, "Acknowledged. Do you have a suggestion for an alternate route of investigation?"

This time, Toman's response took fifteen minutes to come back. He opened with an eye-roll of epic proportions. "Oh, I don't know. Why don't you ask Little Pip's financial advisor?"

Rada gawked. "He had a financial advisor?"

"Yes, he had a financial advisor," Toman continued; the message was prerecorded, but he'd anticipated her response. "*Why* did a backwater wage-slave need a financial advisor? Well, how should I know? Isn't that what I hire you people to find out?" He bugged his eyes at the camera, then clucked his tongue. "Oh, interesting fact number two: Pip only hired said advisor six months before his death. Toman out!"

He signed off. He'd attached a bundle of files to his final response and Rada spent the next several minutes combing through it.

"Okay, back to his life insurance policy," she said. "It looks totally normal. Exactly what you'd expect from a guy like Pip."

Simm shrugged. "Perhaps that's because he didn't want to draw suspicion by taking out a massive policy right before his death. A thorough investigation would turn up his fraud. Dinah would get nothing."

"How much do you think that claim would last her? Five years? With a payoff that modest, why bother faking your death at all?"

"I couldn't possibly know how Pip's mind works."

She inserted her device in the arm of her chair and craned her neck to look him in the eye. "Simm, I know you pride yourself on your unassailable objectivity. But sometimes, you have an idea that you think is so great you start skipping past all the hints that you might be wrong."

"Whether or not that's true, do you have a better idea?"

Rada gritted her teeth. "No."

"So would you rather retire to the Hive and pass the case off to someone else? Or go back to Neucali and speak to Peregrine Lawson's financial advisor?"

She stared at her lap, removed her pad from the chair, and punched in a new course. The ship began the process of hooking back in the exact opposite direction. "When Toman sees our fuel bill, he's going to skin us alive."

"Mr. Tennymore, please." Rada smiled into her device.

On its screen, a young woman smiled back. "May I ask who is calling?"

"Rada Pence. He doesn't know me, but it's regarding one of his clients."

The woman's smile dimmed fractionally. "Hold, please."

The image switched to a gorgeous scene of dust spewing across a bloodily vivid Martian sunset.

Rada muted her device. "How much time do you need?"

Simm glanced up. "It's already in. His system's got virtually no security at all."

"Stick to the plan?"

"Don't see why not. Maybe he'll make it easy on us and tell us everything."

Two minutes later, the Martian sunset switched to a view of a moon-faced man smiling so warmly his eyes all but disappeared in the folds of his face.

"Swen Tennymore. How can I be of help?"

"It's regarding one of your clients," Rada said. "Peregrine Lawson?"

The man's smile began to fall. His eyes emerged like an unamused hazel sunrise. "You understand I can't release any information regarding clients. Past or present."

"I know Mr. Lawson was a client of yours. What I need to know is whether, after his accident, he remained a client."

His eyes were now completely visible. "I am not required to discuss such matters."

"This is regarding his sister Dinah," Rada said. "I'm just trying to make sure—"

"Anyone working toward Dinah's best interests would not need to speak to me." He smiled with as much politeness as he could muster. "Good afternoon."

He signed off.

Simm chuckled. "How much more suspicious can you be?"

Rada turned to find his eyes. "Is he wrong? He's not required to divulge anything. The weird thing would be if he *was* ready to spill his guts about Lawson."

"But as soon as you gave him the name, his whole affect changed."

"Since when were you so attuned to the emotions of regular people?"

Simm's face pinched. "I'm not an idiot. Just because I don't feel like a standard-issue person doesn't mean I don't understand these things you humans call 'feelings.'"

"That's not what I meant."

"Really? Because that's what you implied."

"I was trying to question your assessment of the situation," she said. "I stepped over the line. I'm sorry."

"Accepted," he said after a moment's hesitation. "Now do a little dance."

She scowled and flicked her fingers to the left, then to the right, twisting in her straps. "That's the best you get."

"Did you hear me complain?" His grin settled down. "What's the deal, though? Why are you giving me so much pushback on this? I thought you'd jump at the chance to keep going."

"I'd love nothing more," she said. "And that's why I've got to keep *your* enthusiasm in check."

"Oh. Well. Why didn't you say so?"

"I must have overestimated your intelligence."

Simm laughed. His device pinged. He picked it up and scrolled. "Told you. You bring up Lawson, and as soon as Tennymore clicks off, what does he do? Dives into Lawson's account. Makes sure it's still safe. Convinced I'm right yet?"

"I'd like to be," she smiled. "So Tennymore's handling the money. Where's the money coming from?"

His mirth did another disappearing act. "TransPhere. Security's going to be just a little tighter than Tennymore's. I don't suppose you've any military-grade cracking software?"

"Not on me. But we know someone who does."

Toman frowned at Simm's data, scrolling and scrolling. He reached the end, frowned even harder, then set down the device and stared at the flies dancing on the surface of the pond.

"TransPhere," he said at last. "You could work at TransPhere for thirty years without one good opportunity to dip into their data."

Simm shifted his feet, mud squelching beneath him. "I was sure we had a new trail. Are you saying it's impossible?"

"For mortals? Yes." Toman picked up his device and stood. "That's why I'm lending you the Lords of the True Realm."

"No. Fucking. *Way!*"

Rada examined Toman's face for hints of a joke. "The core team? Why?"

"Breathe, Simm," Toman said. "Breathe, buddy!" He turned to Rada. "As of this moment, I'm a believer. Something's rotten here. To break open the case, all you have to do is track that odor to Mr. Pip."

"And convince him to tell us what it means," Simm corrected.

Toman smiled like a crocodile. "Leave that to me. You will deliver your brief to the Lords at 0330. Do not be late."

He walked toward the dock, heading for the lighthouse/private office he kept on the island in the lake.

"Wow," Simm said. "The Lords of the True Realm. I might have to get drunk before I'm ready to hang out with them." His eyebrows shot up. "Sorry. Joking."

"If it helps, get shitfaced." Rada plucked a purple flower from a reed and flicked it at the water. "I've always told you it's fine if you want to drink around me."

"Maybe just one?" He hardened his face. "No. Too risky. If I said something foolish, I'd never forgive myself."

"Why? Don't tell me you want to join them."

"What would be wrong with that?"

"Nothing. They're total warriors. Virtual gods. I just thought you liked flying around in the *Tine* with me."

"Of course I do," he said. "Someday, though, we might want to settle down. If we do, there's nothing I'd want more than to apply to their ranks."

"Know what? I can see that." Rada reached for his hand. "Stick to the facts. Lay out what we need found. And everything will be fine."

She injected her voice with all the confidence she could dredge up. She checked the time on her device: 4:37 PM, Hive Standard. They had less than twelve hours to prepare.

It seemed like it would take less time than that, yet as with all such projects, it expanded to fill what was available. By the time they were finished, they had reams of reports, pie charts, graphs, video conversations, death certificates, highly incomplete financial records, and bullet-pointed summaries of key findings to date and the methods they hoped might prove Peregrine Lawson was still alive—or that he was, in fact, as dead as reported, and that someone else was paying Dinah's staggering bills.

The hour neared. Rada and Simm packed up their devices, got into a cart, and let it bear them to the other side of the mini-planet. As part of their agreement to live onsite at the Hive, where they could be in immediate contact with each other and Toman rather than on a minutes-long lag that would make multiple-party conversations impossible, the Lords of the True Realm had talked him into letting them reside in Hyrule Castle.

This was an actual, factual castle. A moat. Curtain walls. A keep. Each of its four corners bore a tower made not only of a different stone, but from a different world: cold gray basalt from the Moon; orange-red bricks of Martian clay; warm white limestone from Earth; and the shiny, silver-black pallasite of meteors. At the moment—the middle of the "night," with the dome ceiling devoid of artificial light—the drawbridge was raised.

Simm tipped back his head to take in the towers. "So cool."

"So impractical," Rada said.

"Who goes there?" a deep voice bellowed from above. It had a kooky accent. One that no longer existed, and perhaps never had: the media's stereotype of pre-plague, pre-industrial England. And since there were no silhouettes on the rampart, this voice was in all likelihood being broadcast through a speaker.

Even so, she gazed up in its direction. "Rada Pence and Simmon Andrels."

"And what is your purpose?"

She frowned up at the merlons. "Didn't Toman tell you?"

"Our purpose," Simm said, balling his fists and holding his arms straight down his sides, "is to entreat the lords of this fortress—and of the virtual plane itself—to assist us in a quest of unknown portent."

The voice considered this. "And you claim you were sent by our friend and ally?"

"Sir Toman Benez," Rada affirmed. "Wealthier than a dragon. And twice as clever."

Beside her, Simm mimed applause.

"I see that this is so," the voice replied. "Then enter Hyrule, and step before the LOTR."

Metal clanked overhead. Rada flinched, but it was just the drawbridge lowering into place, revealing the courtyard beyond.

EDWARD W. ROBERTSON

12

The port in the wall flashed, silent, the noise of its fire lost to the vacuum. MacAdams grunted into his radio, leaping backwards. Check that, he hadn't leapt: he had been propelled backwards by the impact of the shots hitting his chest.

Taz yelled out, grabbing for his arm as he spun past. She snagged him and pulled him behind the crates. Small rounds shredded into the wall behind them. MacAdams appeared to be unconscious. Little spheres of blood floated from the wounds in his chest. The lights on his wrist indicated he was alive but maybe wasn't too happy about it. His suit claimed it had sealed shut where possible and that his oxygen was fine.

"What do we do?" Webber yelled.

Taz didn't look up from her examination. "What do you mean, what do we do? He's been shot, numbnuts! We get him on the shuttle and back to the *Fourth*."

Webber gazed at the boxes of cargo. "What about the goods?"

"We're too close to the Lane. No way can we get MacAdams out of here, come back for the defenses, and still have time to load up the shuttle."

"Take him home," Webber said. "I'll take out the defenses."

Taz snorted. "Right, asshole. And what if something happens to you?"

"What do you care?"

Past her faceplate, a genuine smile lit her eyes. "You're on, cowboy. See you in hell."

She got MacAdams under her arm. Keeping low enough to stay behind the safety of the boxes, she crawled along the floor toward the airlock.

"Oh hey." Over the comm, Taz's voice was infuriatingly calm. "In case you haven't picked this up, this ship has gone totally GAP."

"GAP?"

"Genocide Against Pirates."

"So you're saying all I have to do is tell it I'm a viking. Or the health inspector." Webber eyed the wall of boxes. "How do I shut it down?"

"At this point, only Cooper's people can do that. You're going to have to blow it up. As it blasts anything it perceives as a threat."

"Which includes?"

"Don't ask me," Taz said. "Every outfit's protocols are unique. You only need to remember one thing: never get in a firefight with an autogun. They're faster and more accurate than you can dream."

He rifled through his bag of materiel. "I'm starting to regret this decision."

"I'm in the shuttle, but we haven't launched yet. There's still time to come with."

"I got this," he said. "Get MacAdams out of here."

"Roger. Remember, it's a robot. Don't get out-thought."

She fell silent. His device was linked up to the shuttle and a notice popped up that it was being readied for launch. He couldn't see the far wall, but he had a mental snapshot of where the autogun had been — high up, able to command virtually the entire cargo deck. He couldn't get a straight bead on it without exposing himself.

Not a worry. His bag of tricks included a three-pack of pinky-sized missiles. He got one out, linked it to his device, fed it a rough course, and ordered it to adjust to heat/motion (and also not to get confused and home in on him instead). He lobbed it upward. Its tiny engine engaged and it streaked across the hold.

The camera in its nose fed back to his device. He watched as the autogun locked onto the missile and fired. The video feed went blank. With no atmo, he didn't hear or feel a thing from the explosion.

Chatter over the comm. Taz explaining the situation to Gomes. He turned it down, paying just enough attention to hear if his name popped up.

He prepped and launched a second missile. It too was shredded to bits within an instant of clearing the cargo. What was the gun keying on? The missile's heat, its engine sig? Well, he didn't need a guided missile, did he? They were in zero G. All he had to do was bank a grenade off the ceiling.

He ran a few calculations on his device versus the map of the room it had assembled from the brief-lived missiles. Made a few practice throws. When the device agreed his angles were good, he got out a walnut-sized grenade, drew back, and flung it over the wall of crates.

Light flashed through the hold, his visor darkening to compensate. Webber swore. It was locking in on all motion, then? What could he do about that, blast open one of the boxes and flick coffee beans at it until it ran out of ammo? For all he knew, it had a self-filling magazine and could print itself new bullets until it ran out of ship to draw from.

He tipped back his head, searching for answers. And saw bright red globules of blood hanging in the non-air, completely undisturbed by the miniature bullets that were pulverizing everything else that emerged from cover.

With a bit of work, he detached his water supply from his suit and palmed his way up the back of a tower of shipping cans, stopping below the rim. His water was nearly full at six quarts. More than enough to send a thick shield drifting toward the autogun. If it didn't fire on the water, he could spray a second batch and follow it up with a missile or grenade. With any luck, the gun would continue to view the liquid as nonthreatening, ignorant of the explosive hiding behind it.

He poked the tip of the water tube past the top of the cargo cans and punched the ejection button. Water spewed out the end, its release pushing gently against him. No bullets seared through the vacuum. He stopped the flow. Holding his breath, he affixed his device to the top edge of the can and extended its camera.

Shapeless globs of water sailed across the vacant space. The autogun was motionless, but it felt like a predator lying in wait. Some bits of liquid flew off in their own directions, but most was gathering in a super-glob. This headed straight toward the sentry gun. The glob's lower half enveloped the weapon; its upper half broke free and dashed against the wall, scattering in all directions.

The gun flashed. Webber winced, but the weapon wasn't firing—it had caught on fire. Smoke drizzled from the autogun's base.

Webber unzipped his pocket, got out a pen light, and lobbed it over the cargo stacks. The light tumbled end over end. It hit the far wall and bounced off without drawing any fire.

"Webber to *Fourth*," he said.

"This is Gomes." The captain's voice was strained. "Everything okay in there, Webber?"

"Defenses are down. Send back the shuttle and let's steal us some beans."

There was a second unexplored hold below the first that contained nearly 20% of the anticipated coffee, but Gomes told him not to risk it. As it turned out, they barely had time to transfer the last batch from the main hold. With the interdiction threshold dwindling to ten minutes, they strapped in and booked out. MacAdams was being treated in medical, overseen by Taz and Vincent, who had some training for such things. He thought the marine would make it, but there were no guarantees.

They accelerated hard, beelining for the Locker. Once they slowed, and it was more comfortable to speak, Gomes said, "How'd you know that thing wasn't hardened against water?"

Webber explained the sequence of events. "I didn't have a damn clue. Electronics' mortal enemy since time immemorial."

"Ships like that are built to operate in vacuum," Lara said. "No reason to waterproof the hardware."

"Sometimes it's better to be lucky than good," Jons said.

Gomes chuckled. "Saved us a couple hundred thou. Not to mention Ikita's goodwill."

"You think he'd get nasty if we came back empty-handed?"

"I'd rather not find out."

Webber had only been in his suit three hours total, but he was filthy and exhausted. He asked for and was granted a shower. After, he collapsed into his bunk.

They got back to the Locker and returned to their apartment in the treehouses, which no one had decided to leave despite the cost. MacAdams was taken to the hospital, stable but unconscious. Vincent made arrangements to resupply the ship and alter its profile yet again. Gomes set up another Nude Room meet with Ikita. With MacAdams out, she took Jons in his stead.

This time, Ikita didn't try to restructure the deal. He asked how things had gone. Gomes hemmed and hawed a little, then had Webber and Taz relay events.

"Most amusing," Ikita said once they finished. "It sounds as if you may want to invest in some autoguns of your own."

"We'll reinvest in boarding gear," Gomes said. "Even so, proof positive that there's no replacement for the human brain."

"Not yet, anyway. Then again, if such things existed, I wouldn't need to hire you, would I?"

"Until then, am I to assume we're still on your roster?"

He leaned forward, fingertips pressed together. "Indeed. Nothing is official yet, but I may have another venture for you quite soon."

"We'll stay frosty," Taz said.

Once Gomes had the funds in hand, she called a crew meeting. In the hospital, MacAdams was awake and talkative; he attended via device.

"We took a 20% hit to our expected haul," Gomes said. "With medical expenses on top of that. So I don't want to hear any complaints about shrimpy pay."

"You kidding?" Jons laughed. "This could keep me rolling for six months."

Lara rolled her eyes. "That wouldn't cover six days of your bar tab."

"With a face like this, you think I need to pay for drinks?"

It was a huge sum. Enough to make a man want to buy a ride in a horse-drawn carriage while sporting a new hat he'd never wear again. Yet it was less than last time. And Webber had a long ways to go before he was out from UDS' thumb. He sent them another payment, reserving a third of his share against living expenses. Once everything was squared away, he felt a little better.

He allowed himself a few nights out with Jons and the others, then resumed his workouts and training. Six days in, a message popped up on his device. It was from a man named Ko Vostok. He was captain of the *Idle Hands*, and he was interested in signing Webber on.

They met at an open air cafe on a quiet side of the rock. The restaurant fronted an artificial beach, complete with itty bitty waves and fiddler crabs. As Webber sipped his drink, he could smell salt water.

"I'll be blunt," he said. "I'm not interested in jumping ship."

Ko was as thick as one of the dwarves from the *BOGA*. He gestured with a beefy hand. "Yet here you are."

"It seemed like the polite thing to do." Webber lifted his sweating glass. "Besides, what kind of idiot turns down free drinks?"

"Because, of course, money remains money: the heart of every issue. Your captain, Gomes, what is she paying you now?"

"A percentage."

Ko retained a blank look. "I should hope so. What is your exact share?"

"Eight. There's been talk of a bump now that I'm a can opener."

"Talk," the stout man said. "Well, here is another word for you: twelve."

"Twelve?"

"I run a tighter ship. Fewer mouths to feed."

Webber set down his glass. "How did you hear about me?"

Ko waved to the buildings. "Gossip is a hardy creature. Thrives in all environments. Talent, however, is a much rarer beast. When you spot it, you must trap it fast."

"That's a generous offer. What have your last hauls been like?"

"Some good, some underwhelming. On the whole, I am pleased."

"How often do you make runs?"

"For a while, we averaged a new mission every 54 days. Recently, however, we have faced some attrition—two retirements, not deaths—but I plan to resume operations as soon as I've mended our holes."

"No offense, but I'd like to see hard numbers," Webber said. "It's nice to be wanted, but my captain treats me pretty well."

The captain laughed. "And so you see the problem people in my position face. Not only must I beat your current terms, but by enough to convince you to leave a team that you might see as family." He stood and extended his hand. "I will transfer the details. They will be lighter than you might wish, but I am open to questions. I appreciate you taking the time to see me."

"No problem." Webber shook hands. "Like I said, it's just nice to be asked."

He finished his drink. On the tube home, Ko's followup appeared on his device. Webber ran a program to compare the numbers. If Ko was able to get back to his old productivity, Webber would come out ahead by as much as 10% while exposing himself to fewer runs. He got home, gave it some thought, then called Ko Vostok.

"It's tempting," Webber said. "If money were all that mattered, I'd be yours."

"Understood." Ko smiled. "If you change your mind, or find yourself in need of fresh scenery, don't hesitate to call."

Webber assured him he would. He signed off, feeling like an insane person. A year ago, he would have killed for an offer like that. Maybe literally. Well, punched someone, certainly. Committed low-grade assault without a second thought, if that's what it took. How had everything changed so fast?

Later that day, as he was fixing himself up for a rare night out, Gomes knocked on his door.

"You talked to Vostok?" she said.

Webber met her eyes in the mirror. "Have you been bugging me?"

"Your device is routed through the ship. Don't worry, I'm not listening to your calls. I recognized his ID, that's all. So what'd he offer?"

"Twelve."

"And? Don't make me drag this out of you."

"I turned him down," he said. "It was a good offer. But I don't know him. I don't know his people. He'd have to go a lot bigger to turn my coat."

"Twelve," Gomes muttered. "Well, I'm glad you said no. Otherwise, I would've had to promote Jons. We'd never get his stink out of the suits."

It was a pleasant time. Easy. He'd go out to lunch by himself and order food that was grown rather than printed; after years of sludges, pastes, and smoothies, his mouth rebelled at the texture of discrete pieces of food. At the gym, he found himself talking to women. He hadn't been doing much of that lately. Even stranger, he wasn't particularly invested in the outcome. They seemed to respond to that. He began to consider moving out of the treehouse, getting his own place.

That would isolate him more thoroughly than he'd like, though. Easier to pay for the occasional hotel room.

A few days after his meet with Ko Vostok, he was in the common room with most of the others, lounging around, fiddling with devices. There was some talk of going out later, but no one had set a definite course. During one of the frequent lapses in conversation, Harry walked into the room and stopped in its middle.

"What's up?" Jons said. "You look like you just learned your girlfriend was separated from you at birth."

"I'm..." Harry shook his head, gazing out the window at the trees, the fruit-studded boughs, the smudgy glow of the atmo-scrubbing bacteria colonies. "I've been furloughed."

"Huh? For how long?"

"Indefinitely."

Webber swung his gaze up from his device. Jons looked skeptical, Lara angry. Vincent was the only one who didn't look surprised.

Harry drifted forward another step. "Captain said that, given our present line of work, a fixer was no longer necessary. She offered me a retainer in the event our—your—circumstances change. But it wouldn't be enough by itself."

"This was out of the blue?" Webber said.

"I am blindsided. Devastated. Thank goodness I was allowed to stay for our first two ventures or I'd be out on the street."

Lara met eyes with the others. "Was anyone aware of this?"

Vincent frowned at the floor. "She came to me about trimming expenses. Emphasized that I should look at all options. But we didn't discuss anything like this."

"Pretty low to be kicking people out the hatch just as we're getting a taste of the good life. How long have you been with the *Fourth*, Harry?"

"Five years." He ran his hand down his face. "I'm sorry, I need some air."

He turned and strode stiffly from the room.

"Shit," Webber said.

"Hate to say it," Jons said. "But I think Captain might be right."

Lara arched an eyebrow. "How do you figure *that*?"

"What does Harry know about pulling jobs in a place like the Locker? Isn't that why Captain picked up MacAdams? This ain't charity. It's business."

"Putting him on furlough was a good hedge," Vincent said. "You never know. He could be back before we know it."

Lara narrowed her eyes. "I don't think she goes this route unless she doesn't expect to use him for a long time."

Jons rested his elbows on his knees. "Either way, it's more for us."

Webber got up to go to the bathroom. After, he went to his bunk and thumbed up Harry's address on his device. Harry answered, looking wild-eyed, distracted. He was on the move, holding his device at waist height, leaving his head framed by the branches of the trees.

"You okay?" Webber said.

Harry gazed past the device, eyes on the path ahead. "I believe it is premature for me to say."

"You saved, though, right? Didn't blow it all on French wine and Jovian androids?"

The man chuckled reluctantly. "My splurges have been delicate. For now, my nest is well-feathered."

"Good to hear." Webber sighed. "Well, if you need a hand, or you just want to talk, give me a call. Got it?"

"I shall do so. I appreciate it, Mr. Webber."

He signed off. Webber had barely set down his device when it chimed with an incoming call. He picked it up, expecting Harry had changed his mind about wanting to be alone, but it was from Gomes. He clicked on. One by one, the rest of the crew — minus Harry — appeared in the participants.

"Attention crew," Gomes said. "As of this instant, we're back on the job. Gather your things and meet at the *Fourth* immediately. We launch in one hour. You miss the boat, you miss your chance."

"What's up?" Jons said.

"You will be briefed en route. For now, if you have any other questions, you may stick them up your ass."

The screen blanked. Webber returned to the common room, where the others were extracting themselves from their couches.

"Anyone know what's happening?" Jons said. "Vincent?"

The quartermaster shook his head. "Not a clue."

Webber tossed together a bag of essentials and headed to the base of the tree. The others were right behind him. They rode the tube to the elevator and up to the port. Machines whirred around the *Fourth*, making last-second checkups. Inside, the ship was empty. Gomes showed up fifteen minutes later. Ten minutes before takeoff, Taz arrived with MacAdams, who was back on his feet, if a little fragile-looking.

Gomes stayed on the horn until Lara began to count down. The *Fourth* lifted. The next few minutes were spent keeping an eye on its numbers and screens.

The ship kicked into a hard burn. Rather than heading sunward, like normal, they were on a nearly straight path spinward, ripping through the fringes of the settled system.

Gomes spun her chair around to face the crew. "I would apologize for the lack of notice, but this is how it has to be. At this very moment, our target is headed for a rendezvous with its escort. That escort is substantial. Our only chance is to catch it by its lonesome."

"And what is it, exactly?" Webber said.

"What I'm about to tell you is beyond secret. Ikita asked me not to tell you anything at all. I'm choosing to disobey him for two reasons: first, I trust you. Second, I believe that the more you know, the more likely we are to bring this home."

She made them all swear to secrecy before going on. "The target is a ship known as the *Specter*. Unique design. About the size of a corvette or a light hauler." Two images appeared beside the main screen. One was a wireframe of a tube-like, clean-lined ship. The second appeared to be a live photo of the ship departing a large asteroid or small moon. "Very little intel on it. By appearances and context, it isn't a warship, but you can guarantee it won't be toothless, either. Not with its payload."

Jons wiped his nose. "The payload being?"

"Tech. A machine of some kind. Ikita wouldn't even tell *me* what it is. Just the payment: twelve million."

The bridge went dead silent except for the vibration of the engines.

"I'm sorry," Webber said, "but did you say twelve *million*? Like the one with all the zeros at the end?"

Gomes nodded. "And a twelve at the front."

The conversation continued, but Webber had entered a state of shock. Even after subtracting expenses, his cut would come in at right under a million. Enough to wipe his debt in one swoop. To put him in the black. To relocate him to a more profound terra incognita than even the Locker: a world where he'd be able to do what he wished without the constant worry of where the next dollar was going to come from.

The others were arguing about something. The lack of intel. The narrow timeframe. The fuzziness of the cargo. Doubt hung in the air. Fear. He had made enough bad decisions to know how these became self-fulfilling prophecies. Weights you cuffed to your ankles before you tried to leap across a ravine.

"Do you know what we're talking about?" Webber said. "We're talking about changing each and every one of our lives. For some of us, this means getting out of debt for the very first time. For others, it's early retirement. For the rest, it's somewhere in the middle—you may have a ways to go, but the skids will be greased. The weights will lift. You'll have the option, if you want, to give this up. To quit risking your freedom and your life every time you step out into the void."

As he'd spoken, the others had quit arguing. Every eye was now on him. He tried not to meet any of them. "What we all have in common is that this will give us choice. Including the choice to never do this again. Moments like this—where everything can change—they don't come along often." He gazed between them. "We're a team. We've done this before. And we can do it now."

"Fuck yeah," Jons said. "No more naysaying. How long until the action, Captain?"

Gomes glanced at her device. "Eleven-plus hours."

"That gives us eleven-plus hours to figure out how to kick this ship's ass. So let's lace up our boots and go to work, people!"

They shot to their feet and whooped.

As it turned out, there wasn't much they could do to prepare—mostly, this involved close analysis of the *Specter*'s visible components to extrapolate what it was capable of—but the sourness in the air, the heaviness of impending defeat, that had been sucked out like the atmo from a hulled skiff. By the time they neared the action horizon, the crew had provided Taz and MacAdams with enough additional intelligence for them to add three contingency approaches to the two they'd already brought to the table.

In the middle of this, Webber snuck in a brief nap. He was back in the bridge when the monitors warbled.

"There it is," Gomes murmured. Lara pulled it up onscreen: a dark tube plowing through the field of stars.

"Hold up," Lara said. "The scans. There are *people* onboard."

"Bullshit," Gomes said. "This is just like the others. Pure drone."

Lara punched it up on the screen. Bio-sigs appeared beside the ship's outline. Eight, human-sized.

Webber grimaced. "In fairness, that could be a crew of chimpanzees."

Lara fixed Gomes with a look. "Did you know about this? Is that why you were in such a hurry to take off?"

"You think I'm happy about this?" Gomes said. "Their flight plan was for a drone. That ship is not supposed to be manned."

"Does this change anything?" Taz said. "We weren't gonna blow the ship up. Not unless we were planning to collect the cargo with a broom and a vacuum."

Warning messages popped up on the screens. MacAdams rubbed his jaw. "They've spotted us. Decide now. Before they decide to strike first."

Gomes gripped the arms of her chair. "We're committed. Anyone who wants out, state it for the record and recuse yourself to quarters."

The crew met eyes. No one spoke up.

"Noted," Gomes said. "Move in. Initial protocol."

Stone-faced, Lara went to work on her device. The *Fourth* swayed forward, closing. Messages flooded the screen. The last was a simple text warning: "DISENGAGE OR BE DESTROYED."

"Sounds like my ex-wife," Jons said.

Taz's hands flew over her device. A spread of missiles raced from the fore of the *Fourth*. On the screens, orange dots marked their presence. They closed on the *Specter*, spreading out. The translucent green sphere denoting the missiles' effective range expanded from the enemy ship.

The *Specter* launched missiles of its own. The first met the *Fourth's*, detonating in pale blooms. One of the *Fourth's* passed through the net, lancing toward the green field.

The *Specter* turned hard. Harder than Webber had seen on any sim. The missile blew past. The *Specter* launched an array of counters. As the missile turned, a rocket plowed into its side. The *Specter* flew on.

"What the hell was that?" Gomes blurted.

"Umm," Taz said. "That's not possible. A maneuver like that should have turned their crew to goo. Are they still alive?"

Lara pulled up the screen. One of the bio-sigs was moving throughout the ship. "And kicking."

Webber's mouth dropped open. "That's the target, isn't it? We're not stealing meds or coffee. We're taking whatever's letting them do that."

Jons began to laugh. "We are so screwed."

EDWARD W. ROBERTSON

13

Across the courtyard, the doors to the keep opened wide. A knight in full plate descended the steps, visor down, walking stiffly. A scabbard hung at its hip. It stopped before them and inclined its head.

"Greetings." Its voice was a robotic monotone—it was, in fact, a robot. "Please follow me."

It turned on its steely heel and led them up the steps. Simm grinned like a dog. The high-ceilinged antechamber smelled like fried chicken. The automaton clanked across the floor, its steps muffled by the carpeted pathway to the next set of doors.

These opened to a vast hall. A round table commanded its center, but the action was along the walls, where six constellations of screens flashed with readouts and video. Desks, chairs, and shelves sat in support of the screens, covered in devices, food wrappers, toys, and figurines. Behind each workstation, an alcove opened into the wall, hosting a snug-looking cot. A different banner hung over each of the six stations. Some of the heraldry was obvious (a dragon, crossed swords), but others made no obvious sense to Rada (a salmon, a frayed pair of boots).

Four of the stations were presently occupied by two men and two women. None turned to look at the knight. From the back of the room, a young man walked through a door, adjusting his pants. A black cape plunged from his shoulders.

Seeing Rada and Simm, his eyebrows shot up. "People! Our guests have arrived."

Only then did the others turn from their stations. The men were stubbled, the women wild-haired. They were universally bleary-eyed. As they made their way to the table, each carried at least one device. One woman appeared to have four. One of the men pushed a tall, vertical screen mounted on wheels. Its upper segment displayed an animated ASCII face. He set it before a gap in the chairs ringing the table.

"Uh," Rada said. "Hail and well met, my lords."

The red-haired woman snorted. "You can drop ye old-timey lingo."

The man with the cape gave her the eye, then smiled at Rada. His voice was the one she'd heard through the speakers, although not as deep. "I am Liam. Our fun-hating friend is Nora. And you, fair lady, are welcome to speak however you like."

Rada's smile wasn't exactly of the strength to forge legendary blades. "I'm Rada. This is Simm. Thanks for seeing us. I know how busy you guys are."

Liam gestured. "Be seated."

She pulled up a chair. It looked, felt, and sounded like wood, its feet scraping over the floor, echoing in the vaulted stone chamber. Rada winced and laid out her device.

"Here are our files to date," she said. "To summarize, several weeks back, Jain Kayle, an employee of Valiant Enterprises involved in extrasolar travel, arranged a meeting with us. The subject of that meeting was not divulged. When we attempted to rendezvous, we discovered that Kayle had died the day before. It looked accidental. After investigating, however, we believe it was murder.

"For the moment, that branch has dead-ended. What we are currently pursuing is Kayle's final message. We believe it is a code, decipherable only by her son, one Peregrine 'Pip' Lawson. Supposedly, he died in an accident more than three years ago. As our files indicate, however, we have reason to believe his death was staged. If you can help us pin down his new identity, it could be a huge win for the Hive."

Liam nodded over his device. "And so you ask us to play oracle."

"That would be our job," Nora said.

"Do I sound pissed off about it?"

"I am," said a forty-year-old man with a graying goatee. "I'm nipples deep in the Kettinger file."

Nora gave him an exasperated look. "If Toman thinks it's worth a look, I'm inclined to give it one."

"Did I say I wouldn't do it? All I said is I'm not happy about being dragged away from my real work."

"Jain Kayle was a real, living person," Rada said. "This isn't just about decoding her message. It's also about finding justice for her and her family. Unless you can help us, I'm not sure that will ever happen."

The goateed man drew back in his chair, gazing at the table. "The first step is going to be to feed everything into Merlin."

"Already on it," said the second woman, fingers dancing over her device. The back of her left hand was tattooed with three golden triangles. "But I got a bad gut about this one."

"Indeed." Liam turned to Rada. "Our task is perilous. Financial data is often contained within redoubts of terrible strength. The mere act of attempting to infiltrate them may betray the Hive to unacceptable risk."

"I'm not asking you to do anything to endanger us." Rada favored him with her archest look. "Only for the Lords of the True Realm of the Net to show me their moves."

"Shit," the goateed man laughed. "She knows how to throw down the gauntlet."

The six-foot-high screen beside the table began to fill with figures and abbreviations. The tattooed woman muttered to herself, tapping away. The others bent to their own devices.

"We really appreciate this," Simm said. "And if I may say so, I am supremely envious of your castle."

"It's pretty sweet, right?" Liam said without looking up. "Makes it a whole lot easier to be cooped up with these clowns."

A couple of the others laughed. Nora glanced up from her device. "For the next few hours—maybe the next few days—this is all we're going to be doing. Unless you get off on hardcore slack-jawed typing, you may want to find a better way to occupy yourselves."

"Just listen to those lusty clicks," Simm said. "The way you caress that pad."

Nora eyed him, decided he was joking, and laughed lightly. "That reminds me, I'm due for a trip over to the Ring. Before I forget that sex can involve another person."

"Don't leave the Hive," Liam said without looking up. "We may have questions."

"Will do." Rada stood. "Thanks for all your help."

A couple of them grunted. Rada walked from the table. Simm followed, gazing up at the stained glass windows and painted ceilings. Outside, a faint breeze stirred the grass surrounding the castle.

"Yeah," Simm said, blinking like he'd snapped out of a trance. "We *definitely* need to move here."

"I know, right? They get their own cot and everything."

"They have bedrooms, too. Or we could live in the ring and I could come here during the day. How does that sound? Pretty good, right?"

"That could work," she allowed, meaning it could work for him. As for herself, she couldn't see leaving the *Tine* behind. Not any time soon. She had far too much yet to see and to do. She was young: it wasn't impossible that, some day, she could see what lay beyond the Solar System. The thought of rooting herself to the Hive made her want to break into a sprint through the grass.

She supposed it didn't have to be like that. If Simm was that serious about trying to join the LOTR, or of otherwise becoming a permanent resident of the station, she doubted he would object if she told him she would continue to pilot the *Tine* for the time being. Well—he might object, but he wouldn't throw down ultimatums. He wasn't that kind of guy.

She wondered if that was part of why she was with him.

"Hey," she said. "I'm going to walk around. Do some thinking. See if anything new jars loose. Okay?"

Simm waved. "Let me know when you're on your way back?"

Rada smiled. "I will."

She started through the grass, checking the map on her device to make sure she wasn't about to enter forbidden land or stumble into an abyss. According to the reports, that's how Peregrine Lawson had bought it. Stumbled right down a Martian ravine and never came back.

He'd been out on a walkabout. On Earth, you'd call it "camping," but on Mars, the Moon, places like that, you could scratch out a few bucks by broadcasting the trip to piggybackers watching from the safety of their living rooms. It was far from a great living—there were so many videos out there you could spend your whole life experiencing virtual Mars for free—but some people would pay for new footage, or to have people explore areas specific to their interest.

After splitting up with Xixi, Pip had done a lot of those tours. Rada could understand the motivation: to clear his head and earn some cash in the process. If he truly had died, it was possible that he'd been thinking of Xixi and the wreckage of his life when he misstepped and slipped. Thirteen subscribers had received the footage of him skidding down the crack in a roostertail of orange dust. Then the camera went dark. There was a crunch. Heavy breathing. A dripping noise.

Then, silence and blackness.

Such things weren't rare on Mars, where people liked to think that all that open space was their communal back yard, and that if you didn't occasionally get out and take part in it, you weren't a *real* Martian. Yet in the context of examining Pip's death as fraud, she couldn't help wondering if the statistics were inflated. His was the perfect accident: in a desolate, hard-to-reach locale; more than a dozen witnesses; no damage to expensive vehicles or habitats. Neucali authorities had made a token effort to retrieve the body, but the ravine had proven too deep for recovery. A remote-operated probe *had* found a body and taken a DNA sample confirming it was Pip, but that wasn't conclusive. All it meant was Pip's handlers had grown some of his flesh in a vat and stuffed it down the hole.

Meanwhile, if Simm was right, he'd been whisked away as undeclared cargo on a ship bound for who knows where. Any one of the hundreds of moons, asteroids, habitats, and stations scattered around the system.

What must it be like to start over like that? Liberating, she supposed. You could become anyone you want. Step out of your fetters and into your ideal. That would come with a shadow, though; by removing yourself from all expectations and shame, you would be more willing to explore the darker fringes of yourself. She stayed straight and narrow, in part, because her failure would let down many others: Simm, Toman, the Hive, her grandma.

But if she had no eyes waiting for her to slip? She wasn't sure it would be long before she found herself seated at a bar. Three years into her own second life, she still wondered if it was worth it, being a responsible, upstanding human being. Why not do what made her happiest? Even if that meant living a degenerate, abbreviated life? What was best: the quantity of the years? Or the quality?

You only got one life, right? Was it really all that bad to be bad?

She wondered how Pip was using his second chance. Nothing like she was contemplating, she imagined. He'd been a steady worker, sacrificing his money, his relationship, and his very identity for his sister. No doubt he was at that very moment finishing up a hard day of work. Cooking dinner for some lucky woman. By now, it wasn't impossible that he'd have kids, and was kissing their foreheads and tucking them in. She envied those who could be happy with such things.

Rada walked through the grass, trailing her fingers through its soft green tips. Did it know how far it was from Earth? Would it care?

36 hours later, the LOTR bade them return to the castle. The robot knight delivered Rada and Simm to the inner chamber. The room smelled like coffee and the sweet tang of W8KE. The datahounds were scruffy-haired and bleary-eyed. Probably hadn't slept since the last time Rada had seen them. Except for Liam, who was rolling out of his cot at that very moment.

"Hail fellow and all that shit," he said, voice thick with sleep. He slumped toward the table. "I can't say we lived up to the standards of the Lords of the True Realm. Yet I refuse to call it a total defeat."

Rada seated herself. "Anything you've got is more than we walked in with."

He fiddled with his device. Numbers appeared on Merlin, the six-foot vertical screen who was parked beside the table. "We attacked this along multiple vectors. Everything you brought us. The subject. The mother. The sister. We found a trust. Cracking that trust was not easy."

"In fact," Nora said, "it wasn't possible."

"Okay, if you want to get technical, we didn't crack it. But we did...poke it. Pick it up and shake it. And a few grains fell loose." He gave them a bleary smile. "The trust was established six months prior to Lawson's 'death.'" Liam punctuated this with air quotes. "There was not one, but two sources of payments. We tracked one to Peregrine, the other to Jain. When Peregrine died, naturally, a large sum passed to the trust—his savings and life insurance."

"But it was smaller than it should have been." Nora called the figures up on Merlin. "More than can be explained by funeral costs and what have you. We believe the discrepancy is from the payments due to the organization who arranged his…" She sighed and air-quoted as well. "'Death.'"

The goateed man scratched his neck. "The discrepancy also matched the fees frequently charged for such services."

Liam rested his elbows on the table. "Here's where things get interesting. Following Peregrine's death, new payments only arrived from one source—Jain's. About six months after that, however, another source kicked in. This was set up to look like more insurance and things filtering through the system, but we traced this to a front. Then Merlin followed it through about six more fronts. That's where the thread started to get fuzzy."

"Like a ship full of tribbles," Nora said.

"You might say we lost it altogether. However, that's when Merlin unleashed his magic. And delivered us a name."

Rada grinned. "You got his name?"

Liam rolled his lips against his teeth. "Peregrine Lawson's? No. Instead, Merlin traced the payments back to their handler. A Universal Debt Services employee named Collin Winslowe."

"That's it?" Rada said.

Simm bolted from his chair with a scrape of legs. "Don't you see? Winslowe is handling Pip's account. If we find Winslowe, we get Pip. Do you know where he is?"

Liam grinned. "That's the best news—he's stationed at the Locker. Pirate central in Uranus orbit. As far as we can tell, it's a permanent post."

"Thank you," Rada said. "Not to test a gift blade on my thumb, but is this as deep as you can get?"

"You can always dig deeper. What we've got now is from dancing around outside the walls. To get more, we'd have to break into the fortress. Of UD-fucking-S. A project like that could take weeks."

Nora laughed. "Weeks? That's optimistic. Try a Jovian year."

Rada stood. "Then we're on our way to the Locker. Please, if you can, continue to investigate. We've already hit too many dead ends to count on any one lead."

Liam winked. "No worries. Merlin's on it."

Simm bowed from the waist so deeply his forehead bumped the table. "My lords. My ladies. You have secured my gratitude from now until the Big Rip. If I may ever be of service, you have but to ask."

Liam stood and bowed in kind. "The Lords are pleased to be of assistance in this most unusual case. Should your quest bear fruit, please return to drink and feast—and tell us of your story."

Simm's grin was wide enough to swallow Titan. Rada thanked them. As soon as she was outside the castle, she broke into a sprint.

Rada's eyes tick-tocked up and down the dingy street. On the flight in, she'd paged through countless pictures of the Locker. It had gardens, rooftop villas, an inhabited forest. Parts of it were a genuine wonderland.

This was not one of them.

People sat on stoops, rubbing powder on their gums. Others stood on corners, spitting sales patter at everyone who passed. Pedestrians kept their distance, careful not to get jostled and have their pockets picked.

"Explain," Simm said in her ear. "Why did he *choose* to meet you in what appears to be actual hell?"

"Best guess? Sales technique. This place is a reminder of what I, a potential debtor, am hoping to escape."

"That's outrageously manipulative. Well, please, please don't die."

"I'll see what I can do."

A notification popped up on her device; he was near. She affirmed the meet, sending her location. A man in a long jacket and a short-brimmed hat emerged from the crowd.

"Ma'am." He touched the brim of his hat. "Shall we adjourn to my office?"

"Let's."

He led her up an echoing stairwell. The third-floor landing smelled musty, sweaty. His apartment was nearly as barren as the channeled surface of Ariel. He offered her one of the few chairs.

"Your paperwork looks good," he said. "Have you settled on a final figure?"

Rada cleared her throat. "I've lied to you, Mr. Winslowe. I'm not here about a loan. I'm here about Peregrine Lawson."

The man blinked. "I don't know what a Peregrine Lawson is. I do know I don't appreciate having my time wasted."

"He didn't die in that fall. He was relocated—new name, new ID, probably a new face to boot. Your company's been collecting from him ever since. For the home he bought his sister, the care she needs. I know everything except the final piece: his new name."

Winslowe stared at her. His expression was as unadorned as the walls. "If any of this were true, then you should know you'll never get that name."

"Wrong. It's only a matter of time. I'd prefer to skip that, however. If you help me, it will absolutely be worth your time."

"Are you trying to bribe me?" He laughed. "Do you have any idea who I work for?"

"Yeah, I know. And when you're UDS, U Don't Scare. What a saint you are, noble salaryman. By the way, dick, tell your masters 'U' isn't a word."

He leaned his face inches from hers. "One more word out of you."

"And what?" She held out her hands. "Here's the deal. If you don't tell me what I want to know, my people keep digging. Eventually, they'll find it.

And when they do, they'll expose everything else they drag out, too. Every rag of dirty laundry UDS has in the hamper."

Winslowe's face had gone as hard as pallasite. "What is so god damned important about Pip Lawson? He's no-account. Detritus. If he died today, the universe wouldn't miss a beat."

"His mother's dead."

"Boo hoo. So's mine."

"A few weeks ago, she was murdered," Rada said. "She and Pip were estranged. But we have a final message from her."

"So tell me." Winslowe folded his arms. "I'll pass it along."

"Not an option. Your choices are to tell me a single name now. Or, in three months, the entire system will learn the names of everyone you've got."

"I see. And what if you were to disappear right now?"

"Then I believe my employer — Toman Benez — would make it his life's work to tear UDS to the ground."

Winslowe dropped his gaze to the floor and let out a long breath. "You haven't gone to all this trouble to deliver a dying mother's final message to her estranged son. Nobody's that pure. Tell me the real reason or we both walk away unhappy."

Rada clenched her teeth. "The truth is that I don't know. That's what I need Pip for. All I know is that it involves my employer's work — the study of alien life — and that it was worth killing Pip's mom to keep quiet."

"When I was a young man, I would have shot you and walked away. No matter how much money your bossman's got, a thing like that can't be undone. Take enough irreversible steps, burn enough of the fields, and that's how you win." He gazed into nothing. "But that's the problem, isn't it? You can't undo it, either."

"It weighs you down. Until you can't take another step."

He did some more staring, then fiddled with his device, turned it off, and pocketed it. "Outside."

Her device hadn't registered any bugs in the apartment, but she followed without a word. He headed downstairs and into the bustle of the street. People seemed to give him a little more room than most of the pedestrians. Rada kept one eye on Winslowe and the other on the crowds.

"I don't like threats," he said. "But I don't like touching off wars, either. You want Lawson that bad? You'll find him under the name Mazzy Webber." He gestured up at the dome enclosing the miniature world. "If you're telling the truth, though, you better hurry. Your boy's turned pirate. And his ship's on the hunt."

"I'm not here to hurt him," she said. "I hope you know that."

"If you were, doesn't sound like I could stop you."

She smiled, turned away, and hustled through the crowd. "Get that, Simm?"

"Indeed." Simm's voice was accompanied by frantic typing. "He's crewing on a ship known as the *Fourth Down*. When it isn't running up a black flag, anyway. They shipped out thirteen hours ago."

"Just our luck. They file a flight plan?"

"Naturally. But if they're up to no good, it'll be fake."

"Do we have an e-sig to follow?"

"I'll see what I can do."

She took a tube line to the elevator up to the port. Simm launched the moment she was buckled in. There was a lot of wash around the port, but betting that the *Fourth Down* had launched along its initial flight plan, Simm followed this, soon picking up their signature. Rada accelerated as hard as they could tolerate, grunting against the strain.

"What are we going to say when we find them?" Simm squeaked.

"He may have had differences with Jain," Rada said. "But you'd have to be one cold SOB to not want to hear your mother's last words to you."

Despite the extra Gs, she was able to nap off and on. The engine signature grew clearer and clearer. The *Tine* coasted, then flipped around and began to brake.

A screen flashed and the *Tine* lurched, knocking her from sleep. "The hell was that?"

"Debris," Simm said. "Mechanical. It's all over the place."

"Did they hit their mark? Or did their mark hit them?"

"I don't—oh. *Oh.*" He pulled up a new screen. In the far, far distance, the *Tine* registered two ships, the pieces of a third, and thousands of pieces of junk. As Rada watched, an explosion glowed from the darkness.

"Defense systems online," she said, though the *Tine* was already spooling them up automatically. "I've got the feeling things are about to get nasty."

14

As they gaped at the screens, the *Specter* juked again, impossibly quick, slipping another missile. It pasted the hapless rocket with one of its own.

"Orders?" Lara said.

"Too late to disengage," Gomes said. "We're up against a human-crewed ship that can maneuver like a drone. Ideas?"

"Fast and hard," Taz said. "You drag this out? Turn it into a dogfight? Their maneuverability will tear us apart."

"A modest proposal," Vincent said. "We could flee?"

Across the inky gap, the *Specter* dispatched the last of the missiles and began a frighteningly sharp turn. Rockets burst from its belly and soared toward the *Fourth*.

"Nothing doing," MacAdams said. "We've seen what they're capable of. They won't let us out of here with that intel."

Counter-rockets were already flying from the *Fourth*. The autopilot began a textbook three-plane break to get the ship out of harm's way while the missiles duked it out, but Gomes barked orders and Lara veered the ship back toward the *Specter*, which was curling away along a standard path. This left them flying on a more direct path to the incoming missiles, forcing the enemy rockets to tighten their angle of approach, drawing them nearer to the *Fourth's* counters.

Gomes ordered a second slew of missiles to fire on the *Specter*. A screen beeped, suggesting a new course; Gomes accepted and the *Fourth* zigzagged away, sloshing Webber's guts to the point of nausea.

Not that he needed abrupt momentum shifts to help him feel queasy. Sitting there as a helpless spectator while the two ships slugged it out, he finally understood how small he was, how vulnerable to the forces of nature and war. The band human bodies could survive within was so narrow: just the right amounts of oxygen, pressure, and heat. Meanwhile, the number of explosions, projectiles, and high-velocity crashes it could survive was stubbornly set at zero. Leaving Earth, strapping yourself inside a flying metal coffin, doing battle with another flying metal coffin — it was madness pie topped with a cherry of crazy.

The *Specter's* missiles encountered those from the *Fourth*. The two groups became a commingled cloud of heat, light, and dust. Seconds later, the

Fourth's offensive flurry met the *Specter's* interceptors and disappeared in another cloud.

"Good news," Lara said. "Their missiles are Jex-9s. A few years older than ours. From what we've seen, I'm guessing they don't have as many as we do, either."

Gomes considered the screens. "War of attrition?"

"If that's how they want to play it, it's our best bet."

"Proceed. Stick as close as you can while remaining as cautious as you can."

Lara swung the *Fourth* about for another pass. The *Specter* hove about. The two ships approached along parallel paths and exchanged another volley of rockets. As they flew past each other, down to a very low speed compared to that at which vessels crossed the gaps between planets, the *Specter* curved into a fishtailing buttonhook. Lara peeled away as hard as she could risk. It wouldn't be enough to shake them.

"What are you doing?" Gomes said.

Lara glanced across the bridge. "They're going to have our six."

"Fine by me," Gomes said. "Buy us a few minutes, though. MacAdams, Webber, Jons! Get to the rear lock and fill it with everything that isn't bolted down. The harder and smaller, the better."

Webber grinned. "We're going to nail 'em?"

"If they're dumb enough to tail us, I'm happy to teach them a lesson."

The three men unbuckled and popped to their feet. Webber activated the magnets in his soles just in time to avoid being flung across the bridge by a sudden turn. He reeled downstairs toward the aft airlock. This abutted several cabinets of hardware for low-tech repairs. They dumped it all into the airlock, bright steel bolts and pins blanketing the floor, then closed the door.

"Locked and loaded, Captain," MacAdams said.

"Skin of our teeth," she said through the comm. "Grab a seat ASAP."

The three of them belted themselves into the uncomfortable couch at the side of the hold. The ship swayed and veered. Jons messed with his device, pulling up the feed from the tail just in time to watch the *Specter* peel away. As it did so, a tower projecting perpendicularly from its cylindrical body was shredded to raggedy bits.

Whoops filtered through the comm. The *Fourth* began to turn, firing a handful of rockets after the retreating ship.

"She's out of here like we just bit her," Lara said. "Pursue?"

"On your second alignment," Gomes' voice came through. "Don't want them to pull the same stunt on us. Webber! Get another load in the lock, then buckle back in."

"Roger." He stood, leaning against the acceleration. Helped by Jons and MacAdams, they littered the airlock with another layer of screws, scrap metal, and raw solder. Webber grew heavier and heavier. By the time they finished and returned to the couch, he thought they must be pushing four Gs. And it was only growing stronger.

"Jeez, Cap," Jons said. "Trying to give us all spinals?"

"That's one way to retire early," she chuckled. "They're rabbiting. It's going to get worse before it gets better."

"Flood them, Captain?" Lara said.

"If they're gonna show us their ass, I can't think of a better idea."

A steady trickle of missiles fired from the *Fourth*, accelerating as hard as they could, inching toward the rabbiting *Specter*. Swimming upstream as they were, the missiles made for easy pickings for the *Specter's* defenses, but Webber had played enough video games and combat sims to know it didn't matter. What mattered was that Gomes believed she had more rockets than the enemy. Thus all she had to do to prevail was to keep firing hers until the others ran out (or, if the other guy could outrun her, use them to force him to dodge, slowing him down). Explosions dotted the starfield ahead of them like the lights on an airport landing strip.

Jons made a face at the basic visuals on the screen. "Think we can get upstairs without getting crushed?"

"You first," Webber said. "If you *are* crushed, try to ooze back this way so we know not to follow."

Jons smirked, then got a face like a little kid psyching himself to leap over a wide puddle of unknown depth. Before he could convince himself to unbuckle and dash upstairs, the ship veered, rocking Webber's head against the couch's absorbent supports. The fading bloom of an explosion whisked past the screen.

Hard, steady pressure resumed. Webber's pulse muttered wetly in his ears. All the while, they'd been keeping more or less even with the *Specter*. At once, they seemed to leap forward, closing fast. The *Specter* had flipped to point its nose toward them.

"Brake!" Gomes shouted. "Brake brake brake!"

The ship flipped; Webber's head slammed forward into the restraints. If not for the straps and tuff-foam arms holding him in place, he would have flown across the hold. He grunted. They hadn't put on a burst of speed. Rather, the *Specter* was slowing down. Braking harder and faster than the *Fourth* was capable of. They should have seen it coming—the maneuver was as obvious as a mountain—yet deep in the split-second decisions of real-time combat, no one had given it a second thought.

Or maybe they had. The only alternative would have been to let the *Specter* get away. Gomes had taken the gamble. Webber had a bad feeling about the cards he was about to be dealt.

On screen, which was now a view from the *Fourth's* aft, the *Specter* loomed nearer. The *Fourth* began to swerve. The other ship dipped down the screen, then slowly climbed back toward the center.

"Launch it!" Gomes screamed.

Lara choked on the crushing deceleration. "Launch what?"

"Everything! Until we slow down, they can fly circles around us. Tear us to shreds."

"Panhandler Protocol engaged," Lara said. "Launching now."

Missile after missile shimmered on the screen, as bright and numerous as the fireworks at the finale of Evacuation Day. The front of the *Specter* strobed as it launched an ongoing volley. The missiles met between the two ships and burst across the heavens like the formation of a new galaxy.

"We've got penetration." Lara's voice wavered. "So do they."

Bright green dots appeared beyond the galaxy of explosions. Incoming rockets. Others lanced toward the *Specter*. Both ships launched a panicked cluster of counters. Webber wriggled his hands free of the couch's foam grips and, straining with every movement, pulled his suit's emergency hood over his head. MacAdams and Jons followed suit. Over the comms, the crew on the bridge all began to talk at once, questions and orders merging into a slurry of nonsense.

Missiles and counters slaughtered each other wholesale. A lone green dot sailed through the carnage. Someone on the bridge screamed.

Webber fought his arms back into their restraints. The entire *Fourth* shuddered and rollicked like a rock kicked down a cobbled street. Webber squeezed his eyes tight. A deafening bang roared through the ship, followed by the rising, eerie klaxon of a hull breach.

The acceleration-induced gravity dropped to 2 Gs, then one, then half.

"Oh f—" Jons interrupted himself by vomiting into his hood.

On screen, all the missiles had vanished. The *Specter* was slightly closer, but the field of stars had changed. The blunt nose of the enemy vessel was burning, shedding debris into the vacuum.

"Report!" Gomes yelled through comms.

Lara's voice was ragged. "Engine banks B and D are down. As in dead. Multiple punctures on port side. Already sealed off. Missile batteries five and six are toast. Lucky they didn't go off."

"Probably because they were nearly empty. Hold, you all right down there?"

"Jons just showed his dinner to the inside of his faceplate," Webber said. "But we're intact. How about the *Fourth*?"

"Limping. Lost a few eyes. Fortunately, it looks like the *Specter*'s no better off. Lara, give them another poke."

"We don't have much left," Lara said.

"After that last round, they won't, either. It's do or die."

"Confirm. Launching three."

Three new rockets left the *Fourth*, spearing toward the flagging enemy. It launched counters and swerved to draw the rockets into a trap, but the *Specter* didn't have half the zip it had shown previously. The outbound missiles winked off: one, two, three.

"Incoming," Lara said. Lights popped up from the *Specter*, first a handful, then a score. "Shit. *Shit!*"

"Give it whatever you've got left." Gomes' voice was growing resigned. "One way or another, this is the end."

A cannonade of rockets departed the *Fourth*. With both ships slowed, the missiles seemed to zip across the space with terrible speed. On each side, a subset of rockets leapt ahead, exploding in empty space to create a barrier to the others. The remainders adjusted course, struggling to track the burst-walls and the reactions of the rockets on the other side, whipping crazily through constantly shifting vectors. A wave of counters followed both sides in, darting toward any missile that grew too confused by the chaotic flocking. Explosions strung the sky.

Six of their missiles cleared the scrum, continuing toward the *Specter*. Five of the enemy's carried through.

"Full evasion," Gomes said. "Launch flares. Dump the airlock. Put everything we've got between us and those missiles."

The ship rolled and swung. On the screen, pinpricks of light blooped from the *Fourth* and expanded in spheres of white-hot light. Across the bay, the airlock rumbled, venting its debris into the darkness. Two of the incoming missiles vanished in a spray of dumb energy.

"Not how I saw this going," MacAdams said.

Jons was muttering, talking to himself. After a moment, Webber recognized it as prayers. Were they about to die? The others seemed to think so, and yet he felt oddly light. He had established a new life insurance policy, and though it was modest—spacers had outrageous rates—it should pay off the remainder of Dinah's house. That would still leave her care, of course, but their mother ought to be able to handle that much. Dinah would be okay.

Even if she'd be left in the lurch, returned to the road to the poorhouse, he would have been satisfied by the fact he had tried. Given his all. More than most could say. His dad would have been proud.

More important than his concrete effort to make Dinah's life less of an ongoing hell, he was proud of himself in the abstract. He had taken a shot. Lived outside of rules. Outside of law. Tasted freedom and potential and what it felt like when you left worry behind.

His only regret was that he hadn't lived long enough to see what more he could have become.

The counters knocked out one of the two remaining missiles. The other headed straight toward the *Fourth*.

The ship jolted to the side, ringing like a gong. Webber gasped.

Everything became nothing.

15

He was less than six hours from rendezvous with the *Specter* when the message came in. He knew at once that it was an emergency, and not only because of the wrapper the message came inside. Rather, if it hadn't been an emergency, he would never have gotten a message at all.

As expected, it was from Finn. A video message along with attached files. Yon called up the message.

Thor Finn's young, confident face materialized on the device. "Heyo. I think you can guess what this is about, so I'll cut right to it: the *Specter* has been attacked. Single vessel. No definite ID, but our initial searches indicate it isn't one of the heavy hitters. In fact, judging by the sloppiness of its look—not to mention its methods—we're guessing pirates. C'est la vie, right? You do everything right, and then some idiot bumbles in and smashes it to pieces.

"We lost comms during the brouhaha. At this moment, we can't be certain the *Specter* continues to exist. Your mission is to extract it at all costs. If that proves impossible, to destroy it. And, if you have the opportunity, to negate any witnesses."

Finn grimaced, raising his eyebrows in sympathy. "There's no getting around it: this is a mess. One that I could have avoided, if I hadn't been so damn sure our office was leak-proof. Needless to say, while you're cleaning up this mess, I'll be cleaning up the one on my end. Oh—and this may be my fault. I'm aware of that.

"But I'm also self-aware enough to know that, if you can't handle this, I'll blame you as much as myself. As always, Yon, your value to me is beyond my ability to express."

That was the end. Yon called up the attached videos and reports. It was even sloppier than Finn had implied. Yon knew he should be giving his ship new orders, but hot, terrible panic shot through his limbs, followed by the pure and senseless wrath that was the chief reason he traveled alone.

As if aware of his mood, the rat in the clear plastic box to the left of the dash began to scrabble at its walls.

Yon stared at it with raw hate. Of its own accord, his arm lifted. His hand pushed the red button on the top of the box. With a whoosh, the atmosphere was sucked from the box. The rat's mouth fell open. It clawed harder and harder at the wall, eyes bulging, reddening with popped capillaries. It dashed across the box and slammed into the opposite wall. It hopped, frenzied, then crashed to a corner and stayed there, limbs twitching. Very soon, it was at rest.

Yon's pulse slowed, as did his breathing. He punched the second button. The box of the floor collapsed, sucking the carcass away. Nothing brought more clarity than witnessing the death of another being. You couldn't help but understand your own fragility, how brittle the tether that connected you to the universe of physical things.

He closed his eyes and gestured the ship to maximum acceleration. It didn't seem to move at all. In fact, during his first trip out with it, he had assumed that it *wasn't* moving — that it was, perhaps, an elaborate practical joke played on him by Finn, hoping to see him rattled. The instruments had confirmed his motion, however, as had the view of the station receding behind him. It was true: it was real. It was a miracle. The dawn of a new day of human history.

He loved the ship as much as he'd loved anything. As befitting an object of its stature, it had held many names in its brief existence. When it had been nothing more than a dream, Finn had called it the *Amelia*. When it had been a prototype, they had called it the *Protean*, as much for its versatility as for its ability to change its profile. After it passed to active duty, a few called it by its official designation of C4R-898, but most referred to it as the *Ghost in the Machine* or simply the *Ghost*. Some, to his deep confusion and deeper anger, called it *Tim*.

To Yon, however, it had a single name: *Mine*.

It cut through the void like no vessel before it. Now that the initial panic was behind him, he looked forward to seeing what *Mine* would do to whatever remained of the offenders.

16

The hiss of the vents. That was the first and only thing he could hear. Odd, that. Even when the engines were "off," they vibrated lightly, humming through the ship, helping to power the other systems.

No gravity, either. They'd stopped cold. He checked the screen, but that was currently a black wall. Either they'd been knocked into another dimension, or they'd lost sensors.

Beside him, Jons was nowhere to be seen. MacAdams slumped in his restraints, but the man's wristband indicated he was okay. Webber's suit claimed that atmospheric pressure was low, but within the survival band. He didn't take down his hood.

"Bridge?" Webber said. "Captain?"

No response. He unbuckled himself. Every square inch of skin that had been in restraints ached fiercely, as did his head. He felt woozy enough to fear he'd been concussed. He planted his feet on the floor, engaged his magnets, and climbed the steps up from the hold.

The bridge was quiet, but his eye was arrested by the largest functional screen. On it, the *Specter* hung in the void, rotating slowly. A large bite had been removed from its side. A cloud of debris floated around it. As did something far too large to be debris—dark, squat, shaped like a blunt-nosed bullet.

Another ship.

As he wandered forward, Gomes whirled to look at him. She was seated at the controls but had been so motionless he hadn't noticed.

"You're up," she said dully.

"Who the hell is that?"

She rotated to gaze up at the screen. "That is the *Opportunity Cost*. The flagship of Ikita's personal fleet."

The idea was already in Webber's head, but he couldn't get a grip on it for several seconds. "He's here to claim his prize, isn't he?"

"He must have been following us. Saved our asses, though. After that last missile strike, the *Specter* was closing on us. The *Opportunity Cost* zipped past, pulsed 'em dead in their tracks, then swung about."

"That explains why we're not dead." He'd no sooner spoken the words than he noticed Vincent lolling against his restraints, little red drops floating from his eyes and ears. He gaped. "Is anyone else..?"

"Jons is outside working on the comms. Lara's pretty banged up, but Taz is tending to her in medical. MacAdams?"

"KO'd, but in one piece."

One of the smaller screens detected motion and zoomed in. Gomes pushed the camera further. From an airlock on the side of the *Specter*, oblong objects spewed into the vacuum, tiny beside the bulk of the ship. The scanners were on the verge of being served with butter and jelly, but Webber didn't need help to recognize the flailing arms and legs.

"I don't suppose you've heard from Ikita," Webber said.

"Until Jons gets those comms up, we're deaf."

He guided himself to a seat and belted himself in. Along with the drops of blood, loose bits of splintered plastic were tumbling lazily around the bridge. In case they were able to get the *Fourth* moving again, he busied himself with collecting these and stuffing them in the waste tube, which bore them away for safekeeping.

He tried not to look up at the *Opportunity Cost* too often. Something worried him, though. The ship wasn't monstrous, but it was at least twice as big as the *Fourth Down*. A vessel like that would have at least one shuttle, possibly two or three. Yet none had been sent to see how the *Fourth* was doing.

Hopefully, they were too busy salvaging the *Specter*. And spacing her crew.

A half hour later, MacAdams clumped into the bridge, scowling, his pale skin lighter than ever, except where it was mottled and ruddy.

He took one look at the screen and his annoyance shifted to something far more serious. "Who is that?"

"Ikita," Gomes said. "Jons, how are the comms coming? Or are you too busy enjoying the view?"

Jons' voice crackled with static. "Almost there. Would go faster if you'd quit harping on me."

MacAdams guided himself to a chair, strapped in, and rubbed the angry red welts on his skin. "Should I be worried about the engines' unapproved vacation?"

Gomes called up a status report. "Reactor's got power. Life support's fine. We lost some atmo, but the holes are closed up or sealed off. Ikita could tow us all the way back to the Locker and we wouldn't know anything was wrong."

"How's the shuttle?" Webber said.

"Fine, somehow." Gomes laughed. "But if we're counting on that to get us back to the Locker, we'll have to convert it into a generation ship."

"I got first dibs on the baby-making," Jons said. "And I won't brook arguments. Not when I'm the hero who just got the comms back up."

"Dibs granted. Now shut up while I find out what the hell's going on out there." She pulled up a second channel. "*Opportunity Cost*, this is the *Fourth Down*. You out there?"

"This is *Opportunity Cost*," a woman's voice replied. "We've got you loud and proud."

Gomes laughed in relief. "You got here in the nick of time, *Opportunity Cost*. I owe you a drink. Maybe a whole bar."

"Don't repeat that, *Fourth*. Not unless you want someone to take you up on it."

"Advised. Is Captain Ikita onboard?"

"Indeed," the man replied in his smooth tones. "I am most impressed by your work today, Captain Gomes. I only regret we didn't arrive sooner."

Gomes smiled wryly. "Would have been nice to know you were coming."

"I hope you don't begrudge my secrecy. I had no intention of getting involved until it became clear that my intel regarding the target's abilities was incomplete. Are you all right?"

"We lost one. Another's in medical. The rest of us are banged up, but I think we'll make it. Same for my boat—engines are down, but we've got just about everything else."

"Excellent. Transmit me your status and I will take it from here."

"You got it." Gomes called up the *Fourth's* readouts and sent them over. "And please tell me we didn't beat the *Specter* up too bad."

There was no response. Three seconds became five, then ten.

"I don't like this," Webber said.

"*Opportunity Cost*, come in," Gomes said. "Do you copy?"

Another pause. As Gomes opened her mouth, Ikita's voice came through the line. "The goods are intact, yes. Despite what the future may hold, my gratitude for your work here remains genuine."

"The future? I'm not following, Captain Ikita."

"I'm sure you're not. That is what has made you so useful. You see, a heist of this nature—the device's owners *will* come for it. Along with those who attempted to take it. The only way to turn them away is to convince them the item is lost and the thieves are dead."

"You set us up," Gomes murmured. "It was all leading to this. From the very first gig."

"Sometimes—not often, but sometimes—a clever mind is provided its just rewards."

"I get it, Ikita. Whoever you took this from is as big as it gets. Valiant. FinnTech. United Mars. But you don't need to kill us. We can leave the *Fourth* here. Hull it. Make it look like we've been flushed into space. Meanwhile, you drop us off at a backwater rock to live quiet little lives."

Ikita chuckled sadly. "No, you do not 'get it.' If you 'got it,' you would understand that your pleas have no chance of success. The forces in play are too great. More importantly, human emotions and egos are too feeble to trust. One of you would betray me, be it for a reward, or simply to pretend that revenge is the same thing as victory." He clucked his tongue. "I like the idea of hulling you, however. Maximize the evidence for FinnTech to pore over."

"Ikita—"

"Goodbye, Captain Gomes. My regards to your worthy crew."

The channel shut off.

"This is my fault," Webber said. "I pissed him off in that first meeting. He's held a grudge ever since."

Gomes laughed, harsh and hopeless. "We were doomed the second I signed on with him. The worst part is I could have seen the signs. I was blinded by my own greed."

Something detached from the side of the *Opportunity Cost*. Webber flinched, assuming it was an inbound missile, but it was larger, slower to accelerate. A shuttle.

"Is that a boarding party?" he said.

MacAdams nodded, arms folded. "They'll blow us open, let the vacuum do the rest. Leaving plenty of evidence for the *Specter's* friends to pin on us."

"Ikita said it was FinnTech," Gomes said. "I can believe it. The *Specter* has some kind of anti-inertia generator. Something like that could be more revolutionary than artificial gravity."

"Wonderful," Webber said. "Fantastically rich people are about to get marginally richer. In the meantime, what are we going to do to prevent Ikita from making us deader?"

"There's nothing can do. These suits won't last us more than a few hours."

"The shuttle. It's got its own systems, right?"

Gomes gazed at the incoming longboat. "Won't work. They'll pick up your bio-sigs and paste you."

Webber went still. An idea was scrounging around the fringes of his mind. Ready to announce itself. But if he made any sudden moves, it would dash away. "Then we hide by the engines. Their radiation, it overwhelms bio-scans. They'll never see us."

She swiveled in her chair. "How do you know about that?"

"Ten thousand hours in the sims," he laughed. "So long as we load up on radiation meds first, we should be fine. Until we run out of air, anyway."

Gomes swiped at her device, glancing between it and the incoming shuttle. "Webber. Strip."

"Hey, I know it's a good idea, but it isn't *that* good. You can thank me later."

"They'll be here in minutes. You'll never have time to get everyone suited, prepped, and out the door. I'm heading outside. I stand a much better chance against those marines in your fancy suit than I do in my skivvies."

They gazed at each other. Webber nodded and stood. MacAdams unbuckled to help him shuck his pants. Gomes called medical, told Taz and Lara to suit up and grab every anti-rad on the ship.

"Sounds great," Jons cut in. "Bring me a rifle, will you?"

"No way," Gomes said. "This is my fault. It's my job to get you out of here. It's *your* job to get out."

"You won't last three seconds alone. Besides, I'm already out here. What are you going to do, take away my grog privileges?"

"God damn it, this isn't your fight!"

"It never is, is it? The way I see it, the reaper's knocking at the door. Time to do a jig and hope he's laughing too hard to notice when the rest of you sneak out the back."

As Webber had shed pieces of his suit, Gomes had been pulling them on. MacAdams jogged toward the rear of the bridge, magnets sticking him to the floor, and got a standard-issue emergency suit from one of the compartments. He flung the package back toward Webber, who snagged it with one hand, holding fast to a chair to prevent himself from being dragged off by the suit's momentum. He tore open the package and dived into the suit. MacAdams returned and helped the both of them seal up.

"Captain," Webber said. "Thank you for believing in me."

Behind her transparent hood, she grinned fiercely. "You're the best janitor I've ever had."

"Captain," MacAdams saluted. "We'll hoist one for you."

"Can't wait. Now get your asses moving or we won't have anything to celebrate."

MacAdams turned and ran as fast as his magnetic soles allowed. Webber fell in behind him. As he left the bridge, he took one last glance back. Gomes was caressing the ship's controls. Gazing up at the screens, she touched the mouth of her hood, then bolted in the direction of the arms locker.

"Status, Taz," MacAdams said.

"Almost there," she replied.

"I don't need almost. I need ready at the airlock."

"You try getting someone with two broken legs into a suit!"

"Give her a hand," Webber said to MacAdams. "I'll grab our gear and meet you at the lock."

The other man nodded and split for medical. Webber headed down to the hold and gathered up outside gear: lines, clamps, mags, extra cans of fuel for the tiny thrusters on their suits. He packed them up and tethered it to his belt, the sack floating beside him.

MacAdams arrived with Taz. Lara was tied to his back, legs dangling weightless behind her. MacAdams entered the airlock, dropped three anti-rads into the hopper of Lara's suit, then passed Webber a packet. The pills stuck in Webber's throat.

"Party's about to touch down," Gomes said over comms. "Tell me you're on your way out."

"Stepping out now," Webber said. As the airlock cycled, sucking the air from the chamber, he handed out mags and lines to the others. "What side are they coming in on?"

"Top. But they'll plant more than one charge, make sure all our air is lost. Here they come!"

The transmission quit. The airlock opened. Stars stared from beyond. The lock fed out the back of the ship horizontally. Webber walked up the wall and exited at the ceiling, aligned toward the engines further to aft. As the others followed, he set one of his heavy magnets to the hull with a clunk that made no sound yet could be felt through his glove.

He was now standing on the belly of the ship, head pointed down, and he took a moment to realign his perspective. The engines bulged ahead, less than sixty feet away. The hull was barren except for the lumps housing the landing gear and a few small nodes he didn't recognize.

He started forward, hunched low, moving at the dreamlike pace of zero gravity. The line clipped to his belt reeled out behind him. His breath rang in his hood. The others strung out after him. Their suits, set to stealth, adjusted to match the bland darkness of the hull. Would protect them from human eyes. Not the piercing gaze of sensors.

Halfway to the engines, red meteors streaked past the tail, running parallel to the *Fourth* along its dorsal side. Webber stopped in confusion. There was no atmosphere for meteors to be heated by.

Then it clicked: they weren't meteors. They were tracers.

He continued on. He knew he was the only one who could hear the clink of his steps, yet they felt terribly loud. The hull dipped. He crossed the crease between the hull and the nacelle. The engines flared up, hill-like. The counter on his wrist claimed the radiation was negligible. No good. As soon as he hit the engines, the count spiked. It might be enough, but he wasn't a physicist, and standing on the swell of the block, he felt insanely exposed.

He only had one option. Inside. He walked on. Sporadic tracers flew from the other side of the ship. The engines curved inward. Their output was a vast, concave bowl, rimmed by a shallow channel. He climbed into the channel and hunkered down. As soon as the others were in, he cut his line. It retracted toward the magnet set outside the airlock.

Radiation levels were bad. That was excellent. He gazed topside, across the engine blocks, but could no longer see any tracers. On the ship's main channel, heavy breathing rushed in and out. There was no chatter. Shuffling; the grunts of exertion; harder breathing yet. The thump of steps. Rustling, repeated, rhythmic jerks. The person—he thought it was Gomes, but he wouldn't have bet his life on it—was firing a weapon. MacAdams met Webber's eyes. The firing ceased, picking up seconds later.

"Oh God," Gomes whispered. Webber wished he could tell her that she'd done it, that they were safe, but he couldn't risk a transmission. "Oh God, oh please, forgive—"

Thuds. Grunts. Silence. Tucked into the rim of the nacelle, the others blinked at each other.

Lara drew her finger over the device on the back of the left arm of her suit and held it up: "FAREWELL"

Webber nodded, then looked up to the stars, hunting for signs of the *Opportunity Cost*. A few minutes later, the hull vibrated with a small explosion. Two more followed. A geyser of atmosphere spumed from the *Fourth's* flank, settling into an amorphous cloud that dispersed into the vacuum.

Lights blared above. At first he thought it was a final missile, but it was the engines of the marines' departing shuttle.

Webber's readouts informed him that his radiation absorption would reach unhealthy levels in two hours and fourteen minutes. Risk of lethality began another three hours after that. Not to worry, though: his air would give out an hour before then.

Ten minutes ticked past, then twenty. His suit was on the cold side. He thought he should be scared, or grappling with profound thoughts, but he felt empty. He must have burned through his emotional reserves during the missile strikes.

The fat bullet of the *Opportunity Cost* appeared on the edge of the sky, moving closer to the center of Webber's field of vision. His counter pinged.

MacAdams wrote on his arm-mounted device: "Scans."

Webber nodded. The *Opportunity Cost* stabilized its position against the stars, then began to increase in size, nearing. His counter continued to ding. Were they on to him? Had they scanned the ship, found fewer people than they knew had been there minutes before, and were now approaching for a visual scan? That would be the safest approach. The most thorough. Given what Ikita had said—that he was robbing no less an entity than FinnTech, and no less an object than one with the power to change everything—he couldn't blame the man for ensuring that no witness had been left alive.

If anything, Webber should have expected as much.

The man's caution would explain the ship's slow approach. Wary for traps. Not that the *Fourth* had anything left to spring. The ship was brain dead, paralyzed. He might be able to gin up something involving the shuttle, but the *Opportunity Cost* would swat it like a gnat.

The *Opportunity Cost* lurched forward, doubling in size in a matter of seconds. This was it. But it was swerving, too, turning perpendicular to the wreck of the *Fourth Down*. Accelerating.

A minute later, the first of the missiles slashed through the darkness toward Ikita's ship.

17

Adrenaline fired through Rada's veins. Sharp. Painful. Delicious.

She braked hard. "Sit rep."

"Four vessels," Simm said. "Two disabled. And one is the *Fourth Down*."

Far away, the other two ships danced at a distance, separated by a frantic hive of missiles, drones, and fiery bursts. "The ones that aren't?"

"One is a *Titan*-class. Armed to the teeth. To the gums. The other is…" He stared at his device. "Completely unknown. Zero matches to its profile. But its engine signature—it's been modified, but only enough to fool the courts. That's the ship that killed Jain Kayle."

Rada's skin tingled as if she were being burnt alive. Her mind was as clear as the instant before the pain sank in. "Get everything you can on it. The *Fourth Down*, I see power. Is anyone alive?"

Simm made a quick scan. "I'm seeing three bio-sigs. Two are outside the ship, including one floater. Nobody's moving."

"Something's wrong. Besides all the other things that are wrong. Our files say they were running an eight-person crew. Where are the other five?"

"Disintegrated?"

"Simm!"

"It is a legitimate answer to your question," he said. "Alternately, they may have come with a short crew. Or some floated away. Or were taken prisoner. Or joined the crew of the *Titan*-class."

She skimmed the readouts and displays, but there was too much to take in. "Do we have any idea who that is?"

"An enemy of the UFO. Under normal circumstances, I would hazard to say that makes them an ally." He pointed to the screen showing the silent wracks of the *Fourth Down* and the other ship, then displayed e-sig readings on top of that, tangled lines of ionized particles. "See that? It was here before the UFO. An hour, maybe more."

"Rescuing the survivors? Or finishing them off?"

They were coming up on the warm remains of the *Fourth Down*. Simm exhaled through his nose. "You know the only move that makes sense, right?"

Rada shook her head. "We've got to back the *Titan*. Could be it killed Pip. But if it didn't, that's the only place he might still be alive."

"We could Needle ahead. Ask if they've got him, and if so, to provide proof in exchange for our aid."

"Excellent." She pushed the *Tine* forward, began composing her message.

"Hang on." Simm leaned over his device, then hit the brakes. "I'm getting a fourth b-sig. It's on the hull of the *Fourth*. Incoming transmission."

"Attention unidentified ship," a male voice said. "I am the sole survivor of the *Fourth Down*. I am in need of immediate evac. Are you friend or foe?"

The hair stood up along Rada's neck. "Friend. Survivor, please identify?"

The man hesitated a moment. "Mazzy Webber, crewman."

"Webber." She laughed, hot relief flowing through her entire body. "You have no idea how long I've been searching for you."

"Searching for—? Ship, who are *you*?"

"The *Tine*. A family friend. Let's figure out a way to get you off of there. Do you have thrusters?"

"Ship," Webber said. "Give me a sec?"

"Some chatter on the *Fourth*," Simm said to her. "Light encryption. Want me to break it?"

"Please," Rada said.

"Good, because I already did." Simm tilted his head in the universal posture of listening. "Sounds like—"

"I'm not alone," Webber called to the *Tine*. "There are three other survivors. Didn't want to expose them until I knew what you were about, *Tine*."

"Don't blame you." Rada brought the ship about to approach the underside of the *Fourth Down*. "It'll be cramped, but we can do this. Any injuries?"

"We've got one with two broken legs. The rest of us are intact."

"Roger." She turned to Simm. "We'll park under its belly. I'll take the box down."

He bulged his lip with his tongue. "Why not a jump?"

"Too messy. Somebody goes wide, or the person with the legs gets tangled, and we could spend the next hour cleaning it up."

"Whereas you land the box, load it up, and let the auto bring you home safe. Agreed."

As the *Tine* moved to position off the *Fourth Down's* belly, she explained the plan to Webber. Three other bio-sigs emerged from the engine nacelle.

"They were hiding in the engine wash!" Simm cackled. "Brillant. We'll have to zip them back for treatment, though."

Rada grabbed a suit and headed to the back of the ship. The box was little more than its name implied: a miniature shuttle with rudimentary thrusters used for circumstances exactly like this one. She suited up, struggling with the microgravity, and strapped in. The box smelled like fresh plastic. Simm had already programmed its course. She vented its air into the *Tine*, leaving the box in vacuum. A simple red light shined from its dash. Fifteen seconds to launch.

"Rada," Simm said, voice tight. "The *Titan* just went down."

"What's the UFO up to?"

"Recalling all drones. Rada, I don't like this."

"How long do we have?"

"If he goes full burn, six minutes before we'll have to engage."

"Got it." The light had gone green. She punched the launch. "See you then."

The box departed with a clunk. Its screen whirled as the mini-shuttle thrust away from the *Tine* and toward the motionless *Fourth Down*. They were only parked a few hundred yards apart, but it felt like forever until the box landed with a light bump, securing itself firmly with magnets.

She popped the hatch. She'd landed a ways down from the four survivors, who were already making their way to the box.

"Hang on," Simm said. "This can't be right."

Rada glanced up. The *Tine* hung against the stars, slender and beautiful. "What's going on up there?"

"He's coming in hot. *Way* hot. But there's no way this is right. Acceleration like that would crush whoever's onboard."

"You're sure it's not a drone?"

"Negative. Even if it were, that speed should be tearing the *ship* apart. If we don't engage now, we're sitting ducks."

The crew of the *Fourth Down* slogged toward her, slowed by the magnetic soles, comically lax in the lack of gravity. "How long do I have to finish here?"

"None. Launch now, Rada. Get out of there!"

"Not without Pip!"

"How can you think this is worth your life?"

"Because I believe in you," she said, knowing that it was already too late, and if he didn't launch now, there was no hope for any of them. "Keep us safe, okay? We'll be right here."

His voice was monotone, resolved. "Engaging."

As the survivors reached the box, the *Tine* swung about and rocketed forward. The four others looked up, drawn by the motion.

"Wasn't that our ride?" Webber said.

"What do you know about the other ships up there?" Rada said.

"The *Opportunity Cost*—the big fat bullet—that was our employer. Who just betrayed us. And would have killed us, if that other guy hadn't shown up. For all we know, he's a friendly."

"He's not. He's attacking my copilot right now."

"And we're stuck down here?" A woman laughed, her voice harsh. "So what happens if your buddy bites it?"

Rada looked up, but the *Tine* was already nothing but a point of light. "Then he's dead and you're still alive. The *Fourth Down*, is it operational?"

"It's got power," a tall man said. "That's about it. Barely any comms. Engines are dead. Bastards landed in person to blow out our life support."

"We move back to the engines. Hide in their signature until we know my partner's the only bird left in the sky."

"It's glowing with radiation." Webber unzipped a pocket, fished out a packet of pills. "You'll need these."

The suit had a miniature airlock built into its shoulder for the intake of food/water/meds/etc. during long-term survival situations. On their way to the engines, Rada fed the pills into the lock and directed them to her mouth. She wanted to call up the view from the *Tine*, but the connection wasn't a Needle and any transmissions to her would defeat the purpose of hiding.

They climbed over the nacelle and settled into a groove ringing the engine block. Rada gazed steadily upwards, but the *Fourth Down* was between them and the action and there was nothing to see.

"Do you think he's got this?" Webber said.

"What kind of a question is that?" the harsh-voiced woman said.

Rada shrugged. "The only one that matters. And the answer is I don't know."

Behind his mask, Webber closed his eyes. "Let's hit mute, then. No sense giving ourselves away."

The *Fourth Down* wasn't actually motionless — it and the remains of the other ship were humming along at combat speed — but you'd never know it from the stars. They gleamed as ever, promising that they had secrets and that she would never be allowed to hear them. Sometimes Rada felt like they were eyes, looking down on her, and she wanted to blind them.

She had less time to wait than she feared.

"Rada," Simm said. "Rada, come in."

"Simm?" She stood up, scanning the eternal night. "Are you okay?"

"I got him. Tagged him good. Ran him off."

"That's incredible. You're sure he's gone?"

"I think he spent a lot of his weapons during the fight with the *Titan*. He was leaking air. Don't think he'll be back."

"We're hiding in the engines," she said. "We'll wait for you in the box."

"Better not." Simm cleared his throat. "Or you'll be waiting a long time."

"What are you doing? Running sweeps?"

"Well, right now, I am dying."

"Simm?" she yelled. "Did you say *dying?*"

"It's all right. The *Tine's* on autopilot. It'll be in position at the *Fourth Down* inside ten minutes."

"Simm. Just tell me what's going on."

"He shot the *Tine*. With bullets. Just like in olden times. Can you believe that?" He laughed, then coughed. "I caught some scrap. From the hull. Don't worry, the *Tine* isn't as beat up as I am."

"Quit jabbering at me and get into medical, you idiot. I need you in condition to get out of here."

"Listen to me, Rada!" His words boomed across the line. She'd rarely heard him raise his voice and had never heard him shout like this. "I've never died before, but I can tell. It's time. The suit agrees with me. I need you to do two things for me. Okay?"

She stared up into the darkness, searching for any sign of movement. "What's that?"

"The first is the hard one. Promise me you won't give up. That you'll find a way out of this. We've come too far to let it crumble now."

"I swear."

"Thank you." He didn't sound particularly upset or grateful, but she was attuned to his subtle expressions of mood and could hear his relief. "The second would be hard for most people. But not for you."

"What's that Simm?"

"I want you to bury me outside the system. You don't have to do it right away. But I know you've always wanted to leave here. Since you want it, I know it will happen. Put me somewhere…" His throat caught. "Know what, it doesn't matter where you put me. I'll be dead, won't I?

"Maybe so," she said. "But no one knows what comes after. Not even you."

"We're matter. Nothing more. When the electrical charges quit firing between the billions of networked neurons that comprise my brain, then the simulacrum of consciousness known as Simmon Andrels will cease to exist. He will never exist again. The wants of that lost simulacrum will no longer be relevant."

A point of light appeared from the darkness. The *Tine*. Rada tried to wipe her eyes, but her faceplate got in the way. "So what do you want that matter to be a part of when you're no longer Simm? A star? An ocean of methane? A core of molten rock? The Simm I know might be gone, but you can still exist as a piece of something greater. Can't you?"

He was quiet for a long moment. "An icy mountain. Somewhere clear and bracing. Wise men always live on mountains, don't they?"

"And you will, too."

"Just make sure it's hard to get to. I don't want a bunch of neighbors coming around to sell me cookies and raffle tickets."

She laughed, dislodging tears. "Can you be wrong about this? For once, please, just be wrong?"

"I'll try." He went silent again, but she could hear his breathing.

Oddly, she couldn't hear the familiar hum of the *Tine*. She called up the ship on her device. It was unpressurized, breached in multiple locations. The ship estimated it would take five-plus hours for it to seal the holes on its own. That timeline was irrelevant, however, as the life support was completely shot.

She called up the box's long-range scans—they were clunky and crude, but they'd be capable of recognizing if the UFO came back—and started to do some math.

"Hey," Simm said. "Thank you for knowing me."

She snapped up her gaze. "No. Don't you dare."

"I know that I'm not very flashy or sexy. I appreciate that you wanted to be with me anyway."

"People put on flash to distract you from their lack of substance. You might not have glitz, but you've got too much you to miss. And right now, I need you to hold on." The line remained open, but she could no longer hear his breathing. "Simm?"

Silence. Silence; silence; then: "I love you, Rada."

The moving star grew brighter. According to her device, the *Tine* was only two minutes out. "Hang on, Simm! You're so close!"

He didn't reply. She tried to check his vitals through his suit, but there was nothing left to check.

On the hull of the *Fourth Down*, she sat, wrapped her arms around her knees, and closed her eyes. She could feel the survivors walking nearby, vibrating the surface, but no one spoke to her. She envisioned removing her helmet. It didn't seem like such a bad idea. Her device warbled, informing her the *Tine* was in position above.

"Um," Webber said. "Ma'am? Your ship is here."

She didn't reply.

"I don't mean to…interrupt. But our oxygen's getting short. And if that stranger returns, I'd prefer to be gone, know what I mean?"

Rada looked up, found his eyes. "There's no point."

Webber shifted his gaze side to side. "In leaving? I'd beg to differ."

"Beg all you want. Want won't change facts."

"Your ship's pretty shot up. You just lost someone, didn't you? I'm sorry. I am. We've lost people, too. They gave their lives to try to hoist our sorry asses out of here. If you want to sit here, that's your call. But can you at least loan us your ship?"

"My ship won't do you any good," Rada said. "Its life support is trashed. It lost atmo. My suit's only good for a few hours. The box has a few more, but that won't go far split five ways."

"Oh," Webber said. "Shit."

"My new plan is to take a seat and put up my middle finger."

He sat down beside her. Given the lack of gravity, it didn't take any pressure off the joints, but there was something comforting about sitting.

"Who are you, anyway?" he said.

"My name is Rada Pence. I almost knew your mom."

He lowered his voice—ridiculous, since they were on a private channel. "I don't know what you mean. My mom's been dead for years."

She waved a hand. "Forget it. Forgive me if this is too personal, but would you rather die when your suits run out of air? Or would you prefer to climb into the box and prolong things another hour?"

"Thanks for the offer," he said. "But I think we'll make our last countdown in the shuttle. We won't get far, but—" His eyes went wide. "Hey, this is no big deal. But I just figured out how to save our lives."

She wanted to not care. To remain drowned in the molasses of her apathy. With anyone else, she might have—but the look in his eye told her that she had the option to go on. To squeeze some meaning from this bitter rind. If only she could bring herself to stand up.

Rada got to her feet. "What've you got?"

Webber stood, grinning. "You ever see a flick called *Frankenstein*?"

18

It was, in his modest opinion, the kind of idea that deserved songs written to it. To it, and to the person who'd had it.

They went to work.

Rada took the box up to the *Tine*. Taz helped Lara to the shuttle. MacAdams and Webber climbed back inside what was left of the *Fourth*, opened up the hold's main storage, and gathered all the welding equipment into a big floating mass.

Outside, Lara had the shuttle parked over the nose of the *Tine*. The box was waiting for them. Webber and MacAdams loaded up, climbed inside, and were deposited beside the two ships. Webber fired up the torch and made the first weld, painstakingly slagging one of the shuttle's skids to the nose of the *Tine*.

MacAdams grunted. "Don't have to be perfect."

Webber glanced up. "It has to get us there."

"You know, maybe we should shoot for perfect."

It wasn't. It was a nail-biting, heart-jarring mess of scrap, solder, and prayers. Webber knew that if the UFO returned, the *Tine's* sensors would pick it up long before his eyes, but whenever he could afford to look away from the weld, he glanced up at the stars. Rada peppered him with questions about what they'd been doing here. He answered without reservations, beyond care. Halfway through the job, Taz showed up with more scrap looted from the wreck of the *Specter*.

With her help, and that of the *Tine's* autonomous repair units, they had the two ships lashed together within four hours. The *Tine* would do the heavy lifting, rocketing them away to the nearest habitat. The shuttle would be nothing more than a bubble of air that would, with any luck, sustain them through the journey. To Webber's eye, it looked beyond frail. Like an orange stuck to an apple by a handful of skewed toothpicks.

The repair units returned to their mother. The crew piled into the shuttle's cramped airlock and headed for the main cabin. Rada and Lara were already there. Lara's broken legs were packed into a heap of cushions and foam. Webber buckled in.

"If you believe in anything," Rada said, "now's the time to ask it for aid."

She had installed her device in the arm of the shuttle's chair. She gestured over it. Scant acceleration lowered Webber into his seat. Most of the shuttle's displays were dedicated to shots of the struts and welds holding the two ships together. Although Webber stared at them so intently they could have been melted by the heat of his gaze, the connections held.

With the wreck of the three ships fading behind them, and the acceleration steady, Rada eased back in her chair. "If you need to cry, now's the time. Just keep it under five minutes."

MacAdams chuckled. "You always run your ship this tight?"

Rada tried to grin and failed. "I wish I were kidding. We can't accelerate at anything near normal. Not unless we want to tear ourselves loose from our engines. Deceleration will be equally slow. This shuttle wasn't built to handle starship ranges. Oxygen is going to be very, very tight. Can't afford to waste it crying."

"What about calling in a rescue?" Lara said.

"I don't want to risk any transmissions until we're out of here and up to speed. At that point, I'll try a Needle."

"Can't count on anyone to help us," Webber said. "There's nothing in it for them."

"Damn right," Taz seconded.

Rada called their position up on screen: an orange speck surrounded by an ocean of black. "At our current course and acceleration, we'll reach Hoeffel Station in 31 hours. At our current rate of consumption, we'll suffocate in 38 hours. So please — no exercise, no panic attacks, and definitely no post-disaster athletic sex."

"You want me to wait 31 hours?" Taz said. "Better call another emergency ahead to Hoeffel. 'Cause once I get there, they are gonna get *crushed*."

Everyone laughed, welcome for the opportunity to vent a little steam.

Once they settled down, Webber caught Rada's eye. "Now that we're away from immediate threat of death, you mind answering a few questions? Like who you are and what the *hell* you're doing here?"

"What, you're going to test a gift blade on your thumb?" she said dryly. "Like I told you, I've been searching for you for a long time. It was dumb luck I found you before you got ashed. As for why you? We might want to have that conversation in private."

"I don't have anything to hide."

"It's not about you. It's about a kid named Pip."

Webber's mind hit a brick wall and slowly slid down it. "Did you say Pip?"

Rada nodded once. "Get me?"

"I do," Webber said. "And it's okay."

"You're sure of this?"

"The only reason I'm alive is because of these people. They deserve to know why we went through what happened back there."

"I doubt if I can explain all that," Rada said. "But I can fill in some gaps. Your mother. Jain Kayle. Have you heard?"

"Heard what? I no longer have any ties to that name."

"She's dead. I'm sorry."

She stated this so factually Webber thought he'd misheard. He had imagined hearing this news before, as much out of spite as from the chance her murky business would some day get her killed. During these flights of fancy, he had imagined himself to be stoic, vaguely sad, yet ultimately untroubled. Not only because everyone had seen this coming from miles away. But because she had alienated all those who should care most.

Hearing the news for real, however, he found himself unable to speak for three full seconds. "What happened?"

Rada told him about the meeting that had never taken place. About how she and Simm, her deceased partner, had investigated, following the trail to Dinah, and then, through a combination of hunches and full-on data-hounding wizardry, uncovering the fact he'd faked his death. And, finally, had dislodged his name from Winslowe.

"Okay," he said, although it wasn't really okay at all. "Why are you looking for me in the first place?"

"Before your mother died, she sent me a message. One that only you could decode: 'Hey Pip: when the rabbit sees a shadow, where can he go?'"

"I see." Every eye in the cabin was fixed on him. "What do you think it means?"

Rada spread her palms. "I was hoping you could tell me that. I'd say there's a strong chance it's related to the fight that went down over the *Specter*."

"How you figure that?" MacAdams said.

"The ship that killed Jain—it was the same ship that showed up here. That killed Simm."

There had been a lot of pregnant pauses in Webber's life lately, but this one was as total as the vacuum.

"My mom's message," he said. "It's a set of directions."

Rada's eyes snapped to his. "To what?"

He took a shaky breath. "I can't not follow this. Somebody killed my mom. The rest of you, though, you can walk away. So here's the big question: do any of you intend to come with us?"

Taz stared at him. "Who are you, really? What did you know about what was going to happen out there?"

"I had no idea about any of this. I've been cut off from that life for years."

"Then it's a pretty big coincidence that you wind up on the pirate barge destined to collide with your mom's ass-crazy conspiracy."

"It's less of a coincidence than it sounds," Webber said. "Gomes was after the biggest score she could land. And so was my mom."

Taz pressed her lips together, then sighed. "Yeah, I'm out. Even if everything's like you say, it's like you say. I don't have any ties to this."

"I'm in," Lara said. "For Gomes' sake. She pulled me out of a bad place. Without her, I'd be long dead. I owe it to her to find out why she had to die."

MacAdams narrowed his eyes. "I'm in, too."

"Huh?" Taz whirled on him. "What do *you* care? We were in this for the cash, nothing more."

"And that 'nothing more' is why I ain't been happy with my life for years and years. This? This sounds like the chance to do something that means something."

"I don't know about that," Webber said. "But I do know where we're headed next."

Rada leaned so far forward in her chair she was apt to fall from her straps. "Tell me the course."

He shook his head. "Let's land first. Give everyone the chance to make sure they've made the right decision. Once we're patched up and off the station? I'll tell you exactly where to go."

Rada maintained comm silence another twelve hours, then sent a Needle to Hoeffel. They offered to deliver emergency supplies at emergency rates. She informed them that she was just fine, thank you, but would let them know if circumstances changed.

With a backup solution to the oxygen problem in place, MacAdams and Taz took one look at each other and retired to the cargo hold. Webber didn't know if it was spurred by the residual "Holy shit we made it" of the battle or by their impending breakup. All he knew was that it was the loudest sex he'd ever heard.

A few hours later, he woke to zero gravity and the sound of metal groans. The cabin was dark, lit only by displays. The ship was flipping around in preparation for its deceleration. It righted itself and braked, gravity returning.

One of the struts connecting the shuttle to the *Tine* popped like dry spaghetti. Webber's heart leapt from low anxiety to warp nine. Rada eased back, then braked again. The other struts held. The crew let out its breath in collective relief.

"That must have been one of yours," MacAdams said.

Webber swore. "Bet you two hundred it's got your fingerprints all over it."

"Deal. Now pay up."

"We haven't even landed yet!"

MacAdams waggled his hand. "When we installed those, we were all suited up. How many prints you think I left through my gloves?"

Webber rolled his eyes. Losing the bet was the worst that happened to him the rest of the trip to Hoeffel, however. Which turned out to be a standard ring spinning at low gravity in the middle of nowhere. It had once been a safe haven leading deeper into the Outer, but since the introduction of the Lanes, it had diminished. For a time, it looked like it might shrink to nothing. Eventually, however, its slow, easy lifestyle had become a draw, bringing in a trickle of people looking to escape the faster pace elsewhere without having to isolate themselves inside a tiny rock in the Belt.

Most of the ring's circumference was dark, uninhabited, with one main inhabited cluster and several smaller ones dispersed around its curve. Webber was skeptical it would have the facilities to repair the ship, but Rada assured him she'd called ahead and arranged everything. They'd hardly landed when a full brigade of suited mechanics jogged onto the landing pad. The foreman stopped to talk with Rada while the others went straight to work. Rada concluded the conversation and joined the crew inside the terminal.

"They're an unusually enthusiastic bunch," Webber said.

"Money is rocket fuel for enthusiasm." She smiled. "Did I neglect to mention my boss is Toman Benez?"

She put them up in a pair of apartments in a quiet part of town. Not that that narrowed things down; in Hoeffel, everything was quiet. Jons would have stuck out like a corpse on the steps of a church.

With this thought, Webber went to the window and gazed down on the rock garden in the square. Removed from the battle by two days and millions of miles, it felt like a movie, a news clip, some college kid's graphic arts thesis. Yet it also felt as though it was still happening, that he was at that very moment frantically stuffing washers and bolts into the airlock, or staring frozen at a screen while the green dot of a missile grew inexorably closer.

At night, he dreamed about the marines landing on the hull of the *Fourth Down*. Gomes and Jons were there, and they tried to raise their guns but couldn't. They couldn't even scream. The marines opened fire. Gomes and Jons juddered with the impact and were knocked from the hull. At once, they were somehow flash-frozen, their stiff bodies spinning away from the ship, faces hoary with frost.

He didn't see much of Rada. When he did, she looked distant, haunted, as if she were paging through photographs of a childhood she refused to tell stories about.

Lara was sent to the hospital, where the treatment would have her back on her feet by the same time the port crew had the *Tine* back on its fins. Webber visited some. She slept a lot. When she woke, sometimes they said nothing. Other times, they reminisced, or she asked him about his old life, how it felt to have started over so completely.

When he was alone, that's when he got angry. With no other routes open to him, he spent his nights swiping around the net, hunting for pictures or rumors of the UFO. He found a thousand leads, but none felt right.

Four days after reaching Hoeffel, Webber woke and found MacAdams on the balcony, gazing out at the tepid street.

"Taz left," the big marine said. "She waited to tell me she had a ride until after they'd sealed the doors."

"You guys in love?" Webber said.

"No." MacAdams rubbed his jaw. "No, nothing like that. But I would have liked to see her before she left."

"It never goes the way it should, does it? It's always less than. Disappointment. Heartbreak. Maybe the problem isn't with the world, but in ourselves."

"Always wanting more than we can expect to get? Bet you're right."

"I'd say we should be happy with anything that isn't outright disaster," Webber said. "Because usually, it's a bigger mess than vomiting in zero G."

MacAdams laughed. "I think I'm checking out of this conversation."

"The two of you were good, though, right? For a while?"

"We sure were."

"Then what more can you ask?"

Two days after that, Rada announced the ship was ready. They assembled at the port the following morning. The shuttle had been removed, the solder blasted loose, the holes patched. He wouldn't say the *Tine* looked new, but it did look good. Beautiful, even, and deadly, in the way of swords from ancient Ryukyu. Japan, rather; that had been its name in those days.

He climbed in and found a seat in the main cabin. Rada scanned the displays. When everyone and everything was ready, she launched, boosting out to clearance distance and then braking the *Tine* short.

She twisted in her chair, floating against her straps. "Where to, buddy? Inner? Outer? Wherever rabbits go to buy shotguns?"

"Earth," Webber said.

"I hear it's large. Any particular part?"

"I'll tell you once we get there."

"They're pickier than most about granting flight plans. But it'll be another two days before I have to call it in."

Webber waited until both those days were up to let her know. There was no point in delaying, yet he understood exactly why he did it: because, until he spoke it out loud, it wasn't really real.

"Idaho," he said, then laughed. "Of all the places in the system, we're going to Idaho."

"What," Lara said, "is Idaho?"

"The Panhandler virus' ground zero." Rada smiled with half her mouth. "Jain was very into xeno history. Figures she'd hide the answer where we made first contact."

"The rabbit isn't a real rabbit," Webber said. "It was my mom's way of telling me to be creative. If the Swimmers ever came back, the last place they'd look for us would be ground zero."

"Love it. But I do hope you can narrow it down a little further. Idaho isn't exactly small."

"Don't worry." Webber stared at the stars, trying to pick out Earth. "I know exactly where to look."

The mountain loomed above them, green and tremendous. It was early summer but the morning was crisp. Webber scowled. It had been years since he'd spent time outside of a climate-controlled environment. Some people loved seasons and weather, the cycles and unpredictability of a planetary atmosphere, but Webber thought those people were insane. Why not always be comfortable?

Hiking up the mountain was like traveling back in a personal time machine. She had done this on purpose, he knew, directing him to a spot that could only be reached by the slow, thoughtful, archaic process of walking. Thus subjecting him to hours of time in which to meditate on his childhood, when they had been so happy, before Dinah got sick and Webber began to understand that, in the choice between her kids and her work, his mother would always look to the latter first. This place, this trip—it was pure manipulation.

And it was working. The tang of the pines evoked a thousand memories of hikes, of fishing and swimming in the streams, of running through the meadows with their smell of sweet pollen. Wind rustled the grass and the needles.

It was nice, he'd give it that much. Enough to make you think that maybe humanity should have stopped bludgeoning its way forward after the invention of the mill and the plow. The spaceships, the stations, the warrens…all of them put together were less than this one morning on a mountain nobody wanted.

But we had to press outward, didn't we? Because of the plague and the aliens who'd sent it. It was either learn to build hives in every nook of the galaxy, or be wiped out by those who'd left their homeworld behind.

By afternoon, he found the cabin. It looked like it hadn't been used since their summer vacations: windows broken and shuttered, holes staved in the roof, the dirtiness of a thing being reclaimed by the earth it had been torn from. Webber gazed at it a moment, remembering Dinah running in the back door, tracking mud, their mother too exasperated to yell.

The trail was overgrown with thorny blackberries, but Jain must have passed through it not long ago. And unlike her, Webber had friends to help him clear the way.

The trail led to a centuries-old foundation completely hidden by shrubs and leaves and fallen rocks. There was no agreement on the exact spot the Panhandler had started from—in fact, most theories argued that it had to have emerged at dozens of points at once to achieve such complete, swift, worldwide saturation—but the record of the Ancient United States' outbreak began on this mountain, and his mother believed, for reasons he'd never fully grasped, that the precise location was this old house.

He went straight to the crack in the cement where they used to leave messages for each other. There, he found the video chip.

"Can I watch, too?" Rada said. "Or would you rather be alone?"

He shook his head. "Without you, I never would have found it."

He flipped it on. His mother's face appeared on his device. Strong. Resolved. She was smiling, yet there were tears in her eyes.

"Hi Pip," she said, voice creaking. "I'm so sorry you had to find this."

And then he had to pause it, because he was crying too hard to see.

19

Rada's impatience burned hot enough to char her, but she let Webber take his time. After he calmed down, he wiped his eyes on his shirt, blew his nose in the grass, and resumed the video.

"Because it means," the dead woman continued, "that I won't get to see you again. I had more to say to you, though, which was part of what this was about. Trust me, I considered contacting you through more conventional methods. I knew you weren't dead. But I didn't want FinnTech to know that. If they did, I have no doubt they'd hurt you to get to me."

On the device's screen, Jain Kayle glanced down, possibly to consult her notes. "I'm going to explain everything. Everything that *can* be explained, at least. But keep watching, okay? Because there will be something more for you at the end. The most important thing I have to say."

She took a deep breath. "For me, this road started years ago. I'll spare you the personal history and fast forward to where it kicks off in earnest: my involvement with Valiant Enterprises."

As she launched into a lengthy explanation, Rada transcribed a summary into her device, something for Toman to wolf down before tackling the main course. With Valiant, Jain had signed on to a program meaning to answer the most perplexing question of the time: why couldn't probes, cameras, or ships make it out of the system? To attempt to answer that question, they'd come up with a number of plans, including inserting a camera into a comet on its way back to the Oort Cloud. Any transmission could give it away, so it was programmed not to Needle home unless certain triggers were met—the detection of engines, biological matter, other transmissions, and so on.

Meanwhile, Jain relocated to Hoth, a free-floating facility on the fringe of safe Outer space. There, she observed the ice, rocks, and vacuum of the deep beyond. Like so many others, she found nothing.

Months later, she got a transmission.

"That transmission is included in the appendices," Jain said. "It is a video of an encounter between a FinnTech ship and an alien vessel."

There in the woods, the four of them turned to each other, swearing, crying out. Webber paused the video until everyone was coherent enough to resume.

"Their communications—also included here— regard the gifting of a technology," Jain said. "The simplest way to describe it is to say it nullifies changes in momentum. If you have this object on a ship, say, and you accelerate, you won't feel anything. This is even bigger than it sounds, because the *ship* doesn't feel it, either. Not only do you not have to worry about the limits of the human body, but you don't have to worry about the ship's frame. The only limits are its engines and its fuel."

"We saw that." Webber paused the vid again. "That's what was on the *Specter*."

"The UFO, too," Rada said. "We underestimated how fast it could burn. That's why…"

"You're alive," he finished.

He turned the vid back on. Jain was smiling now, lost in the wonder of what she was describing. "Can you imagine what this means? *We can get outside the system*. All we have to do is build a big enough engine. And find someone foolish enough to ride it."

She shook her head, grinning, then composed herself. "It sounds like a hell of a gift, right? Until you think of the questions it raises. Why do the Swimmers—the people who nearly destroyed us—want us to be able to escape our Solar System? If they want us to have it, why do they want their involvement kept secret? Why pretend that FinnTech discovered it? Is this the first time the Swimmers have contacted us, or is this how FT 'invented' artificial gravity, too?

"The secrecy alone would be reason for gravest concern. Our acquisition of this technology demands it be studied and explored in public. Even if it turns out to be a wholly innocent gesture of reconciliation, a blessing, then there is no reason for it to be controlled by FinnTech. It should be available to everyone."

She narrowed her eyes. "That you are watching this, however, strongly implies it is *not* an innocent gift. As does the fact that, when we Needled Valiant to inform them of what we'd seen, they locked us down and immediately dispatched a sanitation crew to purge us of our records. I had to hide my copies in a pebble outside the station. Convinced yet? No? Well, how about the fact Valiant is in merger talks with FinnTech?"

"*Merger?*" Rada said. "No wonder she came to us rather than Iggi Daniels."

"So there you have it," Jain concluded. "One of humanity's largest corporations is striking clandestine deals with our ancient nemesis for technology that will change everything. I don't know what should be done about it. That's why I came to the Hive. Whatever you decide, attached to this message is all the proof you'll need. I trust you to make the right decision.

"In exchange, I ask just one thing: show the rest of this message to Peregrine." She waited a beat, then looked directly into the camera. "Pip, I know you've always resented my interest in my work. I don't blame you. I wasn't there as much as I should have been, especially after Dinah grew ill. But I want you to know..." Her eyes went bright. She sniffed and righted her voice. "I want you to know that the only reason I could pursue this was because I knew that you would always take care of your sister. I'm so proud of you, Pip. I can only hope I've made you proud of me."

She smiled. The recording stopped, Jain's face frozen on the screen, gazing up at Webber. Webber stared through it, cheek twitching. He set the device on a log and walked into the woods.

Rada watched him go, then scribbled more notes onto her device. She wanted more than anything to Needle Toman the news, but she couldn't risk having the evidence intercepted. Not after the lengths Jain had gone to keep it out of FinnTech's hands. No, they were going to have to deliver it to the Hive in person.

Webber walked back five minutes later. His eyes were red, his face puffy. He picked up the device from the log. "Think we ought to see what all the fuss was about?"

He switched over to the attached files. The first was a view of blank space, fixed stars untwinkling on a black field. One by one, they winked off in a line, reappearing moments later. Something was moving across them.

The view cut to a face. Webber shouted and threw aside his device, scrambling back. Rada and the others retreated a step, too. Webber laughed shakily and picked up the pad from the bed of dead leaves.

The face was smooth and egg-shaped. Fist-sized eyes bulged angrily. A thin neck connected the alien's head to a long, tapered body held horizontally above the ground. A score of tentacles, claws, and spindly legs projected from its body.

A nightmare. A Swimmer. The creatures who, a thousand years ago, had smashed humanity's future. Driven them to the brink of extinction. And then disappeared, never to be seen again.

"Holy shit," Webber breathed.

Rada was struck speechless. She had spent years with the Hive, fastidiously hunting down stories, relics, and evidence of aliens in general and Swimmers in specific. Toman had devoted his *life* to it. Now here she was, watching one in action.

The alien gestured, tentacle tips wiggling. A flat, nongendered voice said, "Hello, you who have traveled to meet us. Is this because you have brought us a decision?"

When the view cut again, it was to a human face. One that Rada recognized: the handsome, happy face of Thor Finn, interplanetary magnate of FinnTech.

"The decision was never in doubt," he said. "Only the details. They're always the devil, aren't they?"

The alien face was expressionless. "There is no devil. Only the Way."

There was more — much, much more — but all it did was back the claims Jain had already made. Watching all of it would have taken hours. Promising they could see the rest during the flight, Rada shut it down and led them down the mountain. The silence of the slopes made her feel as if intelligent life had never existed: rocks, trees, insects, nothing more.

With Earth a fading blue dot behind them, Rada stood from her chair and turned to face the others. "I appreciate your help so far, so I'm going to be straight with you. You'll be staying at the Hive until this is over."

"Let me guess," MacAdams said. "You have no idea how long that will be."

"I intend to expose FinnTech as soon as I can. I can assure you that you'll be compensated for your time."

"That's all I need to hear."

Lara raised her hand. "Sounds like you want to set us down like a hammer at the end of a job. What if we want to keep fighting?"

"How do you intend to do that?" Rada said.

"You're going to kill him, right? The ghost in the UFO? Seems to me we may be the only people who've seen him in action and survived."

"I'm not sure how useful that's going to be. I bet this comes down to trickery and firepower."

Lara tightened her jaw. "We're not a bunch of ground-huggers. I'm a pilot and these two are marines."

Rada glanced to the two men. "Does she speak for you?"

"If the price is right," MacAdams said.

"They murdered my mother," Webber said. "I'm in this to the end."

That night, with the others asleep in the cramped bunks, Rada found herself in the tiny galley. She hadn't meant to go there, but now that she was, she couldn't seem to stop staring at the dispenser. She thought she ought to toast Simm. He deserved it. After what she'd been through, she did too. Anyway, without it, she wasn't going to be able to sleep. One drink—slug it back, then go to bed. It wouldn't mean anything. She would wake up tomorrow and be fine.

She got a plastic cup from the holder in the cabinet and set it under the dispenser. Her hand trembled.

Steps shuffled in behind her. She whirled. Though her hands were empty, she put them behind her back. Webber stood across from her, blinking at the hard light.

"Can't sleep?" she said.

"Nodded off for a few," he said. "Then I saw that thing's face. Its eyes. Don't think I'll be sleeping again for a while."

"Me neither. We've all seen the movies. I've seen plenty of drawings. The Hive archives even have three original photographs from the invasion. But nothing can prepare you for seeing them in the here and now."

"It's kind of like sex in that regard." He laughed and leaned against the counter. "Except shocking and horrible and it makes your skin want to crawl off your body."

"So it's like your first time." She grinned, then let it fade. "How are you doing?"

"Fine. Better than fine, honestly. I never expected to hear from my mom again. I didn't *want* to." He looked her in the eye. "Thank you for finding me, Rada."

"Wasn't easy." She put the glass back in the cupboard. "But good things rarely are."

A few hours out from the Hive, she Needled ahead to inform Toman that he would want to clear his schedule. She included her innocuous-looking emergency phrase in her signature. He replied to inform her he would be awaiting her arrival.

At port, she stepped out of the umbilical to the terminal and bumped right into him. She introduced him to the others, who looked starstruck. Even MacAdams didn't have many words. Toman was gracious with them, welcoming them to the Hive and assuring them all their needs would be tended to, but Rada knew him well enough to see the impatience in his gestures. As soon as he could, he shunted the others off on his assistants, hustled Rada to his cart, and peeled out.

In his office—a cluttered place of screens, devices, and bug-hunting paraphernalia throughout the ages—he shut the door, flipped on his security, and turned on her.

"Talk," he said. "Talk talk *talk*."

"We found Jain's message," she said. "She saw something she wasn't supposed to. FinnTech is sitting on brand new anti-momentum tech. Accelerate, turn, stop on a dime, you won't feel a thing."

His jaw dropped in affront. "Thor Finn solved the Jelly Problem?"

"The what?"

"The Jelly Problem. As in, if you try to fly like fun insists, you will be crushed into jelly."

"Don't get too jealous. He had help." Rada bit her lip. "It was given to him by the Swimmers."

Toman developed a Jelly Problem of his own: his face went slack, his hands dangling limply. "Rada, if this is a joke, stop it right now. Otherwise, I'm flushing you out an airlock. Warning: I am not kidding."

"I know," she said, "I'm not, either. We have the transmissions right here."

He took her device, began to open the files, then made himself stop. "Let's take this to Hyrule. Security's better there. Besides, I have the feeling we're headed there anyway."

He drove so fast the cart all but flew. At Hyrule, he ordered the LOTR to lock the building down and gather at the table. Sensing the gravity of the moment, they flew into action.

As Toman fed the device to the room's main screen, his employees fell silent, listening reverently as Jain Kayle spun her story. None of them uttered a word. Not until the first video transmission played and the alien's face popped on the screen. They shouted, leapt from their chairs, exchanged high fives. Liam and Nora burst into tears that were equal parts joyful and scared. When Rada glanced at Toman, she saw that he was weeping, too.

Between watching the extras and hashing out an initial strategy with the Lords of the True Realm, it was hours before Toman rose, rubbed his eyes, and beckoned Rada to follow. He took her to a side chamber made up like an ancient Christian temple: pews, candles, stained glass, statues of saints.

He hopped on the dais and began to pace. "Appropriate venue, considering you just delivered me the Holy Grail. For that same reason, I'd like to offer you three wishes. There's only one problem."

"All I want is to kill the UFO."

"Just so," he nodded. "Rada, I'm so sorry about Simm. I have never found that words make much difference to my feelings. Especially grief. But I hope you know what he's given us."

"I know," she said. "The potential to change everything. But that's your job now, isn't it?"

"And what's yours? To avenge his death? Rada, I think you have a more positive role to play."

"That being?"

He glanced away. "I don't know yet. It's a feeling."

"Then it's beside the point."

"If feelings won't work, here's the rational reasons against. First, going after the UFO could endanger the larger mission of bringing down FinnTech. Second, when we bring them down, the UFO pilot will crash and burn with them."

"Do you honestly believe that? Back with the *Rebel*, IRT killed hundreds of people. What happened to them? Some bad PR?"

"Along with a civil war that replaced the entire government. And a complete collapse of new immigration. *And* system-wide sanctions that have left them crippled."

"We don't have court-worthy evidence that our ghost has killed anyone. Even if we did, who's going to arrest him? The Space Police? We don't even know who he *is*."

He grabbed her by the shoulders. "Then how about this: I don't want to lose you."

"Then let me use the *Tine*. It's either that or I go rent the first bucket of rust I can strap a gun to."

"I could bar you from leaving."

"You don't want to do that," she said softly. "Or you'll lose me worse than death."

Toman sighed and sat at the edge of the dais. "This is the problem with surrounding yourself with talented people. Soon enough, they start thinking they ought to have a will of their own."

"Help me not interfere with your plans for FinnTech."

"That won't be hard. Whoever this guy is, he's a mop. When somebody breaks something, they send him in to clean it up—Jain, the *Specter*. You want to bag your ghost? All you have to do is make a mess."

"We've got more than enough eggs in Jain's files. If we drop one, he'll come running." She rubbed her hands together, realized what she was doing, and stopped. "We've got another problem, though. Simm barely held his own against the UFO after it had already spent itself in a fight with a *Titan*. No way can I take it solo. But if we show up with a fleet, he'll vanish. And he's too fast to chase down."

"Yes, that would be a problem, wouldn't it? Except for one small thing." He nudged her knee with his elbow. "Haven't you ever wondered why I called it the *Tine*?"

20

By any objective standard, the Hive was incredible. All the amenities of an up-to-the-minute modern station combined with a tiny little planet you could circumnavigate in an hour's walk yet spend days exploring.

But it was hard to be happy after they'd taken his device away.

Webber spent time tromping around the grass. Poking around the ponds. People claimed spending time in nature was good for the soul, but since leaving Earth, he had come to believe that mostly all it was good for was getting you dirty, sweaty, and covered in bug bites. Escaping from it with tunnels and habitats was not a new development. People had been building homes to segregate themselves from nature for thousands of years.

After a day of wandering around, he understood he was still angry with his mother. She couldn't have known she'd stumble onto proof the

Swimmers were still out there, manipulating humanity from the darkness beyond the planets. Pursuing that meant she had, in effect, sacrificed him to care for his sister.

Yet what aspect of him had been so special that it deserved saving? He'd lived a quiet, perfectly normal life. No part of it had been as grand as Jain's drive to find the truth. Even after he'd escaped that normality, what had he done with himself? Stolen stuff? It paid better than fixing bikes or swabbing holds, but it didn't exactly qualify him for sainthood.

Hard to blame her for that decision, then. Her life had been worth more than his. Simple math. He didn't know if she'd intended to bury this lesson in her message. All he knew was that he had to make more of himself.

Right now, it looked like the best way to do that was to carry on his mom's work. He didn't know what he could do directly—Benez had a team of eggheads working on the FinnTech/aliens angle—but right then, he had something far more personal in mind.

Killing the son of a bitch who'd murdered her.

Their second day at the Hive, Rada found him in the fields chasing a mouse through the grass.

"You have any experience piloting a ship?" she said.

"About a billion hours of sims," he said. "Sounds more like Lara's gig, though."

"She's in, too."

"What, are we taking a fleet?"

"Covering our bases. If you're not comfortable with the role, I'm sure the autopilot will do fine. But I always prefer a real human behind the device."

He ran his hand through his hair. "Why not bring in a more experienced pilot?"

"Right now, bulletproof trust is far more important than a third pilot." She smiled wryly. "Besides, these days, 'combat pilot' is synonymous with 'drone nanny.' I don't see much difference between that and the sims."

"You're the only one with as much skin in finding him as I've got," Webber said. "If you think I can help, I'm all yours."

"Then come this way." She nodded across the field. "It's time for you to enter the castle."

The building was stunning. Yet it was nothing compared to the sim they had waiting for him.

Four days later, his device buzzed. They were on the move.

At the terminal window, he drew up short. Out on the pad, the vessel awaiting them was bulkier, more of a wedge than a needle. "New ship?"

"Kind of," Rada said. "This time out, we thought we needed something a little heavier."

Its bridge looked the same. The crew was identical, too: Rada, Lara, MacAdams, himself. They took off, Outer-bound.

"You know," Webber said, "at *some* point, we're going to need to know what's going on."

"We're headed to the Locker," Rada said. "There, you will make it known that you survived the battle with the *Specter*—and that you took something back with you."

"The alien tech?"

"No. They'd know that's a lie. Instead, you took one of the ship's devices. On it, you found a schematic."

"Let me guess," MacAdams said. "You want that FinnTech's people should find out about this."

"You are in possession of a great secret. You figure they would like it back. In exchange for a reasonable fee."

Webber squinted. "You're sure they'll send the UFO? And not just pay us off?"

"Since we got here, the LOTR have done nothing but dig. They've gotten as deep as they can safely go. In something like a month—maybe three weeks, maybe six—FinnTech is scheduled to make a huge announcement. One guess what it's about."

"And until then, they're going to do everything they can to keep it silent."

Rada nodded. "Not only that, it was the UFO's job to mop up the spill. He failed. He'll be back to finish the job."

They had a few days to arrival at the Locker. To Webber's delight, Rada had packed a new sim with her. One that included the Lords' best approximation of the UFO.

To his annoyance, then his dread, then his sense of doom, the ship was unbeatable.

One on one, anyway. It was too fast, too agile. There were times it could out-turn the *missiles*. Even if you came at it fully loaded, keeping it under constant fire, it could dart in and out, carve you up piece by piece. If you somehow got lucky enough to hit it, unless it lost its engines, it could simply turn tail and run away. After a day of practice, he brought these concerns to Rada.

She smirked. "Took you that long to figure it out? Come on over here. Lara and I have something to show you."

Together, the three of them still couldn't beat the UFO, and it was only a simulation, the equivalent of a drone. By the end of the third sim, though, Webber no longer thought it was impossible. And by the time they docked at the Locker, they had beaten it—not once, but three times.

"Yeah, but out of how many tries?" Webber said. "A hundred?"

"Ninety-seven," Rada said. "We're getting better, though. Would you rather back off?"

"Not unless it's to try a better approach."

"If I had one, I'd take it."

"Then we stick with the plan."

He and MacAdams took the elevator down to the interior. Rada and Lara would stay with the ship—FinnTech would have her on file as a Benez employee, and if she was seen in Webber's company, the enemy might see through the entire plan.

Before, the tight streets and solid blocks of the Locker's housing had struck Webber as signs of possibility, the promise of endless space to explore. Now, the gray buildings with their out-thrust balconies felt like a foreign jungle of hidden caves and deadfall traps.

MacAdams made a few calls, dropped by a few bars and clubs. At a joint called Balance, which featured what it claimed was the Locker's only null-friction dance floor, MacAdams spoke with a pale, brittle-looking man who arranged a meet later that night. MacAdams thanked him, exchanged a flowing, multi-part handshake, and walked back into the false daylight.

"Good news," MacAdams said. "We're meeting with Pisa Flors. She's practically on FinnTech's payroll."

Webber smiled. "So we can trust her to do the wrong thing."

"Let me do the talking. All you have to do is stand there and look pretty."

They returned after the lights had dimmed to approximate the night. Before, the scene outside Balance had been desolate, nothing but garbage and footprints. Now, people ringed the entrance six deep, waiting to ID themselves and see if they had enough social cachet to be allowed in. MacAdams muttered something and bulled his way up front. Webber followed in his wake, trying to look cool, which was almost impossible when you were scurrying behind the guy who was actually getting things done.

For a bouncer, the guy manning the door was pint-sized. The motionless android behind him looked much meaner. The bouncer gave MacAdams a dubious look and barely offered

Webber a glance. He scanned them, raised his eyebrows, and let them inside.

Bass pulsed like war drums. Vapor swirled from the crowd, smelling of strawberries and orchids. MacAdams made his way to the back. Numbered doors lined the back wall. MacAdams counted down to the one they'd scheduled the meet in. The door opened to a small, mirrored foyer. As soon as he closed the door, the music blanked out.

The foyer fed into a dark room with a couch, a table, and a bed. A young woman sat on the couch, arms spread across its back. She was pretty enough to be one of the club girls hustling drinks in the main room, but the tailored cling of her clothes implied she made more money than that.

"Pisa," MacAdams said.

"You brought a friend?" She smirked at Webber. "Looks like I'm in for more fun than I bargained."

"If this goes down, well show you as much of the town — and ourselves — as you want." MacAdams rubbed his arm. "Although I expect you can do a lot better than us."

"So what if I can?" She trailed her fingers over her neck. "What's the fun in jumping in the same pool every time you get hot?"

"The certainty there won't be any sharks in the depths."

"I am not a shark. Sharks don't let you bite back." She sat up, the archness fading from her expression. "Doesn't it ever get boring being all business, MacAdams?"

"I'll let you know when I retire." He sat beside her, denting the couch cushion. "If I seem stiffer than normal, it's for good reason. A couple weeks back, we were on a job. Things went south. We didn't know what we were getting into. We lost the target. Along with some friends."

"This sounds familiar."

"Word's out, huh? Well, like I said, we didn't know the score. It was a setup."

Pisa pursed her mouth, quirking it to the side. "Are you coming to me to apologize to them?"

MacAdams lifted his palm and spread his fingers. "I'm trying to make things right. They sent a cleaner, but they didn't get everything. We've got a schematic. Straight from the *Specter*. It's the only copy. 200K, and it's theirs."

"Did you ever speak this idea out loud to see how it sounded? Because, to me, it sounds like you want to apologize to FinnTech by selling them back something you stole from them."

"They killed our crew. My friends. 200K is a low price to make things right."

"MacAdams." She lowered her eyes, scowling at the fabric flowing over her lap. "They'll skin me just for *bringing* this to them."

He scowled across the room. "Tell them I made you do it."

"They know me too well to fall for that. This is a no-go, big guy. What you need to do is hand it over and walk away."

"We don't have to do a god damn thing," Webber said. "We didn't knock out the *Specter*.

That means we pulled our loot from a derelict ship. The Law of the Inky Void says it's ours."

She laughed at him. "You think FinnTech will give a shit?"

"If we'd left it, anyone could have come along and grabbed it. Or how about this: if we wanted, we could sell it to one of their competitors for *millions*. Enough to walk away and disappear beyond FT's grasp."

Pisa drew back her head and gave him a long look. "Then why don't you?"

He stared back. "Because disappearing costs more than money. It costs who you are. For some, that's a good thing. For me, right now, I don't want to be anyone else but me."

She chewed the inside of her lip. "I'll make the call. But if I were you? I'd cash out and disappear. I don't think you understand how deep this runs."

"That's our risk to take," MacAdams said. "Thanks, Pisa."

"Good luck."

They exited the room. On their way out, Webber's device pulsed. It was Pisa's contact info.

Outside the Balance, MacAdams strode down the street. He didn't say a word until he got to a white building. On top of providing Nude Rooms, its services also included latest-gen bug sweeps for anyone who felt that might have been compromised.

MacAdams made sure they were clean, then let out a breath. "That was pushing it."

"If I hadn't, we were dead in the water."

"Do you hear me complaining? All I'm saying is it was a gamble. If you hit, you look like a genius. If you bust? You're a maroon."

"I don't think there's any confusion over whether I'm an idiot," Webber said. "But if you don't like having to gamble, that means we need to plan better next time."

"Agreed," he laughed. "I only like gambling with money. Not my hide."

The building included a small number of rentable apartments that were considerably more secure than your run-of-the-mill Locker walkup. MacAdams had reserved one for the next few days. They headed up to it and settled in. Webber fired off a message to Rada about how they intended to see the glowing forest tomorrow—code that they'd had their meet and were waiting to hear back.

Just two hours later, MacAdams' device pinged. He picked it up and scowled. "I told you, Pisa, you can do better. Now ain't the time."

"That offer's long gone," she said. "But I thought you'd want to know they agreed to a meet. Three days from now."

MacAdams snorted. "Boy, three days, huh? If they think I'm such a VIP, I better go hat shopping."

"You don't understand. They're not sending over some local from Saffer Street. They're flying someone in."

His eyebrows shot up. "Flying someone in? Maybe I ought to buy *two* hats."

She had attached the details to her call. The meet would be in empty space further out and anti-spin from the Locker. Hours from the nearest help.

Good place to get killed.

With no more need to move about the Locker, they returned to the *Tine*. Rada plotted in the course. It would take them seven hours to get there under non-stressful acceleration and braking. With no intention of arriving early, they remained in port.

Webber resumed simming with Rada and Lara. Rada was right: they were better than before. Still dreadful, but better. Soon, it became clear that almost everything depended on the opening gambit. If they could damage the UFO in the first pass, they had even odds of eventual victory. If it made it through that first pass unscathed, however, and was able to adjust to what it was up against, their odds dropped to worse than one in ten.

"Don't worry," Rada told him after a particularly frustrating sim in which the crippled UFO had taken them down one by one anyway. "You got lucky blood in you."

Webber rolled his eyes. "You can't walk down the street without bumping into a Lawson. It's like how after the American slaves were freed and named themselves after Washington or Jefferson."

"Who's Washington?" Lara said.

"History." Rada booted up another round. "Now let's get back to work."

One day went by, another. They got a little better as they continued to learn to work together, but there was only so much they could do to counter the UFO's tech. A low but steady panic stole over his nerves.

And then it was time.

The *Tine* launched. Webber managed to grab some sleep, but wanting to be sharp for the meet, he was up three hours beforehand. He went to the tertiary cockpit and sat down.

He wasn't alone long; MacAdams walked up beside his chair. "Mind if I stick with you on this one?"

Webber laughed. "Do you *want* to call it quits on life? I'm the only one who's never been behind the wheel before."

"Yeah, but you've got the luck. If I had to bet on one person making it out of this thing, my money's on you."

"I thought you didn't like gambling with your life."

"I've thought more than once I should have stayed at the Locker," MacAdams said. "But I've never been the type to duck out on his people. Some things are more important than scrimping by to the next day. Like what you see in the mirror."

The *Tine* streamed on, crossing the nothing that made up almost all of the universe. Rada couldn't let herself be known to the UFO—there was a chance he might recognize her—so Webber had been designated as the speaker. He killed the remaining hours going over the script devised by themselves and the Lords of the True Realm.

"Contact," Rada said. "Single vessel."

Webber's eyes snapped to the screen. The ship had modified its profile again, but the basics remained intact. A prolonged shiver danced down his spine. "That's him."

"We'll know for sure once we're close enough to grab his e-sig."

The two vessels neared, slowing. Automated communications passed between them. They were well within comm range, yet the UFO remained silent. Wasn't hard to guess why. It wanted to get close. Close enough to ensure they were alone. And then, to pounce.

"That's him." Rada's voice was thick with loathing. "That's the bastard who killed Simm."

The comm line opened. Everyone jumped, held down by their buckles.

"Greetings, travelers." The man's voice was smooth and soothing. "Thank you for reaching out to us. It is appreciated that you value your relationship with us above money."

Webber gazed into the device. "All we want is a clean slate. We're asking for enough cash to put this behind us. Nothing more."

"Will it go far enough? There are four of you. I was led to believe there were two."

"This is the rest of our crew. They know what would happen to them if they get greedy."

"I suppose I will have to take that on faith." The man was quiet a moment. "How do I know you haven't made backups? That you won't turn around and sell this to everyone else?"

"Because the file's sitting on a device we took from the *Specter*," Webber said, drawing from the LOTR's playbook of plausibility. "We took a close enough look to discover it's set to self-delete if we try to copy it."

"What else did you see?"

"Are you asking if we actually have what we claim to possess?" He laughed wryly. "Trust me, I wish we didn't. I wish we'd never gotten involved. But I can't wait to see what you guys do with this. We can finally make it beyond the system, can't we?"

"Anything can happen," the man said. His ship inched closer, nearing effective engagement range. "The funds have already been transferred. You may check your account, if you like. How do you propose to deliver the schematic?"

Webber glanced at the screen displaying Rada; she was over on the main bridge. "We'll dump it out the airlock. You can pick it up at your leisure."

"Agreed." Another pause. The UFO crossed the threshold. "One last question. I was there, too. There was only one possible survivor, and I do not think he made it out. So: who are you?"

"I am Peregrine Lawson." He gestured the signal to Rada. "You killed my mother. I'm not here for your money — I'm here for your life."

The link went dead. The UFO whipped forward, disgorging drones. Beside him, MacAdams swore.

"Countdown to splinter!" Rada said through the ship's comm. "Three! Two! One!"

The ship clunked and jarred. On the tactical display, the single orange blip representing the *Tine* became three. Each vessel was as long and thin as a rapier.

"Come on!" MacAdams clapped. "Let's fork this prick."

Webber's hands shook so hard he couldn't operate his device. The autopilot took over, curving his portion of the ship—the *Tine III*—into the attack vector that had produced the best results in the sim. The *I* and *II* followed their own courses, dispensing drones, hemming in the UFO. Missiles launched from two dozen different points, including the enemy.

Webber fought to control his breathing, but his heart was out of the question. The *III* launched counters that streaked to intercept the UFO's first wave. As the UFO's drones arranged a picket, it swooped straight toward the *II*. Lara's ship.

"You think I'm chicken?" Lara said. "We'll see who squawks first."

The two ships rushed each other, releasing a hellstorm of missiles. The first waves met and detonated in a solid line of fire. The UFO opened up, unfamiliar dots zipping across the tactical screen—kinetic rounds, utterly worthless unless you had the maneuverability to get tight and close.

Lara jinked out of their way and launched a second spread of rockets. The UFO began to veer, flinging frantic missiles at the *II*, but he'd gotten too close to dodge or outrun the incoming torpedoes. Silent bursts rippled across the screen, one after the other. Both ships vanished within the conflagration.

"Son of a *bitch*!" MacAdams whooped. "We got him!"

"Regroup," Rada said. "Running scans."

There was no need. The UFO whooshed from the flowery carnage, trailing flamboyant wisps of flame. The *II* was nowhere to be seen. The enemy turned hard, readying for the second round.

21

Rada's heart dropped through her guts. Her ship was already reacting, tightening its course to the resurgent UFO, but she had nothing to give. The enemy had survived the first encounter *and* it had taken away one of their ships. They'd never won a single sim with the odds reduced to two on one.

"Hang on," Webber said through the comm. "Check his vector. See how loose it is? I think Lara winged him!"

Fast as she could, she had the computer compare his current course to the previous ones. "Either he's playing games with us, or you're on to something. I don't think we're out of this yet."

As the UFO finished its turn, the front line of drones met and clashed, vaporizing each other. Rockets painted brief conical contrails across the void.

"He's coming for me," Webber said. "I'm going to flood him."

"You sure? If he's wounded, I say we go conservative."

"I don't want to give him any chance to catch his breath. It's time for the knockout."

"Copy," she said. The UFO was making way for Webber, already beginning to pelt him with rockets. "Got your wing."

She moved to close, but the UFO still had plenty of zip. She burned hard to try to keep pace. The *III* let loose a steady barrage of missiles and the enemy was forced to react in kind. The few remaining drones vanished in the wash of fire. As the two ships neared, the *III* swerved away in autopiloted standard maneuvers, keeping its distance to let the missiles do their job. Counters flocked from both vessels. The UFO cut in hard, attempting to stick itself to the *III*'s six, but Webber seemed intent on pasting it with everything he had. The enemy veered off, dropping counters left and right.

Rada, meanwhile, had caught up. She sent sporadic rockets at the UFO, forcing it to back further away.

"I'm almost out," Webber said. "How much firepower does that thing have?"

"More than we bargained for. I'll take lead. Stay close and choose your shots."

She'd no sooner said this than the UFO cranked back toward Webber and unleashed another volley. The *III* scooted away on a straight line, accelerating hard to buy itself as much time as possible for its counters to contend with the rockets. Flares studded the darkness.

"I'm out," Webber said. "Rada, I'm out!"

She swore, fired off a burst at the UFO, and swung toward Webber. On tactical, incoming missiles died at the hands of his counters. She wasn't closing fast enough to make a difference. She moved to reengage the enemy.

Webber cursed steadily, increasing in volume as the rockets neared. His ship bucked crazily, inducing the nearest missiles to collide, taking out those behind them, too. The final survivors burst off his bow, rocking him.

"You alive over there?" Rada said.

"Just a flesh wound. But I'm dry. Want me to decoy?"

"No way." She and the UFO closed on each other, exchanging more missiles. "Next one it sends after you will be your last."

Despite her warning, he hung close. The enemy came at her hard, forcing her to skate away and buy extra seconds. The UFO drifted in behind her. Too late, she understood the ruse: get her to straighten out, then cling to her tail and chew her apart with his railgun.

She turned as hard as she could. The Gs climbed, shoving her into her chair. Her vision grayed at the edges. Still the UFO followed. She leveled out, breathing hard. At once, bullets flicked past her. She pulled the *Tine* into a corkscrew, juking whenever she felt the UFO drawing too tight a bead.

"I can't shake it," she said. She expected to be terrified, but felt numbness instead. "I could try to flood it. But if I dry out too, we're all dead."

"I'm coming in," Webber said. "Keep his missiles off me, okay?"

"You're dry, Webber! What do you think you're doing?"

"Trying. On my mark, straighten out, okay?"

"And give him a clear shot?"

"Exactly."

"This is insane." The *Tine* shuddered; the latest volley had clipped her wing. At least it was only decorative. She deployed counters, sending them toward the nearing *III*. "Tell me when."

As Webber approached, the UFO flung a handful of rockets at him, but stayed locked to Rada's tail. Through the comm, Webber was breathing hard. Accelerating faster than his body could sustain. He came up parallel to them, advancing halfway between her and the FinnTech assassin.

"Now!" he yelled.

She leveled out. He veered hard toward the line between her and the enemy. As soon as he crossed it, the *III* began to wiggle and shuck.

"What the hell?" Rada said.

"Just shaking my ass at him."

The UFO fired on Webber instead. Bits and pieces of the chewed-up *III* fell away. And then she understood. So, too, did the enemy. He veered hard.

White light flashed from his front as Webber's homemade flak tore through the face of his ship. Someone screamed; she thought it must be the assassin, but it was MacAdams, delirious with battle-joy. Rada peeled away, hammer-heading around to nail the UFO with everything she had left.

There was no need. He was drifting, silent, one more piece of flotsam coasting forever on the universe's endless sea.

Rada laughed into the comm. "I don't believe for a single second you thought that would work."

"I was just trying to get him off you," Webber said. "Although this outcome did cross my mind."

"He's coasting. I'm launching the coup de grace."

"Hang on! You can't waste him. Not like this."

"Suddenly you're merciful?" She cued up the launch. "Bad news: I'm not."

"I want him dead as much as you," Webber said. "But I want what's on his ship, too. I'm going to come up on him. MacAdams and I will board. Us marines need a taste of the action."

Rada stared at the screens, suddenly hungry to make this work. "He looks intact. What if he's playing dead?"

"Park a missile on his ass. If he twitches, blow him to hell."

"And if you're onboard then?"

"Then at least I'll die with him."

"MacAdams?"

"Maybe it's the adrenaline talking," MacAdams replied. "But I want in on this, too."

"I'll park it off his engine." She programmed orders to the missile. "If it blows, hopefully that's all it'll take out. But once you light something up, there's no telling how big it's going to burn."

She launched the rocket. It slowed, creeping up to the UFO's rear. As it snugged into place, Webber brought the *III* around to the silent vessel's fore. On high zoom, Rada watched as two suited figures exited their storm-tossed ship, swam through the void, and entered the punctured hull of the assassin's ship.

Webber screamed.

Webber landed on the hull with a thud. He grabbed for a strut, expecting to bounce off, but his magnets stuck with no rebound at all. MacAdams made a similarly fluid landing beside him.

"That ain't normal," the other man said.

"The device is intact," Webber said. "Time to do what pirates do best."

"Catch the pox?"

Much of the hull was far too hot for his suit to handle. Webber navigated to a gash that was only scalding rather than volcanic and eased himself around the rended metal edges. A weak artificial gravity field sprung up, threatening to scrape him over the jagged metal if he slipped. He took his time getting inside, trying not to think about the missile Rada had parked off the ship's tail.

The gash led to a cargo bay. There was no atmosphere, no pressure. The bay held a few containers secured tight to the floors and wall. An old fashioned notepad lay in the middle of the floor. You just didn't see things strewn unsecured around a starship and the presence of the object spooked him worse than a body would have. He bent to pick it up. Block capitals filled the page. The writing was gibberish, word salad. He scanned a few pages and secured it in a zippered pocket.

MacAdams moved swiftly between the clamped-down boxes, gesturing that it was clear. He led the way upstairs, pistol in hand. Compared to the lower level, the upper was a scrap heap. Flakes, splinters, and chunks of metal and polymers carpeted the floor. Huge wounds slashed the bulkheads. A scuzzy haze of smoke fuzzed the corridors.

In the command room, the front wall had been shredded. Very expensive rubble strewed the ground, shifting silently under Webber's steps. A spindly man was seated in the captain's chair. Flak pierced his body. Bright red icicles had dripped from the wounds, but his suit had already resealed itself.

MacAdams made a spitting noise. "Only human."

"Sure he's not a vampire?" Webber leaned in for a closer look. "Maybe one of those stakes hit his heart."

Behind his mask, the man's eyes popped open. Webber screamed and scrabbled back, lifting his pistol.

"Webber!" Rada said over the comm. "You okay?"

Webber steadied his aim. "He's alive."

The man lifted a hand, shards of plastic falling from his suit's sleeve. "Get out. You don't get to be here."

"I'd like to watch you suffer," Webber said. "But I'll like this even more."

He pulled the trigger. The gun's bang was a whisper — there was just a bit of smoke to carry the sound — but to his surprise, he hardly felt its buck, either. A distant part of him wondered how the bullets had even fired at all, but this ran a distant second to watching the man's face go slack.

"He's gone, Rada." He holstered his weapon. "It's over.

Yon felt the bullet enter him — an indescribable kick, followed by numbness — but he didn't mind the discomfort half so much as the disgusting feel of having the two men watching him die. It felt like worms slipping between his skin and the fat beneath. He tried to scream at them to go away, but something had stolen his breath.

Their faces loomed above him like two dim moons. The moment became forever. The light in the command room faded, but as it waned, the two moons waxed. They were no longer the faces of humans — they were the eyes of a Swimmer.

The alien descended on him. He tried again to scream, but the creature was deaf. Its tentacles enfolded him in a moist and sickening embrace.

"There it is." Over the comm, Webber's voice was hushed, reverent. "Are you seeing this?"

She stared up at the screen, conscious that her mouth was actually hanging open. "Sorry, I'm in awe over here. This is like rubbing a lamp and watching the genie come out."

"Except we didn't rub the lamp. We shot it. And now we're going to kidnap the genie."

On the screen, a silver cylinder projected from the floor of the UFO's guts. Minute stars orbited it in complex patterns, distorting the shadows of the room. She suspected the tiny lights were decorative rather than integral to the design, and she feared it had been built by alien claws rather than human hands, but she didn't care. It was beautiful.

"Enough gawking," Rada said. "Load it up and let's get out of here before FinnTech's backup arrives."

While Webber and MacAdams uninstalled it from the UFO, Rada began composing messages. Most were to Toman and the Hive, but she had one for Simm's parents, too. The two men returned in the box bearing the object. They came to the bridge all grins.

"We have got to get that thing plugged into the *Tine*," Webber said. "We'll be the meanest ship in the system."

"Toman will want it," Rada said. "But I bet I can talk him into giving us the first copy."

"He'd better." MacAdams found a seat and settled in with a sigh. "Won't be long before this is the new normal."

She nodded, lost in the idea of the coming future. An era defined not by the weakness of flesh and metal, nor of the might of whatever unseen forces lurked beyond the fringes of humanity, but by the wills of those willing to push into the unknown.

"So what's next?" Webber said.

She grinned at the stars. "Who knows?"

"Surely Toman has a plan. Isn't he some whiz kid supergenius?"

"Oh, what's next for the Hive?" She turned and gave him an impish smile. "Simple. We tell the world."

22

The world, as usual, didn't give a big fat shit.

Oh, there was plenty of hooting and hollering. Some claimed the Motion Arrestors, as they began to be known—much to the consternation of the LOTR, who claimed that wasn't what the devices did at all—were a transparent Swimmer plot to finally destroy humanity once and for all. FinnTech argued there was nothing in the MAs that would suggest such a thing. When various research groups insisted FinnTech release the schemas for independent verification, FinnTech balked, claiming that, given the horrendously lax state of patent protection, a delay was necessary to ensure their proprietary rights were secured.

This opened the door to the sub-argument that they didn't deserve patent rights in the first place. FinnTech argued that it shouldn't matter *how* they'd acquired the technology, only that they had; others insisted that the circumstances of their acquisition were well beyond the scope of existing laws and thus the laws could not apply.

Most of these opinions were forwarded by scholars, pundits, judges, low-level representatives, and so on. The players, the people who mattered, they weren't even paying attention. Not when the new technology meant better, fleeter ships. Not when fleeter ships meant more profit. FinnTech was already scrambling to fill orders. Toman's people had nearly reverse-engineered the MA the *Tine* had brought back and were leaning toward selling their own line of the product.

Like Rada had said, the genie was out of the bottle. Anyone trying to stuff it back in would wind up watching helplessly as they fell behind the culture's newest leap.

Webber was about as far as he could get from the front lines of this politico-economical warfare and received most of his news from Rada. He intended to rejoin her soon enough, but for the moment, he had other business.

It was a long ride from the port. After cruising through an array of neighborhoods, the cab found St. Martin's Street, a quiet neighborhood of single homes. The vehicle whirred to a stop outside a pale blue house. Webber hated himself for caring that its lawn was well-tended, but if the lawn was being seen to, then presumably Dinah was too. He couldn't help smiling: the house was modest, but it was hers.

He was met at the door by Marcel, the live-in assistant.

"Mr. Webber?" The man gazed down, apologetic. "Today, she's not feeling so well."

"Oh." Webber glanced behind him, but he'd let the autocar go. "Maybe tomorrow."

"She told me to see you inside." Marcel stepped back. "I told her you wouldn't mind coming back, but she insisted."

"Stubborn. Blame our mom."

The inside smelled like antiseptic and clean linen. She was in bed, propped up by pillows. She was pale and there was little flesh between her skin and her cheekbones, but the light in her eyes was as lively as the tiny stars that had orbited the machine.

"Pip!" She laughed, spilling tears. "Even when you called and I saw you on video, I figured it had to be a prank."

"On myself, maybe." He sat on the bed and embraced her. She felt light and hot but there was some sinew to her. "How've you been?"

"You don't get to change the subject like that. Why did you do it, Pip? Why did you go away?"

"You were about to lose the house. I tried to get a loan, but nobody would touch me. Not unless I sold them my life."

She reached for his hand. "Why? Why give up so much for me? You lost everything, didn't you?"

"Everything wasn't so much," he laughed. "My life hadn't turned out how I wanted, Dinah. Not at all. I can try to blame Mom, and I'm sure you'll blame yourself, but it was nobody's fault but mine. Keeping you on your feet, and at the same time I get to become someone new...it felt like the only chance I'd ever have."

"It sounds insane!"

"The only thing I regretted was I wouldn't be able to see you again."

"Well, did it work?"

"I'm here, aren't I?"

She rolled her eyes. "Your new life. Is it fun? Are you getting to do everything you imagined?"

He laughed again. "Way more. And it's only getting started."

"Two scoops of wonderful." Her grin shrank. "Faking your death, though—that's fraud. Will you be in trouble for coming here?"

"I've made some new friends. One of them is very generous. He's cleared up everything." He grinned at her. "And there's more. How would you like to take a vacation?"

"Oh yeah? Hawaii? The Sea of Tranquility? The Hotel d'Titan?"

"Idaho. The cabin. Like when we were kids."

"I've missed that so much." This time, her smile was the resigned smile of the chronically ill watching life from within the window. "But you know I can't leave here."

"I don't think you understand," Webber said. "My new friend is Toman Benez. I just got done earning him a second fortune. He's paying for the entire thing."

Dinah stared at him, eyes clocking between his, searching for signs of a joke. She burst into laughter, then tears, then more laughter. "When can we leave?"

~

She was so wrapped up in the fallout from the fight and the taking of the MA that it was days before the grief hit her. When it did, she stayed in her apartment in the Hive's ring for three days. She left the lights off. Didn't shower. Spent hours staring at the tap of her machine. She held out by imagining Simm seeing her pour and consume the glass. In her mind, he wouldn't leave, but he wouldn't speak to her, either. Not until she was better.

But willpower was a resource. Finite. She knew she could only hold out so long. For that reason, and because she was as restless as the comets, she rousted herself. Collected his ashes. And walked to Hyrule Castle.

The automaton lowered the drawbridge and told her to enter as she pleased. Instead, she asked the bot to see if Liam was in. Minutes later, the data hound wandered outside, blinking at the morning light. After their initial greeting and small talk, the conversation dwindled to nothing.

"Did you hear about Simm?" she blurted.

His gaze darted across the courtyard. "We sent a card. Didn't you get it?"

"I did. Thank you." She untucked the box from under her arm. "I have an odd request. His ashes—can he stay here?" She blinked at Liam. "It won't be forever. Soon, I'll take him to the stars. But he wanted to be a part of your team so badly."

"That's..." Liam shook his head, gazing up at the bubble enclosing the rock. "I was going to say weird. But my whole life's weird. Besides, it's pretty cool, too. Where should he stay? The Tower of Earth? Moon? Mars? Or Meteor?"

She gazed up at the four high corners of the castle. "He never cared for Earth; too traditional, too crowded. The Moon is fine, but he thought further than that. Meteors would interest him, but they'd frighten him, too—too unpredictable, and they always crash in the end."

"Please tell me Mars will suffice. We're kind of busy to start work on a fifth tower."

She laughed a little. "Mars is perfect. It's out there, but it's stable. And there's room to be whoever you please. I think he would have been happy there."

"Then the Tower of Mars shall be his." Liam held out his hands for the box of ashes. She gave it to him and he gazed down at its brushed metal surface. "The realm has lost one of its finest knights. Yet not in vain: he delivered our grail."

She wanted to scoff, but if Simm could have heard it, he'd be smiling so hard he'd have to look away. She broke down again. When she finished, however, she felt renewed, as light as hydrogen. She was glad there was a dome overhead in case she started to float away.

After a month on Earth, Webber returned to the port. On the flight up, he had a good long look at Founder's Bay and the remains of the mothership that continued to corrode off the coast.

Once, it had felt impossibly old, like the last surviving brick of a house that had long ago crumbled into sand. Now, however, the ship looked like the fossil of a prehistoric shark, once believed extinct, discovered to be hiding in deeper waters than humanity could navigate.

One of Toman's ships awaited him in orbit. It picked up a few other passengers in the Belt, but for most of the ride, he had it to himself. He made the Hive in short order. A cart carried him across the ring to the rock and then to the castle.

Rada awaited him outside. "How was Dinah?"

"Good," Webber said. "We went to the mountain. We hiked around, explored. After two weeks, she ran. Only for a few steps. But I haven't seen her run in years."

"That's incredible. And no trouble with the law?"

He shook his head. "Toman's a wizard."

"Sufficiently large quantities of money are indistinguishable from magic, aren't they?"

"And how've you been?"

"Getting there." She turned to stare up at the castle's dark, gleaming tower. "Sooner or later, I'll be able to convince my head that it's over."

"Is it?" Webber said. "We killed the assassin. But he was just a cog in the machine. The people who sent him are still out there."

"You mean FinnTech. One of the largest arms manufacturers in the system—check that; after their merger with Valiant clears, *the* largest. Every government on Earth is too busy lining up to buy

Finn's newest gizmos to pretend to investigate his company."

"Toman's no slouch in the arms department. Besides, I know how to get a far more valuable ally than Valiant."

"Please tell me you haven't stolen a page from their book and struck a secret deal with the aliens."

"Nope." A slow grin spread across his face. "The Locker."

"You want to come after Finn with an army of pirates?"

"Privateers," Webber corrected. "Together, their armada will rival anything FinnTech can muster."

She laughed, the noise echoing across the courtyard. "Assuming you can get them under one roof. Call them what you want, but at the end of the day, they're pirates. They won't be easy to unite, Admiral."

"Admiral Webber," he said, testing the words. "I like the sound of that."

"You can dream when you sleep. Right now, it's time to work."

He glanced up. The artificial light hid the stars, but he knew they were waiting beyond the thin shield of the dome. Once upon a time, they'd felt forbidding, a wilderness you could get lost in if you took the wrong step.

Now, though, they looked more like a map—one that would lead him to his destiny among them.

OUTLAW

ABOUT THE AUTHOR

Ed lives in the Los Angeles area with the author-mandated two dogs, two cats, and a fiancee. His hobbies include running, and blowing up fictional worlds.

Outlaw is the first book in the REBEL STARS series. These books are set in the far future, following a terrible apocalypse. If you'd like to read about that apocalypse, please check out the BREAKERS series, starting with book one, *Breakers*.

Made in the USA
Lexington, KY
24 November 2017